THE SURPRISE WEDDING

A FAKE RELATIONSHIP SMALL TOWN ROMANCE

JEAN ORAM

The Surprise Wedding: A Fake Relationship Small Town Romance
© 2017 by Jean Oram
All Rights Reserved
Large Print First Edition

Cover created by Jean Oram

Printed in the United States of America unless otherwise stated on the last page of this book. Published by Oram Productions Alberta, Canada.

COMPLETE LIBRARY OF CONGRESS CATALOGING-IN-PUBLICATION DATA AVAILABLE ONLINE

Oram, Jean.

The Surprise Wedding: A Fake Relationship Small Town Romance / Jean Oram.—2nd. ed.

Large Print ISBN: 978-1-989359-55-6, 978-1-989359-56-3

Paperback ISBN: 978-1-928198-80-2, 978-1-928198-41-3

Ebook ISBN: 978-1-928198-33-8

First Oram Productions Edition: November 2021

ACKNOWLEDGMENTS

I couldn't create a book without the help from the many women on my team. From Donna W. and Mrs. X. who give me early feedback along with Lucy M. (she entertained about eight million ideas that started with 'what about if I..." as I worked through both *The Surprise Wedding* and *The Promise*. (*The Promise* is Devon and Olivia's prequel novella, but you can totally read this book first without any issues if you haven't read that one yet.)

I honestly thought Devon was going to be super easy to write! It turned out he was a complicated man with quite a past due to the woman who'd stolen his heart so many years before we first met him in *Whiskey and Gumdrops,* and then got to know him better as a best friend and flirt in *Tequila and Candy Drops*.

As well, special thanks to Rachel B. for pointing out inconsistencies and to Margaret C. for her fabulous line edits. And finally, for the final proofing touches that always prove to me just how fluid and fussy the English language is between people, regions and countries—thank you Erin D. and Emily K.

I'd also like to thank author Julie Farrell for letting me post book description after book description into our Facebook chat box as I planned out the entire seven book series in one go! You're awesome and your feedback was always on-point, kind and generous. Just like you.

XO,

Jean Oram

A NOTE FROM THE AUTHOR

Thank you to my readers—from those just discovering my books from the first time to those who picked up my first book, *Champagne and Lemon Drops,* back in March of 2013 and have been reading my works ever since. The last four years have been a wonderful adventure and I'm particularly excited to start this new series as it is set in my fictional mountain town of Blueberry Springs which is where I first started my publishing journey.

Blueberry Springs isn't real, but it feels that way to me, likely due to the fact that it is a mix of all the small towns I've lived in over the years—including the mountain town of Banff, Alberta. Over time Blueberry Springs has evolved and grown as I've brought in new characters, changing the dynamic and focus of the town. Over the various books more than 100 characters have been mentioned in Blueberry Springs. Interesting fact, 100 was the population of the hamlet I grew up in. Not including cats and dogs, of course.

This new Blueberry Springs series, Veils and Vows, is going to be a little different from the original because I'm going to dive into my own version of catnip. (Say what, girl? Just stick with me for a moment... You know that romance trope or type of story that always gives you a little thrill as a reader? Such as a secret baby or a marriage of convenience or a wealthy man coming and sweeping a regular woman off her feet? Yeah, that fun stuff! Reader catnip!)

So, my catnip happens to be marriages of convenience (reasons for marrying other than love). I didn't even realize it was an actual romance 'thing' I could search for as a reader until about a decade ago, but I still remember the first time I read a marriage of convenience romance. I even remember where I was when the book found its way to me. I was in the crabapple orchard at home and I was about seventeen, maybe eighteen. (The 'orchard,' in case you are envisioning something grand, was actually about ten trees in two rows beside the schoolhouse I grew up in that my parents had bought in an auction. We lived in one half and ran the family's beekeeping operation out the other half.)

Anyway, my guy friend's grandfather had written and self-published a book and he presented it to my mom while we ate supper in the orchard. (My mom was a great supporter of artists of all kinds and she's the main reason I published *Champagne and Lemon Drops* when I did—I wanted her to see me start my publishing journey before she passed away.)

Being the book hound that I was, I, of course, picked up the book. It turned out it was a historical romance set in the frontier days. A farmer, shy and reserved, ordered a strong bride from Russia. It was intriguing and I found myself transported by these two characters that were obviously falling in love with each other even though they didn't speak the same language. It had a heartbreaking ending, but it was definitely one of the most memorable books I read that decade.

Writing the Veils and Vows series, which is about marriages of convenience, has reminded me of that book. It's long gone now, as is my friend's grandfather, but in some ways I wish I could read that story again. My hope is that this series makes you feel that same way about my books.

Happy reading,
Jean Oram
Alberta, Canada 2017

The Surprise Wedding

CHAPTER 1

*D*evon Mattson straightened his tie and stood in the doorway to the large banquet area. He'd lied to get into the private gathering for Carrington Cosmetics and Cohen's Blissful Body Care. Lied to give himself the opportunity to ask a favor of the last woman on earth he ever wanted to see: Olivia Carrington—the woman who, ten years ago, had broken his heart when she'd punted him out of her life.

That's how desperate he'd become.

But she hadn't returned his calls. Nobody at Carrington had and he was running out of time. Olivia would be here, mere hours from his hometown, for only six more days as a part of her company's business retreat—an annual brainstorming affair that the company shared with Cohen's

Blissful Body Care which was owned and operated by their close family friends, the Cohens. According to Carrington's corporate website, in six days they'd all go back to South Carolina and at the rate things were changing in Blueberry Springs, he didn't have much beyond that. He needed a miracle and he needed it sooner rather than later.

He spotted Olivia across the room almost immediately. She was sitting near the head of the enormous table, the chandelier above sparkling like the diamonds in her ears. She was smiling, one elbow on the linen cloth as she listened attentively to the person beside her. She was still as beautiful as ever, her smile just as alluring. A deafening flood of emotions roared through Devon.

Anger. Loss. Heartbreak.

He had believed she was different. Not just a rich princess type, but a woman who was kind, fun and creative. Someone he could give his heart to and she'd hold it safe.

He'd been wrong, and all he could see was their shattered past, the way she'd pushed him away, rejecting all he had to offer during a time when they should have held on tighter, become a family.

Was he really going to ask her for help?

He could still slip from the room, unnoticed, and leave the pain in the past.

But he needed her. She was the last stop on his personal train of desperation.

Olivia's father stood at his chair at the end of the table, clinking his glass, commanding the attention of his guests.

The elite group fell silent in sync, all eyes turning to Jack Carrington. Olivia's cascade of blond curls stood out among the heads of gray. She was even more gorgeous than she'd been in college, and back then she'd been able to take Devon's breath away with just one tentative smile. She still drew his eye as if their souls were connected.

Which they weren't.

She'd severed that link, made it clear she didn't need him in her life.

"As you know," Jack Carrington boomed in a smooth voice that held a hint of southern drawl, "we've gathered here this week to discuss new opportunities, proposed mergers of cooperation and quite possibly a *union*."

He paused to smile, letting everyone in the room take in the last part of his statement. A tall, lean man Devon recognized from years ago stood up across from Olivia. He was smiling like he had claim to a million-dollar lottery ticket as he looked upon Olivia, possessiveness marking his gaze. He began fishing through his suit jacket's inner breast pocket as though in the search of a ring. Devon's heart began to thunder. Luke was every bit Olivia's match, their worlds lining up in a way Devon's and Olivia's never had.

Instinct told Devon to intervene. Luke was going to propose, he could feel it. He needed Olivia before she said yes. He didn't know why, exactly, only that Luke, as a fiancé, would interfere with Carrington helping Devon's hometown of Blueberry Springs.

Olivia pushed back in her chair as she apparently realized what Luke was doing, her fingers gripping the edge of the table. She looked pale, uncertain, her eyes wide as though she were facing an oncoming train while tied to the tracks. Pastel-clad older ladies at the table began tittering, hands covering their mouths as they speculated about the possibility of a marriage proposal, eyes gleaming.

Without thinking, Devon strode into the room. "Sorry to interrupt, but I need to speak with Olivia Carrington."

All eyes turned to him, and Olivia stood so suddenly her heavy chair teetered. Her face registered a flash of relief mixed with shock before she did a double take. She dropped back into the chair, mouth open, her hand missing her wineglass as she reached to clutch it. Her lips frowned ever so slightly as she took in the room with a sweeping glance, reading expressions, reactions, and undoubtedly realizing how it all reflected back on her.

Yeah, yeah. He was a painful memory from her past, the last person she expected to see crashing her public soon-to-be engagement, someone she had probably hoped to never see again.

"Olivia?" he prompted gently.

She stood again, opening her mouth to speak, their eyes meeting. A flash of pain, bright and strong, surged between them, spearing him.

He shouldn't have come.

"This is a private gathering," her father said in a loud, stern voice.

"We won't be but a moment," Devon said kindly, trying to act unaffected, calm. "If you don't mind, Olivia?"

Her cheeks were flushed and her tablemates gaped at the two of them, trying to decipher what the interruption meant. He knew that, as always, Olivia wanted to get every detail right, make the right impression. She glanced uncertainly, apologetically, at Luke, while lightly touching her neck just under her ear, revealing her nervousness.

She stepped away from the table and her father put out an arm to stop her, saying, "This isn't a good time."

Olivia halted.

"Who is this man?" Luke asked. He smoothed

his suit jacket, standing taller as he came around the table as though Olivia was in need of protection.

Little did the man know Devon had absolutely no designs on his fiancée-to-be. That ship had not only sailed, but been plundered and sunk offshore. This was about business, his town, and absolutely nothing more.

Olivia said in a soft, placating tone, "Why don't we set up a meeting, Mr. Mattson?"

Mister. Wow. She was playing the proper heir to a T. Not that he was surprised. That was the real Olivia, not the one he'd fallen for.

But a prearranged meeting? He knew if he agreed, she'd never show up for it. Her father would personally guarantee it.

"I can pull up a chair until you have a moment." He tipped his chin toward a waiter who was standing by, a white linen cloth draped over his left arm. "A chair, please." The man jolted into action, but froze when Olivia's father put up a hand to stop him. The waiter gazed from one to the other, conflicted about how to proceed.

"You are not welcome here," Mr. Carrington stated. His face had turned red.

Yup, he remembered Devon. Any father in his place would have, and Devon didn't blame him for the wall of anger, his primal need to protect his daughter. But Devon had never meant to hurt her, never meant to put them in a position where everything could fall apart so easily.

He carefully shifted his weight, knowing the Carringtons didn't want a scene and were waiting for a valid excuse to toss him out.

"I only need a moment to discuss something with Ms. Carrington. Or anyone who knows about her organic line, really." He gave a bland, disarming smile. He casually leaned against the wall, glancing up at the ornate ceiling. Talk about getting a crick in the neck, painting those little cherubs on the plaster like that, the wispy clouds and fancy gold whatever-you-called-it. And he thought trying to keep the current mayor of Blueberry Springs in line was a tricky job.

Devon checked the room again, knowing appearing aloof would aggravate the Carringtons, forcing them to act. Olivia had her head tipped to the side, studying him. He raised his eyebrows and she flinched, looking away.

The women near Devon were chatting loudly now, clearly speculating about who "the stunner in the cheap suit" might be. This was his most expensive suit and it was most definitely not cheap. At least not by Blueberry Springs's standards. But here in the posh mountain resort where the wealthy held their retreats, maybe it was. Nobody had had to mess around with his inseam to get the fit right.

He shot the women a disarming smile, which they returned, their already pink cheeks brightening. Oh, they loved a little drama, didn't they?

"I thought you promised to never speak to him again," Devon overheard Mr. Carrington say quietly to his daughter.

Olivia placed a hand on her father's arm and began discussing something with him in hushed tones. Devon caught him saying, with a hint of exasperation, "This pet project of yours..." before Olivia addressed the room at large.

"I'm sorry for the interruption," she said smoothly. "Please, enjoy your desserts. I'll return momentarily."

She gracefully swept away from the table, her cocktail gown clinging to the curves Devon remembered like a blind man recalls the steps leading up to his own home. He had a fleeting thought that she might still have the ability to break his heart and that coming to see her had indeed been a very, very bad idea.

OLIVIA CARRINGTON WAS both upset and eerily relieved as she hauled her ex-boyfriend out of the elegant dining room. The heavy doors swung open as they approached, reducing the restricted feeling in her chest as she set foot in the wide hallway. It soon gave way to a generous lobby where the setting sun came streaming in. She wanted to start running and never stop. And yet she knew she'd soon return to that room, knew that Luke would ask her to marry him like their families had been expecting for years, and knew herself well enough to foresee a "yes." A yes that would help save her family's business, because marrying her childhood friend, Luke Cohen, the new CEO of Cohen's Blissful Body Care, would raise Carrington's stock. She would live in a beautiful home with a wonderful man, working in a company surrounded by family. What more could a woman ask for?

Love. She could ask for love.

But the pain of seeing Devon standing there reminded her just how powerfully devastating true love could be. How it could seep into every crevice of your soul, breaking it wide open when you failed.

And she didn't have that with Luke.

Which meant he was safe. The perfect choice.

Love was dangerous and she knew she wasn't strong enough to survive another heartbreak.

She should say yes to Luke. Protect herself from

the pain of losing, the agony of being wounded if things didn't work out.

She found herself out on the sidewalk, sucking in the warm mountain air, hands dug into her waist as if she'd just finish a mile-long sprint.

"You okay?" Devon asked, his deep voice unexpectedly gravelly and kind.

How could he even ask that?

She was *fine*. Her life was *perfect*. Couldn't he see that?

She had moved on long ago, blotted him and how she'd behaved out of her every thought, scoured the heartache and pain from her soul. He had no right to act like he cared. She'd shattered their hearts when he hadn't trusted her to make the best decision for the three of them, to be an adult and discard their idealistic dreams, face reality.

Not that it mattered. That was so long ago, and the universe had taken everything back, from Devon's love to their unborn baby, forcing her to start over again.

And she had. She was now the head of public relations at Carrington Cosmetics and about to create an organic, all-natural cosmetic line that would ensure the health and safety of millions of women. No toxins, no more carcinogens.

Olivia did not look back. She did not lie awake at night regretting the way she'd ended things, worried about him. No. She'd made a plan and moved forward, knowing Devon Mattson was better off without her.

"Why have you come here?" she asked, her voice shaking as she focused on him again.

"You haven't returned my calls." He crossed his arms, his suit jacket straining over his biceps. He studied her in that intense way that had always made her feel as though he saw her. Not just her appearance, as everyone else did, but really *saw* her. It was unsettling.

His phone messages had said he wanted to talk about cosmetics, but what did he know about the business? Thanks to their common alma mater's reunion update booklet she knew he was working as Blueberry Springs's property manager. Exactly as he'd planned.

At one time she'd been a naive, starry-eyed woman in love for the first time, consumed by the fact that someone was in love with *her* as a person, and not the things that came with being an heiress, a model, The Face of Carrington Cosmetics. She'd actually thought she might follow Devon to his hometown, design wedding dresses, instead of take her outlined path into the heart of the family empire.

Thank goodness reality had given them a wake-up call, because she knew now that it wouldn't have worked out.

Different worlds.

Insurmountable differences when it came to dealing with life.

She hadn't been able to bring herself to call their intoxicating, whirlwind relationship a mistake or a lapse in judgment, because it hadn't been. It had been every bit as real as her Gucci handbags and her Louis Vuitton sunglasses. No, it had been more a case that she hadn't felt she was using her own volition when she was around him. He got under her skin, freed her mind and became the lift that caused her to fly on wings she had no right to even take out of the airport hangar.

And now he was here, after ten long years, hinting that he might have the very thing she'd been searching for.

"You're not in the cosmetics industry," she pointed out. She gave the cartoon character tie a pointed look. Devon was still that carefree, unaffected man, not a potential business partner.

"I can offer what you need," he said.

"What *I* need?" Her heart thumped madly and she felt the sequined surface of her gown against her palms as she bunched the loose material in her hands, as if it could somehow anchor her.

"What Carrington Cosmetics needs," he corrected.

She released the dress, crossing her own arms, her heart still racing. "Really?"

"Blueberry Springs can, yes."

"I don't see how a small mountain town in the middle of—"

"Send someone to Blueberry Springs this week and I'll show them everything you need to make your proposed All You line a go. You need a stabilizing ingredient?"

"How did you hear about that?" She'd mentioned it to the press here and there, but how did he know? He lived on the opposite end of the continent and was supposed to be completely out of her life. Not following her in the news or whatever he was doing. And definitely not popping up at the dual company's brainstorming retreat. "Why are you trying to help me?"

"This isn't about you. Anyone at Carrington will do."

She felt the sting of rejection even though it made absolute sense that he wouldn't want to be anywhere near her. She finally allowed herself to truly look at him, to try and figure out his intentions. Devon Mattson was still lethally attractive. The hollows under his cheekbones were more pronounced now, giving him a honed handsomeness that she figured had landed him more than his fair share of admirers. The youthful muscular bulk she'd originally been drawn to had been replaced with a more refined, more virile manliness. And that humorous sparkle in his eyes she'd once adored was still there, although she also detected a tinge of sorrow and hurt.

Because of her.

"I don't understand," she said. "Why Carrington?"

"We're only a few hours down the road," he replied, "but what you need won't be there for long." Their eyes met, his uncharacteristically serious. "I'll keep turning up all week until someone comes to check out this lead."

"I won't be coming to Blueberry Springs, so don't bother interrupting me further unless you want to be banned from this hotel." She tipped up her chin. Whatever it was he thought he had couldn't possibly be worth ripping open old wounds, or giving each other the chance to blame the other for a romance that hadn't been meant to last.

Besides, she knew her scientists had been thorough in their search. Yes, they believed the stabilizing answer was out there, but the odds that Devon had found it were incredibly slim. He was up to something. She was sure of it. But what? And why?

"I don't expect *you* to come," he reiterated lightly.

"Good." Because she could feel him already pushing her life off the rails, interrupting Luke's proposal and causing members of the company's board to speculate about the two of them. She needed Devon out of here. "Carrington isn't interested."

I'm not interested.

She turned to reenter the grand hotel, feeling off balance, and his hand brushed hers as he beat her to the door, opening it. She flinched at the contact, at the jolt of warmth that filled her from his touch. She was close enough she could feel the heat from his taut frame and she found herself wondering if he'd traded in the white tees that used to stretch across his chest, and thrown out the tattered old Converse sneakers that had taken him so many miles.

Not that it mattered. Devon Mattson was from her past and that's where he had to stay. She didn't need reminders of how she'd failed them both, how she hadn't been strong enough and had ultimately broken their hearts.

"Send someone to Blueberry Springs," he said evenly, not breaking eye contact. "I guarantee you'll find exactly what you've been searching for."

As Olivia returned to the banquet, she had a

chilling suspicion that Devon Mattson was not going to remain in her past where he belonged, but was going to upset her entire life once again.

CHAPTER 2

On Saturday morning Devon rounded the corner to his house, waving goodbye to the town's only lawyer, who'd joined him for the last quarter of Devon's weekly half-marathon-length run. Devon was drenched in sweat and ready to take his dog out for the final mile—a nice cool-down in the late morning sun. After that he'd hit the shower, before trying once again to convince his ex-girlfriend that it was in her company's best interest to add a little industry and employment to his hometown while saving it from a hydroelectric dam, which was slated to destroy several local hikes as well as the town's familiar landscape in a matter of weeks.

His heart sank at the idea of facing her, and feeling the pain, once again. Hers had been floating there, fully evident to him, bringing his own to the surface. It was almost too much to handle.

But all he needed was one quick deal. He could stomach a few minutes of pain to help people who mattered to him.

And if Olivia did decide Blueberry Springs was worth checking out, she'd send a minion so the two of them wouldn't have to face each other again. Win-win.

He just had to convince her to send someone.

As Devon drew closer to his house, his feet slowed and his heart rate picked up. He might not have to make the drive, after all, seeing as in front of his little two-bedroom home was a silver Porsche Cayenne. He knew only one person with a love of that specific color and model.

And it wasn't one of Olivia's minions.

She'd personally come to Blueberry Springs. Not what he'd expected. Heavy dread weighed on Devon at the same time a swirl of relief swept through him.

As far as he could figure, her quick arrival meant one of two things. She was either desperate for product help or... Well, that was probably all it could mean, seeing as he was fairly certain her father had set up roadblocks against her coming here. And given their past, as well as a decade of silence, they weren't exactly searching each other out for anything beyond career-related desperation or last ditch attempts.

Plus, she'd likely come in person because she didn't want any of her minions touching him with a ten-foot pole. She'd kicked him out of her life because he didn't make the "Carrington cut," as he liked to call it, and he'd be a fool to believe his status had changed. So she was here because she was desperate to see what he'd found, and she wanted to minimize how much of her life he could taint.

He could live with that.

Olivia was tapping her phone's screen, her charcoal-gray dress pants making her legs look impossibly long. Or maybe that was the effect of her killer heels combined with her purposeful walk as she came to greet him. She gave a definitive nod, not meeting his eyes. "Devon."

She was uncomfortable and didn't know what to expect. Ditto for him on that account.

"You came." He was unable to keep the surprise from his voice.

"Despite what you think, my parents don't run my life."

He bit back his reply, knowing that they once had—to the point of helping her shut Devon completely out of a life that he had more claim to than they did. He'd held it against her during

19

their breakup, and obviously she had a good memory.

"That's awesome. So how'd you find my house?"

"I don't have a lot of time. Shall we?" Her mouth was set in a stern line, so much like her domineering father that Devon did a quick reassessment. She was no longer the young woman he'd once kept hovering on the brink of laughter. Now she was shutting him out, trying to hide her hurt behind walls thicker than any he'd ever seen.

He'd done that to her.

But she'd done the same to him.

He supposed in some ways it almost made them even.

"It was a four hour drive and I want to be back for supper." She squeezed a hand around her smart phone, her once kind, soft brown eyes uncharacteristically closed and shuttered.

Wow. Talk about walls.

Devon couldn't help glancing at her ring finger. Still bare.

Not that he cared. It was just easier to make a deal with his ex without a potentially jealous new fiancé in the background.

"Let me shower and I'll show you everything." He resisted the urge to waggle his eyebrows and make an innuendo.

He opened his front door and his golden retriever, Copter, bounded out, knowing it was his turn to run.

Copter went straight to Olivia and sat on her feet, gazing up with his soulful eyes. She looked startled, then reached down to gingerly pet the dog's big head. The canine collapsed onto his back to reveal his vulnerable underbelly.

The traitor. Didn't Copter sense she shouldn't be trusted?

Devon whistled, bringing him back into the house. Inside Olivia's Porsche a dog appeared at the open window, barking once before hanging its shaggy head over the glass, its crooked bottom teeth jutting up over its top lip. Wow. That was one ugly mutt and not at all the type of pet he'd ever imagine Olivia owning.

"Nice dog," Devon said to her, closing the door on Copter so he wouldn't get it in his head to go say hello to the smaller animal and scratch Olivia's car in the process.

Devon wasn't poor, but he had no desire to spend money on a new paint job for someone else.

He pulled his damp shirt off his pecs and stomach, then, without thinking, tugged the garment over his head, leaving his chest bare in the June breeze.

"Come on in for a coffee while I rinse off," he told Olivia.

Her gaze was stuck to his chest, her cheeks pink. She turned away, her movements jerky. He glanced down. He was cut, he admitted. Worked out almost daily—swimming, running. He'd forgotten how she used to admire his muscular chest, the broadness of his shoulders, the bulk of his biceps. It was cute that he still affected her. The new crisp, serious Olivia still found him attractive.

That made him inexplicably pleased.

He flexed for her with a grin. She was dutifully avoiding looking anywhere near his chest.

Aw. Life was supposed to be fun. So much of it was beyond one's control—why fight it? There was enough sadness and anger in the world already. People needed to let go, enjoy the ride and live a little. The hurt would never leave, but you could distract yourself from it for a while.

"I'll wait in my car with my dog. Thank you."

"It's welcome inside. I also have a fenced backyard."

He caught sight of someone coming down the sidewalk and groaned inwardly. Mary Alice Bernfield. If anyone could mess this up for Devon—besides himself—it was the town's biggest gossip.

Sure, he wanted to slip past Olivia's walls like a ghost, but Mary Alice would use dynamite, not caring what the consequences were. She loved people, loved secrets, and considered herself a helpful soul. And mostly, she was. But sometimes…sometimes she was a bit tough to take.

"Come on in, both of you," he coaxed Olivia.

"We're fine here, thank you," she replied primly.

He nudged his chin in the direction of the approaching woman, and said casually, "Suit yourself. But I should warn you that around here people wait inside unless they have a gossip-worthy reason not to. You know, such as stalking." He raised his brows, expecting Olivia to give in. She had an image to keep, after all, and he'd put good money on her not wanting to tarnish it with some wildfire gossip in a small town she might need to work with.

Then again, she might not realize that her flashy car and fancy attire—ugly mutt of a dog aside—said things. A lot of things, considering all the irons he was currently wielding in an attempt to save Blueberry Springs.

"I'm sure she'll find out everything she wants to know about you in the time it takes me to shower." He winked at Olivia, figuring that would get her bounding up the steps to his house. Even if he was shirtless.

"I'm trained to handle people," Olivia said, hands on her hips.

Nuts.

She was that uncomfortable around him. He

got it, he really did. Especially with him poking at her. But they needed to cooperate here.

Meanwhile, Mary Alice had not only seen Olivia, but had increased her pace. The woman possessed a bloodhound's ability to sniff out romantic backstory tidbits, scandals and the like. She was insatiably curious, and Olivia stood out like a new story to be told—especially when she kept flashing pained looks in Devon's direction. There were fewer than last night. Olivia seeming to have tucked most of her discomfort behind the walls of Miss Businesswoman today. But there was still the odd bit that made it past the gates, and Devon knew Mary Alice would latch on to it like a treed cat in a hurricane.

"Hey, Mary Alice. Nice day, isn't it?" he called as she bustled up to them. Maybe he could outtalk her, spin her off her rails. Act as a human shield, so Olivia didn't go running before he had a chance to save the town.

"Hello, Devon." The woman stopped a few feet from Olivia, making her dog bark.

"Where's *your* dog?" Devon asked Mary Alice. "Walking without him? He's going to know you left without him and pee all over the carpet."

She ignored him, her focus locked on Olivia. "Now, who is this beautiful woman and why have you been keeping her from us?"

Olivia shushed her dog, while giving Mary Alice a strained smile. "Olivia Carrington." She held out her hand, crisply shaking Mary Alice's. "Pleasure to meet you."

"Oh, you must be from the big city, with those lovely manners and those gorgeous pants. Look at how they hang."

"Thank you," Olivia said politely.

"You must be busy, with all the tourists in town. All that extra gossip," Devon said to Mary Alice. She ran the local convenience store, which seemed to be an excellent hub for gathering morsels that didn't come from her sister, Liz Moss-Brady, also a gossip, as well as a reporter for the local paper.

"I have extra help," Mary Alice replied, and Olivia backed away slightly, unconsciously toying with her necklace as the curious woman began scrutinizing her features. "You look very familiar. Have you been to Blueberry Springs before?"

"Mary Alice, when are you going to race me around the old paddock track? I bet that little SUV of yours goes like greased snot."

The woman gave a deep laugh, the sound rough and rich from her prior years of smoking, her large chest bouncing. "I'll leave that to younger, more foolish kids—such as yourself. I love that little car too much to put it through such abuse."

Devon pretended to pull a dagger from his

chest. He swung his front door open, giving Copter the hand signal for "stay." "Well, it was nice seeing you, Mary Alice, but Olivia and I have a meeting."

"Is that what you're calling it these days?" She gave Devon's bare chest a pointed look and laughed again, then said in a low voice to Olivia, "He's single, you know. Quite a catch, even though he is a bit of a daredevil." She raised her voice again, taking on a slight scolding tone. "Not that anyone can manage to hold him still for longer than a minute or two."

"He's not my type," Olivia said weakly.

Tell me about it. He'd been good enough for the fun times, but as soon as things got tough she was suddenly no longer interested.

"Mary Alice, if you were only twenty years younger," Devon teased. He waved Olivia toward the house, but she was still playing with her necklace, slowly edging away. He needed a distraction. Something big and worthy like a...like an explosion or an alien invasion. Because for all Olivia's people training, she obviously wasn't prepared for the powers of Mrs. Bernfield. Although, to be fair, Devon didn't think even hostage negotiators would be equipped to deal with the woman.

Mary Alice caught sight of Olivia's bare ring finger. "You know, I'll bet you have exactly what it takes to tame that man over there. He's actually quite sweet and kind." She waited for a reply from Olivia, her eyebrows raised in question, but Devon was already down the steps and extracting his ex-girlfriend.

"She's here for business, Mary Alice," he said lightly, his tone carrying an undercurrent of warning. "Nothing more."

Definitely nothing more.

"Devon, honey…" Mary Alice's focus was on him now. "You flirt with anything that moves, and if you don't want me chatting with her that means one thing. You two have a history, or something is going on in secret."

"No!" Olivia and Devon both sputtered.

Mary Alice broke into a grin. "Thought so. And I'll bet the two of you are married by the end of the month." She waved her hands in excitement. "Oh! In fact, I'd better call Liz and place that bet before she does." She scooped her fingers down the front of her shirt, pulling out her phone. Within seconds she was off, chatting to her sister and making a wager Devon knew she'd never win.

He could guarantee it.

***

OLIVIA STRAIGHTENED her soft gray cardigan wrap, cinching its belt. Devon was in the shower, less than twenty feet away. She was in his kitchen, an untouched cup of coffee on the table in front of her. Her late grandmother's dog, Mr. Right, a gassy mutt she'd taken in after the funeral, was curled up at her feet, having already made friends with Devon's dog, Copter. Her parents had tried repeatedly to take the dog to a shelter, but Olivia had held solid on her claim. Her grandmother, who'd been Olivia's personal rock in the stormy sea of life, had loved Mr. Right, and the poor thing had mourned her loss like he was part human. In Olivia's mind there was no way he was going anywhere but with her.

She pushed the coffee aside. She'd been wrong to come to Blueberry Springs. Wrong to think Devon might actually have something that would help the company and her project. Wrong to get out of her car and let that woman, Mary Alice, pluck assumptions from thin air.

Yes, she still felt a conflicting buzz, a special pulse of attraction, whenever she was near Devon. And apparently it was strong enough that others could see it.

But married by the end of the month? Wow.

She pressed her trembling fingers against her temples.

That was crazy talk.

Devon had apologized for Mary Alice, assuring

Olivia that the entire town wasn't as kooky as she was—although Olivia tended to doubt that—then hit the shower, after slamming things around in the kitchen as he brewed her a quick cup of joe. Black. Disgusting, in other words.

The few minutes had been awkward. So many minefields for them to dance around. And judging from the way Devon had shoved his hands into his longish hair, giving it a tug—a move she recalled meant he was stressed—he didn't want anyone bringing up their past and waving it about any more than she did.

Which was good. She was here for business, not about their crash-and-burn relationship and all the festering wounds she thought had healed years ago.

She should have sent her assistant, though, or one of the scientists working on the proposed organic line. Or even her sister, Emma, who knew enough about the project and had been acting as though she needed a break from her usual management duties, stress lines marking her usually cheery face. But Olivia had come herself, feeling the need to control what might be said to those she worked with about her and Devon—their past, and specifically, the ill-fated pregnancy that even her sister didn't know about.

The good news was that she needed to stick around only long enough see whatever stabilizing agent Devon thought he had for Carrington Cosmetics, check its viability, then go. If she was super quick she could even still make her six o'clock tee time with her father on the golf course of his dreams—the entire reason he'd chosen the Rockies for this year's retreat despite her varied arguments against the location.

All she wanted was an all-natural lipstick that didn't make people sick.

Was that too much to ask?

She rubbed her temples again and sighed.

This was crazy. Every last bit about today was crazy.

And returning to the dual-company retreat wasn't going to be any less crazy, seeing as she'd have to face Luke and the big, life-altering question she'd managed to dodge last night.

The safe side of her wanted to say yes. She'd be marrying a man who was a loyal, protective friend. He was perfect, lovely, kind, generous and connected. Add in rich and handsome. Not exactly a hardship. Plus their union would help both companies, both families. Hardly a losing situation for anyone.

However, her more romantic side wanted to say no. Despite her fears, Olivia wanted more from marriage. She wanted love and passion. Something she knew she and Luke didn't possess.

But maybe that would come in time?

The bathroom shower turned off and Olivia pulled her mind back to Blueberry Springs, staring at the door off the open traffic area on the other side of the kitchen island. Moments later, Devon stepped out, a towel around his waist, his chest ripped, waist tight and narrow. Entirely lickable.

She quickly looked away, her body tensing with what felt an awful lot like unwanted desire. Mr. Right, apparently similar of mind, went trotting over and licked Devon's bare legs.

"Forgot my clothes," Devon said, entering his adjacent bedroom and closing the door, completely unfazed. When it came to anything emotional the man's middle name may as well be Unfazed. But then his initials would be DUM and that wouldn't do.

Mr. Right sat outside the bedroom door and whined.

Even Mr. Right thought Devon was hot. And he was definitely every bit the man Olivia remembered. Relaxed, casual. Everyone liked him and nothing ever seemed to weigh on him. He took things as they came, problems rolling off him as if they didn't exist. She'd used to admire that about him, wondering how she could get a piece of that for herself. But now? Now she just found it annoying. This was real life, full of adult stuff that needed realistic plans of attack. Dreaming and hoping didn't make life happen.

He appeared again, this time in faded jeans and a loose cotton shirt. Mr. Right bounded to his side.

"Ready?" Devon asked.

Mr. Right barked and Devon chuckled. He reached down and rubbed the mutt's shaggy fur, which never looked neat and tidy no matter how much grooming Olivia sent him for.

Mr. Right let one rip and Devon plugged his nose. "Wow."

"I know. He smells." Olivia's tone dared him to say more, suggest she trade her pet in, leave him behind. She'd spent the past year trying different diets and nothing had worked. The dog had un-solvable gas. End of story.

"We should put an air freshener on your collar," Devon said, and Mr. Right barked once, then grinned, his bottom teeth covering his upper lip, shaggy brown fur falling into his eyes. "You're awe-some." He looked to Olivia. "Shall we go check things out before we meet with the others about the plants?"

Olivia had already abandoned her coffee.

Get in. Get out. Today's motto.

She followed Devon to the driveway, where he was hoisting the garage door, revealing an old, white car. He glanced at her Porsche. "Not sure that would like some of the gravel roads we have to take. Why don't you ride with me? Awesome Dog can come, too, if you want, or we can leave him in the yard."

"He doesn't like to be separated from me." She locked her car after retrieving her Gucci bag, then climbed into Devon's beater as Mr. Right jumped in the back. The car not only had rust ringing its wheel wells, but it smelled like dust and running shoes. The dust was obvious—there was a coating all over the passenger's side of the dash. She hugged her bag and tried not to lean too deeply into the seat cushions, curious about how long a vehicle would have to go without detailing to accumulate this much grime.

Devon chucked a tattered nylon backpack and some clipboards that had been on her seat into the back, and cracked a window for Mr. Right. Then he climbed in beside her, the car so small they practically rubbed shoulders. She pressed herself against the door, pretending to be interested in their surroundings.

"We're going to head just out of town to a meadow," Devon said as he steered them through a sleepy downtown. "Part of it used to be a buffalo paddock."

Olivia nodded silently, concentrating on ignoring how familiar it felt to be riding in a car with him.

It was almost noon and there were a fair number of pedestrians walking through the quaint movie-set-like downtown, Devon getting waves from other drivers and pedestrians alike as they passed. She noticed she received long looks of curiosity, and so far the town was almost exactly like Devon had described it in college. Cute and nosy.

"Do people here know about us?" Olivia asked.

She watched Devon out of the corner of her eye as his grip tightened on the steering wheel.

"No."

"Nobody?" She felt affronted. Not even his family? She'd mattered that little to him? All those hours worrying about him after their breakup had been for naught?

"Just Ginger." Ginger had been Olivia's roommate in college and knew pretty much every sordid detail Olivia had kept from everyone else. "Blueberry Springs is open to outside business and industry."

He was trying to change the subject, obviously, but she couldn't let it go.

"Not even your parents know we dated?"

"Well, Mary Alice just figured it out, so it should be across town by now." Devon tried for a smile, a joke. Yeah, she wasn't feeling it. She wasn't in the mood to have her personal life and past impact why she was here. It was about the All You line and nothing else.

"We don't have factories here," Devon continued, "but it's not out of the question to build one if you needed one close to the plant source. Mandy bakes and distributes a ton of brownies out of town each week without issue."

"Your sister, Mandy?"

Devon nodded.

Olivia still remembered the woman's brownies —well, Mandy had been a teen when she'd sent care packages to her brother across the continent —and Olivia had been the lucky recipient of many shared, mouthwatering treats.

Those were good times and her heart started to warm as memories flooded her, but she clamped down on the feeling, choosing instead to remember how it had all ended. She wasn't getting hurt again, and Devon had a way of loosening reality, convincing her to be someone different. Someone free.

A few minutes later they pulled into a small gravel parking lot at the edge of a massive meadow. Mountains loomed like old stone warriors beyond, laced with hiking trails that led off into forests and up hillsides. A river flowed past to the left and not an inch of asphalt was to be seen anywhere. Basically, it was a beautiful place to hike, not show up in high heels looking for a modern day miracle.

Olivia stayed put as Devon climbed out, after patting the only dust-free part of his dashboard and she assumed it was some sort of superstitious tradition left over from his car racing days.

"I'm not dressed for a hike," she said, when he leaned back in with athletic ease, grinning at her, his enthusiasm sparking her hope.

He tipped his head toward the meadow. In the distance, she could make out worn tire tracks marking the more northerly perimeter. "It's close and it's flat. You'll want to see this, trust me. Oh, and careful with the door handle—it's finicky."

Get in. Get out.

What if this was it?

"What is it we're looking for?" she called through his open door.

"Come see. Your stabilizing agents covers the whole meadow with blooms from the end of June right through to September."

Knowing she was about to ruin her shoes, her ankles or both, she climbed out with a sigh, leaving Mr. Right in the vehicle. The loose gravel immediately sent her wobbling as she tried to stay vertical on what amounted to marbles. She'd dressed like a businesswoman expecting a meeting, not a hike. She'd wanted to ensure that Devon took her seriously, treated her like the manager she was, not an ex-girlfriend he could sway with a wink and a smile.

"Want to borrow a pair of sneakers?" Devon asked, glancing into his car. She took in the gym bag Mr. Right had claimed as a bed—the item she suspected was responsible for the vehicle's "eau de man" scent—and shook her head.

She gingerly followed Devon through the parking lot and down a dirt trail littered with large stones, grateful to discover oddly spaced, occasional spots to land her heels. As they walked, the parking lot behind them began to fill with nature-seekers heading off on hikes, their vehicles hybrids or small cars suitable for saving Planet Earth from extra pollution. They were part of her future market. She was in the thick of it, and she felt her steps become buoyed.

As the head of public relations at Carrington Cosmetics, she knew it was time for the company to own up, step up. Take the lead when it came to protecting the environment, as well as the health of their customers. And her new line, which she'd been working on as a side project after wearing her father down, would do both. Yes, it was expensive and risky and sometimes confusing, but the payoff could be huge, her sense of accomplishment unrivaled.

Her chest thrummed with excitement as she tottered after Devon. He hung back to urge her to go faster. To spite him, she stopped, tipping her head back so she could inhale the clean, fresh air. It smelled like pine and water. Around her, birds were singing, calling to one another. Beautiful.

"We have a meeting in fifteen minutes," Devon said, "but we'll never make it if you don't hustle."

"If you'd told me we'd be hiking," she said, staggering as her heels sank into the path again, making her purse fall off her shoulder, "I would have chosen different footwear."

"Where did you think you'd find valerian? In a window box?"

"Valerian?" She stopped walking once more, and her heart clenched with disappointment. They'd already tested all varieties known to man. It was a wonderful natural antibacterial and stabilizing agent, but not quite suitable for her needs.

She'd just wasted a day of her life, as well as ruined a perfectly good pair of heels, for something her scientists had already looked into. That was just like Devon. Draw her in with a dream, cause her to forget to check reality, then dash those dreams when her hopes were at their highest. She should have known. She should have asked more questions before driving out to the middle of nowhere.

Wouldn't she ever learn?

Devon pointed up to the surrounding hills. "The dam is going to go there."

"The dam?"

"Yeah. It's slated to wipe out this meadow, which is full of valerian. Carrington can not only stop that dam from being built, but can find the plants they need to create a stable product. Win-win."

So there was his angle. He needed her to stop a dam. She'd known he was up to something and she'd still trotted right along after him.

"Sorry, I can't help." She tucked her cardigan, which was much too thin for the brisk breeze, tightly around her. A dam there would indeed flood the whole meadow and the hikers that had arrived after them would have nowhere to go, and the town below would be under constant threat from a breaking dam, the beautiful vistas tainted by concrete walls and power lines.

But that wasn't her problem. Creating a longer shelf life for an all-natural lipstick was.

She turned, starting the daunting walk back, her heels sinking into the earth with an irregularity that made her teeter like a drunk. Devon reached out and caught her just as her ankle rolled, righting her again and sending a hot current of need straight up her arm as they connected. She jerked out of his grasp. She didn't want his help, didn't want him touching her. And she most definitely didn't want him edging his way back into her life as she suspected he might still have the power to do.

It was a good thing he'd brought her out to look at the wrong plant. Now she could go home and shake this off. Live her life. Without him.

"Where are you going?" Devon asked.

"To go play golf with my father. We already tested valerian."

"This variety isn't in the plant guides."

"I'm sure my very thorough scientists have already tried it." She attempted to stride away, wishing she could walk faster.

Such a waste of time.

"Here." He caught up to her, handing her a bloom. "Test it. I'm certain it's different than anything you've tried."

She took the flower, waving it at him, frustrated at how easily she'd allowed herself to be sucked in. Like her father said, you didn't build a company on hopes. "We need to test the roots. The whole plant, not just a bloom or two. And even if this valerian is different and useful, I need about a million of these. All year long. Not just a meadow of them." She softened her tone, knowing he'd meant well in bringing her out here. Her foul mood was about her past failures, the way she'd hurt him, not his current attempt to help her. Help she didn't even deserve, after shutting him out and breaking his heart. "I'm sorry, Devon."

She lengthened her stride, nearly twisting an ankle yet again. The parking lot had filled with protesters, not just hikers as she'd assumed earlier. They were chanting and holding banners high and pretty much the last thing she needed to top her morning—especially since she was pretty sure the guy toting a camera was from the media.

Devon came up alongside her, his eyes sweeping her outfit. "This might not go well. These guys have been camping out and protesting every slight against nature ever since the possibility of the dam being approved was announced several weeks ago."

"They don't scare me." She stormed ahead.

"Greenhouses could be made," he said uneasily, falling back into his sales pitch. "The plants like this climate, our soil. Jill says this variety is different from the rest. I really think this is something Carrington could use. Are you sure you want to walk through this crowd?"

She glanced at the protesters. So far they were just marching around the parking lot. Nobody was chained to anything. No riot police. All was well, in other words.

"Who's Jill?" She hated that she was curious for reasons that might not be business-related.

"She's been working with the Ute people and developing a few of her own products for the local market."

"Oh, so you're looking to pitch a product for your girlfriend? That's why I'm here? We're not interested."

What a sucker she was. Allowing herself to be dragged out here so he could pitch some home-made products his lady love had concocted. It probably gave people incurable rashes and smelled like Devon's gym bag. Or worse, Mr. Right.

No, that wasn't fair. Olivia was just so angry with herself.

For this she'd missed a full day of activities at the company retreat and was still lacking the magical ingredient that would lift All You off the ground. Plus she was going to have to deal with Luke while in a terribly bad mood.

No, she *wanted* to deal with Luke. He would brighten her mood. He was lovely and wonderful and never stirred up her emotions. He was perfect.

She was going to say yes. Definitely.

He was the best thing out there.

"I'm not pitching a product," Devon said, his earlier cheer gone. "All I'm saying is that she has a lot of knowledge in this department and can help you out if you'd be a little less hardheaded and more open-minded. There are other options besides whatever you've planned."

She noticed he hadn't corrected her on the girlfriend assumption.

And, she could tell by his dig about her plans, that he still didn't understand why she'd had to shut him out all those years ago.

What had she expected? Him to be sitting here, pinning for her a whole decade later? Ha! It wasn't like she'd lain awake thinking about him or their past, either, and wondering what-if.

She narrowed her eyes, hands on her hips, facing off. "Go ahead and insult me and fight old battles, Devon. Get it all out of your system, because your little town does *not* have what I need—what Carrington needs—and so I'm leaving."

"What else is new?"

She glared at him.

Up ahead, the protesters yelled about the dam, drowning out the sounds of the nearby river. She wished she'd risked her paint job and driven her Porsche out here so she wouldn't be dependent on Devon for a ride back into town.

"Olivia," he said, his tone contrite now, "you're not even trying to see the possibilities."

She spun toward him. "Be realistic, Devon.

Being a dreamer isn't going to make this work and both you and I know it. This is real life!"

"It can work," he said stubbornly, his jaw set. "Call your scientists."

"And tell them what?"

"To check into it. Jill says it's a reliable stabilizing agent. Completely safe."

Completely safe.

Olivia struggled against her anger, her urge to throw up barriers and shut him out.

She needed this and she'd never forgive herself if she walked away from the right ingredient just because Devon was getting under her skin. She was bigger and better than that.

"Fine. But I'm sure they'll tell you they already did." She pulled out her phone, punched a number, then looked at the device in surprise when it wouldn't connect. "There's no cell signal."

"There's better service in town."

She began marching again. "Fine. I'll inform my people that a property manager and his girlfriend say we didn't check every strain of valerian on earth. Happy?"

"Yes." He kept up with her, pulling a piece of paper from his pocket and handing it to her. "This is the local name for the meadow's variety of valerian. And after we talk to Jill we can dig up a plant for you. For testing."

Olivia snatched the paper. "Fine."

She could handle this. Another hour of being around him? No problem. She was strong. Totally past him and their relationship. She was a professional. An important employee of Carrington Cosmetics. Spending more time with Devon would only reinforce all the reasons she'd made those impossible decisions all those years ago.

She mentally dusted her hands as they reached the edge of the parking lot. Closure. That's what they were going to get.

A protester came closer and she smiled and said hello.

"The Face!" he yelled, recognizing her from one of the hundreds of ads she'd been in promoting her family's products. He pointed at her, hollering, "Down with Carrington Cosmetics! Down with the use of p-Phenylenediamine! Down with packaging not made from recycled materials! Protect our planet!"

As Olivia gaped in surprise, the chant picked up volume and speed as more people recognized her and joined in. They definitely knew the environmental hotspots Olivia was currently working on, from toxins that hurt aquatic life to nonsustainable packaging and ingredients.

She looked at Devon, wondering if he'd set her up. He appeared pale but determined as he slipped in front of her like a shield, as they continued to shout.

"Hey, now," he said mildly. "Be kind. She's only trying to help Blueberry Springs and the environment."

The cameraman Olivia had noted earlier took a few shots of her and Devon.

"I agree! Carrington needs to do better," she said over his shoulder. He was edging her back toward the meadow and she pushed forward. It wasn't the first time she'd come across protesters. She could take care of herself. "That's why I'm here. I'm looking into developing organic, all-natural cosmetics. Carrington cares about the earth, sustainability and its customers!"

"Down with big corporations, raping the land!"

Why did she even bother? There was always something. Three years ago it had been that their models were too skinny—one of the models being herself, a size fourteen, and her sister, who was slim, yes, but not unhealthily so.

Some days it made Olivia wish for an easier life. One without so many people or…well, definitely without this kind of irrational confrontation.

Now she was going to have to write up a press release to combat this bad PR. Reactive releases were the worst—she always felt so dirty, trying to redirect the public's attention and smooth over legitimate concerns such as these. But the worst was that she was going to have to deal with her father, who had told her not to come and would no doubt scold her about her All You "hobby."

"Stop the dam! Stop Carrington!"

Devon kept deflecting angry people when they got too close, and she muttered to him, "This town is crazy."

Using his body to block others from getting too close, Devon maneuvered them the final few feet to safety, Olivia's hands gripping his strong shoulders. She managed to get into the car, her body shaking with adrenaline. That was intense. Too intense. What was with this town? First Mary Alice and now this. A decade ago, Devon had painted her a picture of a peaceful town. She'd seen glimpses of that as they drove through earlier, but this was nowhere near idyllic.

She stared out at the triumphant faces shouting through the windshield as Mr. Right went wild, barking, growling and racing around the backseat, sending Devon's things to the floor.

"You okay?" Devon asked as he climbed in.

She nodded.

This wasn't going to stop her. Women like her grandmother, who had been affected by years of exposure to the chemicals found in cosmetics, deserved change, and Olivia was one of the few people who could make it happen.

It was time to make a difference and it was up to her.

———

DEVON CHECKED OVER HIS SHOULDER, taking an extra second to look way down the road to ensure they weren't being followed. The protesters camping out in Blueberry Springs had been right up in Olivia's face, unlike anything he'd seen to date, and his body still surged with a protective need to react. He was already toeing a very fine line with her thanks to Mary Alice—although Olivia had truly taken it like a champ—and he feared that any further kind of confrontation would give her an excuse to walk away from a potential deal. Assuming he was right, and not a dreamer like she'd said, and the valerian was all his ex-girlfriend Jill Armstrong had claimed.

"They protest the dam almost every weekend, and since the building project will be undergoing the expedited approval process in less than two weeks, they seem to be ramping up," he explained.

"They weren't receptive to Carrington." Her dog crawled into the front, settling in Olivia's lap even though he was a bit big for it. He growled under his breath, still stirred up from the protesters. She cuddled the mutt and it let out a horrid smell. Both Olivia and Devon reached to crack the windows. It was not the kind of pet he ever expected someone like Olivia to have, that was for certain.

"I'm sure once they understand what you're trying to do for the town—"

"Except my scientists have already checked into valerian."

"—they'll lighten up and start giving you patchouli-scented hugs instead of banging on the hood of the car." He tried for a smile. Let her know that he, at least, was on her company's side.

"And what exactly am I trying to do for the town?" she asked, eyes narrowing as she looked up from sending a text that had hardened her expression. Her dog gave her chin a reassuring lick and her fingers trembled as they hovered over the phone's screen.

She seemed calm, but the confrontation had definitely shaken her. Devon had to do something. If she walked…

He needed to lighten things up. A lot.

"Maybe we should stop for a drink or something? Take a breather?"

"Didn't you say there's a meeting? My scientists want to know more."

Devon absorbed that tidbit. He mentally high-fived Jill for her find. There was definitely something to be said for amicable breakups and staying friends with an ex.

"And what *exactly* is your vision for Carrington?" Olivia asked.

This was all going to be perfect. He'd save the meadow and ranching lowlands from the dam and he'd bring along more industry and jobs. "The upcoming new mayor will be receptive to Carrington and will—"

"What are the town's expectations, Devon?"

He sighed. She was all about the business, wasn't she? He still saw flickers of hurt in her big brown eyes, but those walls she'd arrived with proved to be sturdy and reliable. Impenetrable. She was putting him and their past behind her in order to do her job for the family company.

Respect. That was the word he was looking for. He respected that.

Then again, her family had always come first. Not him.

Still, even if he did respect her work ethic and ability to shove everything into the past where it belonged, it didn't mean he had to trust her or forgive what she'd done to him back then.

But they could probably work together without

anyone being charged for murder. And that was always a plus.

"Industry. Jobs," he said. "A small tax break for local businesses, since they won't have to carry the entire load for things such as civic improvements. The usual." He shrugged like it wasn't a big deal, even though he knew those few things could have a major impact on the small, isolated town and wouldn't make a dent in the bottom line of a company Carrington's size. Not only that, it would save his sister's café and his brother's three small businesses from death by taxes.

"So you expect Carrington to pay big taxes and hire tons of locals?"

"Will you?" he asked hopefully, his tone light.

"After you just handed me a PR nightmare back there? You really suck at this."

"The protesters are mostly harmless. They were just being difficult."

"I deal with difficult people every day. That was pure crazy."

"In regards to difficult people, are you referring to your father or your PR job?"

The corners of her mouth almost turned up. Almost.

He considered it a win. She wanted this as bad as he did. That was why she was here.

Man, that was a relief.

"And hey, I got to play hero to a damsel in distress." He waggled his eyebrows and she folded her arms across her chest, causing Awesome Dog to nudge her for affection.

"I was *not* a damsel in distress."

Devon smiled. "Most women swoon over that kind of stuff, you know."

Her glare deepened, but he saw a flicker of her old self in another hint of a held-back smile. He could win her over. And he would.

He found a place to park near his sister's café despite parking being tighter than usual due to the startup of a ten-day music festival his overly pregnant friend Nicola Samuels—now Haber—had organized. He shut off his car's engine and patted the dusty dash, as was his habit whenever it successfully got him from point A to point B.

Olivia was texting again and he took the opportunity to send a quick text of his own to his friend Logan Stone, who dealt with private security. It wouldn't be a bad idea for Olivia to have a shadow, with the protesters acting so volatile. Just in case.

Devon told himself he wanted her protected for the town's sake, not some messed-up personal reason.

"We're going to talk to Jill about this strain of valerian?" he confirmed, slipping his phone in his pocket.

Olivia nodded and waved her device. "I have a list of questions. We'd also like five complete plants to take back to the lab. Roots and all."

"Consider it done."

"My scientists want to personally dig them up, as well as take tests while collecting environmental data."

"Okay."

Demands meant progress. Progress meant hope.

"But that's only if they're satisfied with what I learn in this meeting."

"Of course." The tightness in his chest eased off.

Things were going as well as could be expected. And the two of them? Downright civil for people who hadn't spoken in a decade. He didn't even foresee the need for a protective cup to cover his family jewels, nor the impending misfortune of waking up to find she'd placed his head on a spike at the gates of her company.

He was going to win this one.

But even so, he knew he couldn't fully relax, couldn't trust that she had his or his town's best interests at heart—not when she had proved in the past that hers and those of her family always came first.

CHAPTER 3

Olivia watched Devon as he waited for a pickup truck to lumber by his parked car, coughing exhaust as it went. He'd almost made her smile, poking fun at things, warming her, subtly coaxing her to let down her guard. But she couldn't. She already felt herself on the precipice of being won over by him, which would only lead to disaster. She just wasn't strong enough. Never had been. She could not allow herself to slip into a position where she might hurt him again—especially if this valerian was The One. Too much was on the line.

Through the car window she saw a bright red Closing Sale sign on a shop. Another hint of how much the town needed Carrington?

She smiled. She was starting to think like her

father. It used to bother her how he kept the bottom line in mind for every business dealing, but now she understood the reasoning behind doing so, even if it yielded a certain heartlessness. When you were negotiating something important, you had to keep your eye out for whatever might help or hinder.

She scooted Mr. Right into the backseat, then told him to stay as she gathered her purse and went to let herself out of the car. As the door clicked open, the handle came loose in her grasp. She heaved a sigh, climbed out and marched toward Devon, who was waiting on the sidewalk, texting someone. She waved the handle at him. "Seriously, Devon. It's called buy a new car. It smells and it's falling apart."

He took the metal object from her. "It's called you break it, you buy it."

Oh, he'd love that, wouldn't he?

"And your dog smells worse than the car," he added.

"He can't help it and you said the handle was finicky. That means it was already broken."

"Then…" he paused, his expression playful "… it's called don't break my car, it's paid for." He opened the clunker's back door and tossed the handle inside before slamming it shut again, causing Mr. Right to let out a bark of alarm.

Nothing fazed Devon, did it? Nothing mattered. Nothing broke through the "it'll all work out" idyllic dream he lived in whether discussing an ill-timed pregnancy or a falling-apart vehicle. He didn't even dress like a proper adult. He was outfitted as if he was about to help paint someone's house in his faded jeans—faded beyond fashion. How did anyone take him seriously as the town's property manager when he walked around on weekends looking like the town's maintenance man?

"Don't look at me like that," Devon said lightly, as he reached for the door of a restaurant that claimed to be for sale, and held it open for her. "There are things more important than money and appearances, you know."

She ignored him, taking in Benny's Big Burger. The establishment looked more like a hodgepodge family Italian joint than a fast food place as the name suggested. The town was quirky, that was for sure. She excused herself to head to the washroom to freshen up before Devon's girlfriend arrived.

Wiping down her Manolo Blahniks with a piece of damp paper towel, Olivia sighed at the scratches and dirt that had accumulated. Devon's girl-wonder better have something amazing to make their destruction worth it. Because yes, money and appearances weren't everything, but these were very nice shoes. Power shoes. Take-me-seriously shoes.

Olivia looked in the mirror, fixing her lip gloss and tucking back her curls, while giving her outfit a once-over. She looked every bit the professional she was. She'd go out there and have a to-the-point meeting, then report back to her scientists, leaving them to handle details—if there was anything to handle.

Then no more dealing with Devon or this town. It would be back to her real life. Nice linens, no dirt or dust. No messy thoughts or guilt about the past.

And Luke.

What was she going to do about the perfectly wonderful Luke?

Later. She could worry about that on the four hour drive back. Right now she had this to deal with.

She threw the soiled paper towel in the trash and headed to the table Devon had chosen at the back of the restaurant. Across from him was a pretty woman with a long dark brown ponytail, her smile open and fresh.

Interesting. Not sitting side by side? Was she trying to act professional?

Olivia could respect that.

"Hello," Olivia said, introducing herself and

shaking hands with Jill Armstrong, who had stood along with Devon. She was tall, slim, and dressed with an eye to detail. According to Devon, Jill had been working with local tribes to learn more about medicinal, natural ingredients for her homemade soap and skin care line.

Devon placed a light palm at Olivia's lower back, guiding her into a chair he pulled out for her. The touch felt intimate, and she felt a spark of un-comfortable appreciation for his manners, which had always surprised her even back in their college days. She wasn't sure why, just that she supposed she didn't expect him to care about social niceties when his attitude tended to border on cavalier. But he did. And she'd always liked that about him.

"Thank you."

She caught Jill giving Devon a quick look, and Olivia's ex-girlfriend radar blipped. She'd bet her wardrobe that Jill and Devon weren't current but that Jill still had a small thing for Devon and was feeling slightly threatened by Olivia. That was sure to make things complicated if the woman thought Olivia still had any sort of designs on the man, other than the urge to murder him in his sleep for acting so cool and unaffected about the past. Why didn't he yell at her? Say all those things he must have bottled up inside?

Sure, she'd see a hint of hurt in his eyes here

and there, and, despite her wishes not to, she'd spent many a sleepless night wishing they'd ended things on a better note. And that was even though she knew she'd done the right thing, protecting him. It was something she wouldn't change even if she had a time machine. But he just…didn't seem as affected as she was. Had none of it been as big of a deal to him?

Maybe he understood now. Maybe he knew his plan wouldn't have worked, because there was no way they could have floated through marriage after only three months of dating. And with their college degrees incomplete, they wouldn't have been ready to be parents, either.

She'd needed her family and their help, and he'd taken it as a personal rejection, instead of seeing that she'd been seeking solid support in a situation she was wholly unprepared for and that had scared her beyond belief.

Olivia settled into her spot at the table, her heart banging with old pent-up emotions, wishing she was meeting with emotionless, unknown CEOs right now.

"I heard you had issues with the protesters," Jill said, her voice filled with genuine concern.

"Devon exaggerates," she assured her as the waitress poured them all cups of coffee. "The past is in the past and I'll be better prepared to deal with them next time." She folded her hands on the tabletop.

"I heard from Liz and Mary Alice that they were quite confrontational."

Mary Alice. That woman was everywhere, wasn't she? Maybe that was why Jill was looking threatened. Mary Alice had probably already announced her crazy marriage prediction to the entire town.

Olivia opened a small notebook she carried in her purse.

"Is that a Gucci? It's beautiful." Jill's blue eyes were wide and she almost drooled.

Olivia felt the same way about the bag and smiled. "Thanks." She poised her pen over the notebook. "I hear you're the expert on the local strain of valerian and its properties."

Jill blushed. "I've learned a lot from the Ute medicine men. They've been very generous with their knowledge." Olivia couldn't help but like her. She was so sweet and unassuming. So unlike the type that would try to murder Devon in his sleep.

Before long they were deep in discussions about the plant's medicinal effects and more. Devon hung back, flagging down a middle-aged waitress in a tight polyester uniform to refill their cups as they ran low.

Olivia glanced up at one point, deep in thought.

The Blueberry Springs variety of valerian sounded as though it was exactly what they needed for a longer product shelf life. The only problem was volume. How could she get enough—especially with the dam about to destroy the biggest field of it? She tapped the table restlessly, then frowned as she recognized someone across the restaurant. A very large, fit man was sitting alone at a table with a cup of coffee, his vibe suggesting he was protecting the place simply by being there, on guard. He looked just like Logan Stone, the man her old college roommate, Ginger McGinty, had had her arms wrapped around in her recent wedding announcement.

"Is that Ginger McGinty's husband?" Olivia asked quietly, still watching him. She'd never met the Australian, but had heard plenty about their whirlwind romance and quick marriage from Ginger via video chats. Hardly surprising considering the way Ginger had swooned over anything with an accent and a Y chromosome back in their undergraduate days.

"Yes," Devon said.

The man in question glanced over and gave a faint smile and nod, then turned his attention to the front windows that overlooked Main Street.

Beside her Devon shifted uneasily.

Jill was asking her something, her ponytail

slung over her shoulder, her fingers tangled in its ends in what Olivia knew was a nervous habit.

"I'm sorry, what did you say?" Olivia asked.

"Why organic?" Jill repeated, her face bright with the joy of getting to speak about what was obviously her passion.

Olivia felt a familiar crushing sensation inside whenever she thought about how the doctors had found toxins in her grandmother's bone marrow, chemicals commonly found in stage makeup from decades past—and even more modern products.

"My grandmother had a few health issues doctors believed resulted from extended exposure to toxins found in certain cosmetics."

"Not Carrington?" Jill asked quietly.

Olivia shook her head. The party line was that Carrington didn't use banned ingredients, but honestly, the regulations weren't as tight as they were with food and drugs, leaving plenty of loopholes and exceptions that allowed carcinogenic and other questionable ingredients into cosmetics— Carrington's included. But the particular one that had been found in her grandmother was not used by the family firm.

Olivia gave a small, practiced smile. "My grandmother used to be an actress and wore a lot of makeup." She sucked in a deep breath, ready to deliver the party line. "She wasn't always a Carrington customer." She found herself adding, "The fact is, Carrington could be more careful, too. The whole industry could."

She shut her eyes for a second, making a quick wish. *Please don't let Jill use that the wrong way.* What she'd just said was practically a confession. Then again, anyone could find out the truth by reading product labels and performing a few quick online searches.

Jill placed a hand over Olivia's, surprising her. "I'm so sorry. Will she be okay?"

She kept a smile on her face she didn't feel. "Thank you. She passed away last year of bone cancer."

Jill's own face sagged with sympathy. Olivia didn't dare look at Devon to judge his reaction. He'd once been insightful and caring, but he also liked to break tension with a joke and she didn't think she could handle that right now.

"I admire what you're attempting," Jill said. "If there's anything I can do to help, just let me know. My knowledge—the knowledge of the Ute—is yours."

"I have to admit, given the dam issue, the timing of this find isn't great," Olivia said, pushing her coffee cup away in favor of water with a slice of lemon. She'd practically been drenching herself in caffeine for the past two hours, and it was time to switch to something else so she didn't vibrate all the way back to her family tonight.

She wouldn't need FDA approval to use valerian, but she'd need a toxicology report. That was doable, as her head scientist, Vintra Badami, could whip one up in a day or two. He would also discover how strong the various properties of this particular strain were. All good information to have.

And the bonus was that her father had brought him to the retreat this year to discuss ingredients which meant she could get him to come check things out with her.

But if the valerian worked…she'd need land, greenhouses, a processing plant. No, she was getting ahead of herself and into that technical stuff she'd despised in her business management courses. She could get someone like her sister to deal with that headache—assuming Emma's recent stressed-out behavior didn't prevent her from wanting to take on more.

Olivia made a mental note to check in on her and make sure she was okay.

"I need to talk to my scientists," she said, closing her notebook. "But I'd like to bring one of them out here."

"When?" Devon asked.

"As soon as possible." She smiled at Jill as she

stood, then reached out to shake her hand as she and Devon stood as well. "Thank you for taking the time to discuss this with Carrington Cosmetics."

"We need to stop Barry Lunn," Jill said abruptly. "He doesn't know what's best for the town."

"Who's Barry Lunn?" Olivia asked, glancing at Devon, who was acting as if the tabletop was a piece of abstract art in need of immediate deciphering.

"He's running for reelection as mayor." Jill was watching Devon. "His version of progress is giving our town away to the hydroelectric company. Nobody wants that monstrosity looming over the town and flooding everything upstream."

"Barry wouldn't know progress if he slept with it," Devon said lightly. There was a tightness in his jaw that suggested he might actually care. A lot.

"His mother has him like a puppet on a string," Jill muttered. "She knows nothing about running a town, but he listens to everything she says, then takes it up a notch. Completely misguided."

"So tell me more about this," Olivia said. "He's the current mayor?"

Jill nodded. In the car, Devon had said something about this. A change in guard could impact things.

"When's the election?"

"A week from Monday."

"In nine days?" Olivia stared at them both. "Nine?" No wonder they were in a panic. But if this Barry Lunn fellow gave the town away to companies, maybe she stood a chance. Other than the fact that he planned to bulldoze and flood the areas where the most valerian grew. But still…she might be able to cut a deal with him. It wasn't beyond the realm of possibility. But it was still a long shot, seeing as her needs conflicted with the dam's and this valerian wasn't officially registered as rare or endangered, just more difficult to find in large quantities, by the sounds of it.

"He's planning on hustling the dam approval through in the first week of his new term," Devon said. "He tried to get it done before the end of this current one, but I convinced the council to wait, that we needed more reports."

"And?"

"And I managed to win an extra four weeks."

She turned to Devon, hands clenching. She didn't *have* four weeks. It was already the second to last Saturday before the Monday election. After that, hello hydroelectric dam.

"Don't blame me," he said lightly, reading her mind. "I've been trying to get in touch with you for weeks."

All those unreturned calls. She'd ignored them, assuming…well, she'd assumed the worst.

Time to sort out some backup plans. She turned to Jill who was fussing with her ponytail. "How common is this strain? Outside of the meadow?" These plants had to love more than one little mountain location.

"I—I'm not sure," Jill said. "I've only seen it around here and there. Nothing like in the meadow."

"Can you ask the elders?"

"Blueberry Springs is receptive to Carrington Cosmetics," Devon interjected quickly. "And land is cheap here."

"What happens if Mr. Lunn doesn't win? No dam?"

She was going to need to meet him and the other candidates if this valerian was all it was touted to be.

"The dam will go through only if Barry wins," Devon said firmly.

"Great. Who are the other candidates for office?"

He glanced at Jill again, sharing that meaningful look that made Olivia want to smack them both for having secrets. Then he gripped the back of his neck and peeked at Olivia through his lashes. "Just me."

Devon? Running for mayor?

She stared at him, then blinked. He was serious.

Not a joke. In fact, this was probably the most serious she'd seen him all day. Funny, since it made her feel like laughing.

"So," she said, taking a slow breath, "you have to win if I want to preserve that meadow long enough to figure things out?"

"Pretty much."

There was no longer any "get in, get out," was there? She was stuck. With Devon. The one man she wanted to avoid.

Olivia sat back down, the wind rushing out of her sails.

She had a feeling this news changed everything, and wasn't sure if that was a good thing or if it was bad, bad, bad.

DEVON AND OLIVIA were both quiet as they headed back to his car. She was doing something on her phone, gnawing on her lower lip, relying on him to prevent her from bumping into lamp posts.

Things looked good with Carrington so far, but it didn't mean Devon could relax. Not yet. Especially seeing how Olivia had reacted to the news about him running for mayor. She didn't think much of it, that was obvious.

He stopped beside his car and Olivia came up alongside, studying him quizzically. She kept flicking her gaze across his face as if looking for cracks, hints, anything to prove he was a liar, that he had ulterior motives. That he'd suddenly burst out of his skin and reveal himself as an alien.

"I really can't see you as mayor."

"Thanks." That stung.

"You just don't..." Her gaze drifted over his chest, then over the rest of him. He tried to resist subtly flexing. He failed. "You're cavalier, unaffected by everything. Mary Alice called you a daredevil and you're dressed like you're going to go paint a house. That doesn't convey a mayor-like image, Devon."

She was still studying him.

"And here we were doing so well," he said drily, opening his car door. "No dead bodies or anything."

"Devon..." She gave him an unimpressed look, then sighed in exasperation as the wind brushed a strand of her fine blond hair across her cheek. She was disregarding him as well as the insult she'd just dished out, and it lit something inside him, releasing old hurt.

"I'm enough for the people of Blueberry

Springs, and dressing up won't change a thing." It sure hadn't convinced her family years ago. "People know me, know what I stand for." He pointed at himself, then her. "They're my family, not yours. This town accepts kind people even if they're imperfect."

Devon turned away, disgusted with the way he'd blown up, acting like he cared about Olivia and her opinion. He hadn't been enough for her and her family long ago, and having her standing in his town, talking to his friends, all the while looking down her nose at him? He didn't appreciate it one bit.

He didn't have to act and look like Olivia Carrington expected him to in order to help his town. He turned back to her. "I have heart, Olivia. Heart." He thumped his chest.

She blinked twice. He was certain her eyes were welling up.

"Are you...?" She was struggling not to cry, which was wholly unfair. She was the one who'd shot the first arrow.

He didn't know what to do. He wasn't taking back his words, but he sure wasn't going to comfort her, either.

He shoved a hand in his hair and she slowly composed her features, turning brisk and professional even though the quaver in her voice told the truth. "Do you have a hotel recommendation? I don't see any rated hotels on my travel app." She waved her phone in the air, squinting at the screen while she sniffed and fanned her eyes. "I think I'm allergic to something." She sniffed and blinked again. "I can't get cell service."

"It's better on the other side of the street," he said grudgingly. "The mountains block the signal on this side."

She slipped her phone into her purse with a sigh so full of resignation he'd expect it from a prisoner of war, not her. Once again, her walls were firmly in place when she looked up.

"We're obviously going to have to figure out how to work together without killing each other or wrecking each other's lives in the process."

He nodded once in acknowledgment, moving around to his side of the car. Then he snapped his head up, attention back on Olivia. "Wait...you're staying in town?"

"Vintra is coming tomorrow morning to check out the plants, so there's no point in me driving all the way back, just to return first thing."

"Oh, right. Well, I'll find you something then."

Devon gave his sister a feeble wave as she headed in the opposite direction with the day's deposits from her café. Mandy sent him a curious look, but didn't come over to chat. He bet her place was crazy busy with the music festival currently going on and serenading the sleepy town from a few blocks away. Tomorrow night a band he'd been waiting to see would be playing, and he hoped this valerian business didn't interfere with him using his ticket to the sold-out show.

"Still on the clock?" Logan Stone murmured, walking past them.

"Please," Devon replied, putting one foot in the car. "Let's go," he said to Olivia. He really didn't want her discovering that he'd hired someone to protect her. She'd argue that she didn't need it and he'd feel foolish trying to explain that she was probably right. Plus it would make it seem as though the town was more dangerous than it was.

And it might look like he cared.

Well, he cared. But not in a possessive I-want-you kind of way. The town needed a deal, needed her company, and he'd do whatever he had to in order to make it happen. And if that meant keeping protesters at bay so she could do her thing, well then...so be it.

Plus knowing that Logan Stone was hanging around would remind Devon to behave—basically, not push Olivia to the point of her marching out of town. But she was so darn Miss Perfect and Cool and Sophisticated Business-woman. It made him want to poke at her with humor until he got far enough under her skin that the facade cracked and she had an outburst and revealed what she was really thinking and feeling. Or just acted like the fun person she'd been back in college. The woman he knew and understood.

Well, at least thought he had.

Olivia gave Logan a confused look, and before Devon could distract her, she'd stepped into the man's path, hand outstretched. "I'm Olivia Carrington, Ginger's friend. We haven't met, but I've heard a lot about you."

Logan halted, then engulfed her dainty hand in his, his Australian accent thick. "Lovely to meet you."

"We should get going," Devon said.

"How's Ginger?" Olivia asked, ignoring him.

"Fine." Logan gave a brief nod.

"And your daughter, Annabelle?"

"Also fine."

"I'm in town for a few days. I'll have to look them up." Olivia was warm, friendly—more so than with Devon, and he was reminded of how easy it was to hang out with her when she didn't have a solid brick wall raised between them.

Logan gave Devon a meaningful glance and began directing Olivia toward the car, suddenly a bit more open and chatty. "I'll let her know you're around. You're at the same number? I'll get her to text you." He smiled and opened the door for her.

As he did so, Awesome Dog popped out to greet them. The dog backed away from Logan, but the big man was fast for his size and scooped him up, giving his ears a good rub before passing him to Olivia, who'd settled in the passenger seat.

"Guard dog?" Logan smirked at Devon over the roof of the car.

Devon shrugged, noticing that behind Logan a few protesters were walking in their direction, chatting, signs idle at their sides.

"Mr. Right is very protective," Olivia said from inside the car, petting the dog.

The two men shared amused looks. "Mr. Right?" Devon said, as Logan shut Olivia's door. Talk about being burned in love, to name a scraggy, stinky mutt Mr. Right.

No. Wait. Devon's humor died. That name might be because of him.

He climbed into the car and started the engine. Logan patted the roof and dust sifted down from the ceiling. He'd have to ask Logan not to do that again.

Olivia sneezed as Devon pulled away from the curb, doing a U-turn in the middle of Main so as to avoid the protesters, who might begin an impromptu demonstration.

"Logan is so..." Olivia searched for the right word to describe him. "So..." Her smile had turned into a frown. "He's...nice."

"Yeah, nice." The man had worked some sort of secret, special ops security detail before marrying Ginger. He was likely the most deadly person either of them had ever met. Devon supposed if you were being polite you could call that...nice.

He turned down a side street before circling back toward the highway, where two of the hotels were located. "Let's find you and Awesome Dog—" There was no way on earth that he could refer to the mutt as Mr. Right, as he was fairly certain that would result in an automatic loss of his manhood. "—a place to crash. I'm sure you have a lot of calls to make." He reached over to give her a playful nudge. "And let Luke know you haven't run off with your ex despite what Mary Alice has predicted."

Olivia looked up from her phone, her expression stern, her cheeks pink. Not amused.

He was smarter than to poke at her. But despite it all he found himself smiling, flexing his biceps and waggling his eyebrows. "I swim twice a week. I'm quite the catch. I can see why he might worry."

Never mind that where the two of them were concerned with each other, Devon may as well be a monk.

Again, ship sailed. Plundered. Sunk.

Done. Over.

But teasing her was so much fun.

"Luke swims three times a week." She swiped a finger through the dust on the passenger side of the dash. "You need to get this thing detailed."

"And pay more for cleaning than it's worth? Nah."

She let out a long-suffering sigh. "These pants are dry clean only."

He glanced at her outfit. The pants fit her beautifully, enhancing every curve he'd once had the honor of exploring. "They're nice pants."

She blushed and crossed her arms. "A hotel, please?"

"Good plan, since we both know neither of us would survive you crashing with me."

OLIVIA WAS SPENDING the night at Devon's.

Her ex.

The man who had barely stopped flirting and poking at her since she'd arrived in town, taking off his shirt, not-so-subtly flexing his muscles here and there throughout the day, and intentionally trying to worm his way under her skin.

What had she done in a past life to deserve any of that?

Never mind. She knew what she'd done and it was all in this lifetime. She'd shut him out, kept a massive secret from her closest ally—her sister—shamed and embarrassed her parents, and more.

"You're absolutely certain there's nowhere?" she repeated. Devon had driven her around the small town from hotel to motel to bed-and-breakfast. Nothing. Every last spot was filled up, thanks to the local music festival.

There was nowhere.

Absolutely nowhere.

Panic was welling up inside her and she felt as though she was about to go under.

"What about Ginger!" Olivia cried. She began scrolling through her phone for her number. Anything but walk into the cute little house in front of her —Devon's home. It felt too…personal. Too intimate.

"She lives in a glorified storeroom above Veils and Vows."

"That's fine."

"It has no doors and is literally a storeroom stuffed with boxes." Devon looked pained. "You'd be lucky to score an air mattress or an armchair."

Olivia sighed.

Spending the day with Devon? Fine enough. It

was oddly familiar, yet uncomfortable to suddenly be in his life, at his side all day while they dodged the past and all the words they wanted to say. But having to socialize until bedtime? Share meals? Sleep on the other side of the wall from each other? Not fine. Not fine at all.

"I have a guest room with a door and everything," Devon said. "If Luke's okay with you staying here."

"He doesn't run my life." He was barely even a boyfriend, compared to how things had been between her and Devon. But he *would* be bothered by her staying with Devon. How twisted was that? Luke was ready to pop the question, but the two of them hadn't been intimate in over five months.

Why was that?

Because they were more friends than anything else, and it felt like they should just get on with it, already, and marry to make their parents happy, since they were in their thirties and nobody else had come along to claim them.

Olivia massaged her temples. Too many problems to think about right now.

It was early enough in the day that she could drive all the way back to the retreat, then return in the morning. However, staying in town made so much more sense—especially with Vintra being a morning person. He'd practically be here before she was out of bed.

She was being silly. She was mature enough to sleep in Devon's guest room. In fact, *not* staying with him would suggest that she wasn't over him. And she was. Had been for years.

"My sister's then?" Devon suggested. "She has a couch."

She was *not* sleeping on a stranger's couch.

"Fine." Devon's tone was curt as he read her expression. "*I'll* crash on her couch. You stay in my guest room and borrow a T-shirt or something to sleep in."

"Devon," she said with a sigh. "We're being ridiculous. We're both adults and I'm sure we can survive sharing a house. Plus wouldn't you staying somewhere else give the gossips too much to run with?" She raised an eyebrow and went to open her car door, planning to march into his house. But the inside handle was gone. Right. It was now somewhere helpful, like on the floor of the backseat.

"And would you buy a new car already?" She was trapped in here, inhaling the same manly cologne she'd convinced him to buy eons ago. Why was he still wearing it? It was yummy, but seriously. There were hundreds of scents out there and this one was laden with memories she really didn't want filling her head before she slept in his home—

even though there was no need to wear his T-shirt to bed seeing as her sister had stuffed a few just-in-case items into an overnight bag for her as well as a bag of Mr. Right's food. Smart woman. She'd have to be sure to thank her later.

Devon rubbed the bare spot on the dash. "I can't get rid of my Honda. It's sentimental."

"How can it be sentimental? It's an inanimate object."

"I meant I am. In the backseat I lost my—"

"Oh!" She sputtered. "Don't say it!" She definitely did not need visions of her still-attractive ex-boyfriend who smelled like something she'd love to…no. Just no.

He grinned. The man had a way of getting under her skin in a way no other person on earth did. She wanted to simultaneously laugh at his insane ribbing while stuffing a pillow against his face.

"And would you let me out, please?" She folded her arms across her chest, giving him a glare she didn't quite feel. He was already melting her walls as if they were made of ice and not stone. If she let him in, she was certain it would be game over for the both of them.

"Roll down the window and open your door from the outside. And you can stay here as long as you don't snore or eat all my yogurt," he said, reading something on his phone. His seemed completely unfazed by the fact that she was being held hostage in a rusted old tin can and would be sleeping under the same small roof as him.

She fiddled with the spot where the handle was supposed to hook into the door, and broke a nail instead. She let out an "ow" and sucked on the tender, wounded finger. "You know...your go-with-the-flow mentality is rubbing me raw, like a cheap leather sandal."

"Nice. I like sandals," he said absently.

The urge to make him feel something—anything—was strong. He seemed so unaffected, so removed from the turmoil roiling inside her, ready to burst out. She wanted him to feel as much as she did, but she also knew she needed to play nice and not ruin everything.

"I think Blueberry Springs is a very nice town."

He slowly looked up, his face emotionless.

All right. She'd try harder.

"I'm sorry for earlier," she said gently, trying to make up for her jab about him not looking like a mayor. He didn't, but she hadn't needed to say it. "I'm sure Blueberry Springs knows what you stand for and there's no need to..." She looked him over. He was sexy, that was for sure. But too darn casual for a candidate. "...dress up." He would look amazing and professional in a suit and a fresh haircut. People would definitely take that seriously.

She waited for him to apologize for the smarting, veiled dig he'd made about her family not accepting good people if they didn't look and act just so.

"That's right," he said.

"And…you care about people. I'm sure that really shines through when you're campaigning."

He nodded and scratched his ear before going back to reading his phone, his jaw flexing.

She leaned back in the seat. How were they going to survive sharing a roof when they could barely manage a conversation?

Try harder. Be helpful.

"If we're going to work together maybe I could help. I've spent years in PR and I—"

He opened his door and got out, slamming it shut with more vigor than a man should if he was keeping the ancient machine around for sentimental reasons.

She leaned back in the seat. Okay, so maybe she could have handled that better.

But she hadn't.

Kind of like their breakup.

CHAPTER 4

*D*evon let himself back into his house after his early morning run. He normally took Sunday off, but after a night of tossing and turning due to his questions and doubts about the project, as well as Olivia's statements about his image, he'd been ready for nothing but the sounds of his footfalls to fill his head. That and a little distance from the woman whose subtle perfume had filled his house, bringing back unwanted memories of how his bed would smell like her after a night together.

He didn't trust her. He didn't want her close.

So even though it had been before 6:00 a.m. when he'd gone for his run, he'd already called all the accommodations in town asking about any fresh vacancies—leaving messages at the places where the sensible staff were still asleep—in case

Olivia had to spend another night in Blueberry Springs.

There were no vacancies, but she was now on every possible waiting list.

Back from his run with Copter, he tiptoed past Olivia's room, relieved when Awesome Dog didn't make a peep. Devon's mind, which had managed to quiet around mile four, started to stir again. He'd played nice last night, but wasn't sure he could keep that act up for much longer.

You're never going to win the election.

You don't convey the right image. People don't take you seriously.

That had been the gist of her words, even though they hadn't been quite that pointed.

He didn't have to be überserious for people to know what he stood for. Blueberry Springs's citizens knew him, trusted him. Unlike her. She didn't trust him and the feeling was mutual.

He'd made a mistake bringing her here. Because what if he didn't win? Not only would he have egg on his face, but it meant Barry Lunn could swing in and cut some type of side deal with Carrington, one that would *hurt* the town instead of help it. Devon had no control over what Olivia decided to do and she'd choose her family, the company, her image, over him and what he wanted or needed.

Proven fact.

He rummaged through his closet with more energy than was required to find a pair of clean jeans. He tossed them on his bed, then ditched his damp shirt and turned to find something long-sleeved. He planned to help Olivia's scientists in any way they needed today, which meant he could be spending most of the day messing around out in nature.

He noted Copter's ears perking before he heard the sound of someone behind him. He turned, spotting Olivia in his doorway, wearing a delicate nightie made from sin. Her brown eyes were open wide and, with trembling hands, had a canister of hair spray aimed straight at his face. Since she was a good seven feet away, he turned back to his closet, choosing a pair of socks while nudging Awesome Dog away from his sweaty legs.

"Are you planning to do my hair for me?" he asked Olivia.

"I thought you'd left."

"I came back. I have a way of doing that."

He didn't want to turn around again, didn't want to see what she had worn all night long while sprawled out, warm and soft, in his guest bed.

"I thought you were an intruder."

"I run in the mornings." His gaze, as much as he tried to school it, kept darting to her frilly little nightie. It was a short, short dress that showed off her killer legs and dipped low over her tanned skin, bunching up with a little ribbon above her rounded breasts. Delectable. And it was sending a pounding signal to his groin, impossible to ignore.

They stared at each other for a moment, taking each other in, heat pulsing in the air around them.

"Why aren't you wearing a shirt?" she asked. She was eyeing his seminude state like a hungry dog after a juicy steak.

Okay, maybe not quite like that, but the thought of her eye being irresistibly drawn to him shored up his ego. Unfortunately, she had the manners to resist the powers of his man chest. Some women seemed to have unjustified strength in that department.

He ran a hand over his bare flesh. "Because I live here and this is my bedroom. Shirts are optional." He raised his eyebrows while allowing a meaningful gaze to drift down her sleeping attire, feeling the heat of longing ratchet up between them. Why did she choose to wear that number while crashing at her ex-boyfriend's? Was there something he wasn't picking up from her body language or tone? Because that garment definitely sent opposing signals.

Not that he'd ever go there again. They were from different worlds and she'd proved to him loud and clear that what he had to offer was nowhere near enough for her, that if she was having a family it wouldn't include him.

She let out a snort and crossed her arms, enhancing her cleavage. "I'm not going around shirtless."

"Your choice." He shrugged, allowing his gaze to drift south of her neckline once again, enjoying the view greatly. "I recommend something warmer than that if you're helping your scientist today." She seemed frozen in place, so he hooked his thumbs in his running shorts as though preparing to drop them. "If you like the show, there'll be another at bedtime. I'm here all week."

He grinned as she bolted from the doorway, the two dogs following in joyful pursuit.

Maybe it wouldn't be so bad if she got stuck here for an extra night, after all.

WHOA. Olivia sagged against the closed door of Devon's guest room, clinging to her can of hair spray. What on earth had that flash of heat been about? She was *not* attracted to Devon Adam Mattson. Nope. No way. He hadn't trusted her to take charge of their relationship, their lives, and make the big decisions that impacted the both of them. He'd believed their idyllic, make-believe dream world could continue to exist even when cold, hard, unforgiving realities were staring them right in the face, forcing them to grow up.

Married? Babies?

She'd been twenty. They'd been in school.

She'd need a man with a plan, not a dream. Because how could she have finished off her semester while suffering horrible morning sickness? Let alone complete her degree with a baby when Devon planned to return home before the due date? She couldn't just have a child and step off into an unfamiliar world, pick up an elusive career designing wedding gowns when she had no experience, no...

Olivia sighed, shaking her head. She'd wanted him to trust her, to support her need to be with her family. She'd wanted a man who was bigger than the two of them combined, not a dreamer.

Oh, but seeing his bare, sculpted chest with that streak of dark hair leading to the waistband of his shorts made her remember each and every way he'd proved his manhood during their good times. Yes, she'd considered his bare chest moments ago, but it wasn't because she wanted it pressed against hers, warm and moving. It was because it was... right there. Taunting her with its distracting rippled form.

She shook her head. Obviously, her body and

heart weren't on talking terms, as her body cared not one bit about how much pain they'd brought each other in the past.

But how he'd just stood there, buff and strong, with hunger and longing burning in his gaze, practically baiting her as heated flashes arced between them... If he could go there, to a place of longing, after everything they'd been through, well...it was just proof that he hadn't cared as deeply as she'd thought he had. Otherwise he wouldn't be able to put it all aside so easily and look as though he wanted to devour her.

Why was she even thinking about him? It didn't matter. She was wiser now, and despite his gaze, knew she wasn't stupid or forgetful enough to venture down that path again.

But what a fool she was to have stood there like a doofus in the negligee her sister had jokingly selected last Valentine's Day—then packed on her behalf—gleefully assuring Olivia it would bring a hungry look to any man's eyes. Well, Emma had been right. It had done that to a hot-blooded ex named Devon. Olivia had packed the nightie for her retreat, thinking she might use it to kick-start a relationship with Luke again, but now she was running from his impending proposal.

No, not running.

Just...taking time to think. Making sure they

did things the right way while she took care of company projects. Nothing more.

Pulling herself together, she searched her small suitcase for something appropriate to wear while wandering through mountain meadows. Knit sweater, casual slacks, hiking boots. Right. She definitely hadn't brought anything like that to the five-star retreat and definitely didn't have anything like that in her overnight bag.

Slipping into a lavender lace bra that did wonders for her cleavage, along with a pair of barely there panties, she felt slightly uncomfortable for donning something so sexy in her ex-boyfriend's little man cave. The guest room served double duty as a home office, its walls blue, the black futon matching a small desk. One wall was covered in running bibs, medals and photos, some even from his car racing days.

In a lot of ways his life looked exactly as he'd planned it. Kind of like hers did.

But if this was what she'd planned, why did it feel as though a piece was missing?

She reorganized her suitcase. It was just the project bugging her. Once she had it under way, with a launch date, she'd feel better, she was sure.

Shaking off her thoughts once again, Olivia slipped into a square-necked dress that fit her curves, ending just above the knee. She managed to get the zipper halfway up, but without her zipper-helper from home that basically allowed her to reach the unreachable, she found herself stuck. She sucked in and stretched, her cheeks heating with the effort. She tried reaching with the opposite arm. Not happening.

Emma had recently tried to convince Olivia to join yoga as part of her recent "earthy" kick that had her not only drinking weird juices and smoothies, but also abandoning makeup unless she was going into the office. At the moment Olivia regretted skipping out on an activity that may have given her the flexibility to get the zipper's job done.

She fell onto the futon and groaned.

No. No, no, no!

Today was off to a really crappy start.

Get in. Get out, she reminded herself. Right. She could do that. Unless, of course, it was this dress.

She slipped on a pair of her prettiest heels, collected her purse and the suit jacket she planned to wear over the still-open dress, and went to beg Devon for help. Thankfully, he was now dressed—his typical attire of jeans and cotton shirt sporting a logo from a long-ago race. Definitely not giving the impression of a serious candidate. She found herself wishing he'd accept her help, because just a few minor tweaks would make a huge impact and give him an edge he was currently neglecting.

He looked up, handing her a cup of coffee.

Black.

She accepted the cup, then set it down. She placed her jacket and purse on the wide island and turned, revealing her half-exposed back. She swept her long curls over her shoulder so they'd be out of the way, and using a curt voice so Devon wouldn't get any ideas, said, "Zip me up."

They were both adults. They'd seen more of each other than this.

She didn't feel a tug on the zipper. "Devon?"

She heard him grumble under his breath before the metal teeth started grabbing as he jerked the fastener up to the nape of her neck.

Not meeting his eyes and hating the way she felt her cheeks heating, she turned, picking up the cup. "Do you have cream and sugar?"

Wordlessly, Devon passed her a bowl from the cupboard. The sugar had hardened in the shape of the dish and all he had was skim milk.

Better than nothing.

Her eyes flashed to Devon's in silent horror as realization set in. If she didn't make it out of town tonight and no openings came up in the local hotels…he was going to have to help her disrobe tonight.

Nope. No way. She'd rather cut her way out of

the pricey garment than feel the heat of his hands against her back once again.

"When does Vintra arrive?" Devon asked, after clearing his throat and looking uncomfortable—almost as though he'd just had the same realization about her dress.

"About an hour."

His eyebrows lifted in surprise.

"He's an early riser, hence my desire to stay in town." She sniffed the air. "Something smells good."

Devon leaped into action, opening a small, cylindrical appliance on the counter. He plated something and waved it in her direction, not meeting her eyes. "Breakfast sandwich?"

She scooted up onto one of the tall stools lining her side of the kitchen island. "I didn't know you cooked."

"This isn't cooking."

She took a bite of the hot English muffin, egg and cheese meal with some sort of sauce. It was delicious. But she wasn't going to tell him that. His ego was already large enough without her adding to it.

"You cook and your house is homier and better kept than your car." In other words, at some point he'd had a serious woman in his life. Feminine touches sprinkled the decor, giving it a cozy feel, and she really didn't think Devon was the type to think of placing marathon bibs in shadow boxes. He was much more likely to shove them all in a drawer somewhere.

In this house, she could almost picture him as a husband, a father.

An unexpected spear of regret ripped through her.

"Was that a compliment?" he asked, while stocking the appliance for another sandwich.

"Take it as you will."

In her purse her phone buzzed with an incoming call. She fished it out and checked the caller ID: Luke. She sent him to voice mail, sipping her coffee. Luke could wait. Right now she had a bothered Devon on her hands. It was subtle, but she knew him well enough to sense it could become a significant problem. They may have dated for only a few months, but it had been intense and they'd become incredibly close in that short time.

So what was it that was bugging him? Her dress? No, his mood had started in his car yesterday. He really hadn't like her comment about him not looking like a real mayor.

That and having her in his house.

But was it more than that?

Was it about the valerian? What if he was having second thoughts about a deal with Carrington? Maybe hers was one of several companies he was wooing. She wasn't the only one trying to hone in on the all-natural market.

He seemed desperate enough to ditch her if a better offer came along, and their decade-ago parting had been unpleasant enough that he definitely didn't owe her anything.

Her dog, having finished the breakfast she'd set up for him in the guest room, trotted in, placing himself at Devon's feet. Mr. Right liked hardly anyone but her, but apparently even he was fallible when it came to Devon's charm.

Join the party.

A smokejumper's helicopter passed by overhead and Mr. Right trembled beside Devon, who reached down to pet him.

Olivia set her cup down, lining it up with her plate as though arranging a place setting. She needed to protect the company in case Devon and the town were accepting other offers.

"I'd like to sign a first right of refusal agreement between Carrington and the town and county for access to the local strain of valerian," she said. "One that provides rights to test and snoop around, no matter who the current mayor is or where we need to go. With the exception of environmentally sensitive areas, of course. I'd like at least a year of discovery access—even if the dam washes away the currently best known source." She picked up her phone, mentally composing all the things she'd need to outline in an email to the company lawyers. It was shortly after seven and a Sunday, but she figured they could have an agreement by the afternoon, crossing one more worry off her list. "Anything beyond discovery we'll take from there."

When Devon didn't reply she took a moment to study him.

"I can take care of that," he said finally, sitting down one stool over from her. The heat that had surged between them in the bedroom was gone and she breathed in relief. It was all about the business again. "I'd like to add a clause that if Carrington needs to hire, rent or lease anything, they do so locally wherever possible."

"Fine." Labor was likely cheaper here, anyway.

The tension that had been riding in Devon's shoulders slowly dissipated, making him look more like the man she used to know. He reached out to shake her hand, sending a current of warmth all the way up past her elbow and down to her core as he locked his sunny blue eyes on hers. He was still the hottest man she'd ever met, and when he looked at her in that special way of his it made her feel taller, seen, cared for.

Which was ridiculous. He was just...nice. Happy to make a deal. That was all.

It certainly wasn't personal.

DEVON WAS BUOYANT. A deal. Olivia was serious about the valerian, about Blueberry Springs. As soon as they were done with breakfast, he would talk to John Abcott, the local lawyer, about getting an agreement whipped up. Then he'd finally, officially have a little something in his back pocket to take to voters. True, it didn't solve much. It didn't save the meadow or anything like that, but it showed that he was serious about his campaign promises. He would help Blueberry Springs grow and prosper, while preserving what its citizens loved most.

Only eight full days until next Monday's election. He could do this. He could beat Barry. The man was a schmuck who kept running for mayor because it made his eighty-year-old domineering mother proud to have her son in charge of the town—and the pay was good—not because he actually knew what he was doing or cared to learn.

But still, Olivia's implication that Devon didn't have what it took to win ate at him.

Was she right?

He turned to study her. She was just about finished with her breakfast sandwich and had a tiny piece of melted cheese stuck to her full bottom lip. She'd be bothered if he didn't tell her.

"What?" she asked. She flipped her phone over, checking the screen before placing it facedown again.

He brushed the spot on his face where she had the cheese and she quickly patted the area clean.

"Who do I need from Carrington to sign the agreement?" he asked. He'd have to figure out how to contact them, get them to sign right away, so he could start using his mini coup as part of his campaign.

"My lawyers will take care of all of that, as well as arrange for the mayor to sign."

No way. Barry could take it over, mess it up, shoot it all down.

"I have the authority to sign," Devon said, which was mostly true, seeing as a majority of the agreement would fall under his department's authority. "Wait...*your* lawyers?"

She looked at him over her cup, as innocent as pie. A cream pie angled at his face. "Yes."

"No. We'll use the lawyer here in town. Less bias."

"And yours isn't biased?"

"Yours are going to cover your butt while exploiting ours."

"And your lawyer won't do that for you? If not, maybe you should find a new one."

Devon slung his nylon backpack over his shoulder, resisting the urge to push his hand through his hair in frustration. It felt like she was calling him down again. "My lawyer will take care of drafting the agreement. Yours are welcome to suggest additions or changes after that. Where are we meeting Vintra?"

"He says he's running late, and that bag isn't helping your image, Mr. Mayor."

She just couldn't resist poking at him, pointing out his shortfalls, illustrating how he wasn't enough and never would be.

"I like this bag, and the people in town appreciate me for who I currently am." He placed his hands on his hips. If she thought she could turn him into one of those pretty men with the fancy everything that made them look "just so" she could just think again. Blueberry Springs wasn't the city.

"I'm sure the town likes your youthful, affable, cavalier self just fine."

That felt like an insult. Yes, he was pretty sure it was one. Except she was sucking in a smile, enjoying herself as he reacted to her words.

"You don't think I'm mature enough for this job, do you?"

She stood, the height of her sexy heels making

her almost as tall as him. Almost. "I'll have something for you and your lawyer to sign by this afternoon."

He didn't back away when she came closer, in a showdown. The heat from her body was warming, radiating from her chest. A chest he knew was covered in pale purple lacy—nope. Don't think about it. That zipper...it had practically burned his fingers.

Still thinking about it.

He met those warm brown eyes that were full of determination—just like he was. He replied, "And I'll have something even better for you by noon."

OLIVIA SAT in her car outside the bridal store Veils and Vows. Her friend Ginger had taken it over from her grandmother fairly recently, and Olivia was hoping her old college roommate could help ground her, settle her. She didn't want to talk about the past, though, just something simple, like Ginger's recent marriage and new store. Something to take her mind off Devon and the conflicting emotions roaring through her.

One minute she'd wanted to lick his pecs and the next she'd wanted to make the man feel something—anything. React. Prove she wasn't the only one struggling with their past.

She'd informed him she had a few errands to run before the two of them were to meet up with Vintra in the meadow. And as a result of her needing to be able to keep Devon in the loop, she now had his cell number in her phone, and wasn't sure how she felt about that. Immediate access to a man she didn't want in her life. And that highway went both ways.

She shook off her apprehension and finished the call with her lawyers—telling them she needed the agreement urgently.

She'd show Devon. There was no way he was coming up with a draft in this sleepy little town before late tomorrow. She was the adult with the plan —that was her role. She wasn't going to depend on him. She had to take charge.

A woman came up to her car and rapped on the window. Olivia felt dread seep through her. Mary Alice.

At least it wasn't that young man in camo she'd seen stroll by twice, watching her with more than passing interest. The town was full of oddballs and she'd be happy to skip out of town as soon as she had Carrington's best interests secured.

"So you spent the night at Devon's?" Mary Alice said, as soon as Olivia's window was down a few inches. Mr. Right was already barking at the woman. "Has he put a ring on your finger yet?"

Olivia felt her jaw drop before she schooled it back into place. "Everywhere in town is booked. Do you know of any vacancies?"

"Other than in Devon's bed?" the woman asked with a massive grin. She caught Olivia's expression and burst out laughing, reaching through the window to pat her shoulder. Mr. Right bounced into Olivia's lap, trying to force himself between her and the gossip. Olivia shushed him and sent him into the backseat.

"Oh, sweetie," Mary Alice said good-naturedly, "you don't get teased much, do you? But it's obvious you two have something."

Olivia shook her head. They most definitely did *not* have something, unless it was the urge to bury each other under ten feet of sand. Okay, maybe that was a little extreme. It was probably more like five feet.

But there was nothing to speculate about other than how much Devon must work out to have such a ripped chest. And those big, strong arms. She'd always been such a sucker for them. That and his sense of humor and the way he made the whole world seem like a fun place when he was around.

She cleared her throat. "Do you know where I can purchase a briefcase?"

Maybe he'd allow her to give him a small makeover. Just to take that immature edge off, so he'd look like a real contender and not someone playacting at adulthood. Because the more she thought about it, the more she realized her only hope for securing the meadow of valerian long enough to figure out if it was what she needed was to ensure Devon won the mayoral seat. And that meant she had to intervene a teeny bit.

"In town?" Mary Alice gazed up the street as though mentally checking each store. "Now that's a good question. That's not something we need much here in the mountains." She glanced at Olivia's Chanel dress.

The woman reached down the front of her own floral blouse, digging around until she pulled out what looked like a tin of mints. Olivia leaned away from the window, trying not to appear bothered by her lack of boundaries.

"Mint?" the woman asked, offering the tin.

"No, no thank you." She glanced at Ginger's store. The lights were on even though the sign said Closed Sundays. "Is she open today?"

"Not officially, but she's often in there puttering about."

"Great." Olivia left her windows open an inch or two for her dog and got out of the car. She shivered as the cool mountain air hit her, and pulled her suit jacket tighter around her. It was a chilly morning, the town still shadowed by the nearby peaks, some of which were still snowy despite it being mid-June.

Mary Alice made a comment about how a classic A-line gown would suit Olivia, and led her to the bridal store. As Olivia opened the door she paused, taking in the rows upon rows of gleaming, pristine gowns as their flood of possible happily ever after dreams rushed over her. New lives. Love and expectations. It all hit her like a surprise punch to the gut and she couldn't figure out why. She stood in the doorway, not quite inside and not quite out.

She wanted a happily ever after. She did. But she couldn't see Luke as the man waiting for her at the end of the aisle. Why was that? What was wrong with her? He was perfect and her parents adored him.

Mary Alice gave her an encouraging shove forward, breaking her stream of thoughts.

"Hello?" Olivia called, realizing with relief that Mary Alice had abandoned her. The last thing she needed was the town gossip trying to outfit her in bridal wear.

A woman with auburn curls was adjusting a gorgeous trumpet-skirted gown in a raised display case. She turned, a friendly smile in place.

"Good morning. I'm not officially open except for brides with emergen—Olivia!" Ginger's eyes lit up and she bounded over, arms open, squealing in delight. She engulfed Olivia in a hug. "I can't believe it's you! Logan said you were in town, but he was being so secretive." She rolled her eyes and waved a hand through the air, and Olivia caught the flash of her new ring. "He's so overprotective and acts like everything is such a big drama. How are you?"

Olivia snagged her friend's hand to take in the spiral Celtic knot design of her ring. The knots were woven in around emeralds and diamonds, possibly the most unique piece of jewelry she'd ever seen and totally Ginger.

"It's beautiful. Where did you two meet?"

It was girlie-girl chat time.

"At this amazing corporate retreat. I learned so much about the wedding industry, matched up three couples *and* came home with a husband. It was a good week."

"A week?" Olivia asked in disbelief. She hadn't heard that part of the story. Then again, she knew that when love struck, it moved like lightning, quick and with an unrelenting force.

I'll bet the two of you are married by the end of the month.

Ha! And pigs were going to learn to fly, too.

"A week," Ginger confirmed with a grin. "He's got the best accent in the world."

Olivia laughed, thinking back to college parties. It felt so long ago, but some things never changed —such as Ginger's taste in men. "So was it a whirl-wind fairy tale romance?"

Ginger beamed, just about hugging herself with happiness. "Totally. And his adopted daughter is fantastic. She's fitting in here in town which is a big relief since Annabelle has special needs and was doing really well back in Indigo Bay." She paused, her expression expectant. "So? I heard Carrington Cosmetics brings you to Blueberry Springs?"

"We're looking into the local strain of valerian."

"Those stinky white flowers?"

"Those are the ones."

"Ew."

Olivia laughed at her friend's honest reaction. There was no pretense with Ginger and never had been. She was a bubbly open book. "They don't stink once you boil them. Then they actually come in quite handy."

"Come! Let's talk. We have so much to catch up on." She began ushering Olivia toward the back of the store, through rows of gowns whispering promises of a lifetime of love and devotion as they passed.

"Don't you have to work? I mean—"

"Oh, shush! How often do I get to see you in the flesh? Two or three times a decade?"

Ginger led her into a room littered with boxes. There was a beautiful antique table with four chairs set in a corner, at odds with the dented green fridge and stained laundry sink that sat behind it. Really, the room was like a massive, disorganized, disjointed kitchen slash storeroom.

Her friend began moving boxes out of the way so she could get clean cups from a cupboard. She then poured two coffees, placing them on the table along with cream and sugar.

Ah, she was a good friend. No awful coffee served straight up around here.

"So I heard Devon tracked you down?" Ginger had a sly look in her eye. She'd been there when everything had collapsed between them and knew how destroyed Olivia had been, and how she'd even transferred universities, unable to face seeing him again. Ginger was one of the very few people who knew everything, but that didn't mean Olivia wanted to go anywhere near memory lane just because she happened to be in the same town as Devon and sort of working together temporarily.

"Let's not talk about all that. Tell me about you. You own the store now?"

Out of habit, Olivia idly flipped over a dog-eared wedding magazine that sat on the table, checking the back cover. Not surprisingly, it held a Carrington Cosmetics ad. And naturally, being from a few years ago, it featured her and her younger sister—the faces of Carrington. Somehow seeing herself in glossy ads still caught her by surprise, but this time it was more what she saw in her photographed expression that took her off guard. Emma was as vibrant and full of life as ever, but Olivia looked…resigned at best.

She quickly turned the magazine over again. That couldn't have been right. She loved her family, loved being part of the company, and the sense of independence and power her current job instilled in her. There was no sense of resignation there. The picture must have been taken by that awful photographer Vaughn, who'd always complained that Olivia wasn't skinny enough, and had tried to hide her behind Emma whenever possible.

Ginger was chatting animatedly about the challenges and excitement of taking over her grandmother's store, and she struggled to focus. At one point Olivia had hoped to get a minor in fashion design, with her business degree a backup. She'd been silly to think she could design something as intricate and fussy as wedding dresses for a living, that she could step away from her family and her real life to be with someone as carefree as Devon.

To work in a small town, in a store exactly like this one.

"Are you okay?" Ginger asked softly.

"Yes, of course. I'm sorry." She gave her friend a reassuring smile and sipped her coffee.

She'd definitely taken the right path with her life. She most definitely could not see herself working in a place like this. All those dresses and fabric. The pretty lace and pearl beads just waiting to be sewn onto a gown to make a perfect finishing touch for a glowing bride. That wasn't something she could do.

"So?" Ginger was asking. She was leaning forward, her green eyes wide.

Olivia had lost track of the conversation again. "I'm sorry. I have a lot on my mind." And coming in here had been a big error. She couldn't *not* think about Devon with Ginger around.

"It must be hard being around him." Ginger's hand rested over hers in sympathy. Her friend knew exactly where Olivia's thoughts had strayed.

She slipped her hand away, grasping her coffee and taking a sip. She hated that the emotions she was struggling with were so obvious. "It's fine. We've both moved on." Her cup was empty and she carefully set it down, keeping both hands wrapped around it.

"Have you?" Ginger prodded gently. "You're both still single."

"It's fine. Really. Just because he didn't trust me and my plan, and thought his little dream world would be enough for us to—" She caught herself. She smoothed her dress over her thighs and tried for a smile. "Sorry. That's all in the past. I'm in PR now and developing a new line of cosmetics. Let's talk about our lives, our futures."

Ginger nodded. "How long are you in town?"

"Maybe another night. It depends how today goes."

"Did you find a place to stay? The town's pretty booked up with the music festival."

"Um, yes."

Ginger gave her a sidelong look. They'd lived together for a few years while undergrads and she apparently still knew Olivia well.

"I stayed with Devon." She felt herself blushing, images of Devon's chest floating through her mind, that spark that had surged and flashed between them starting to burn through her again.

Ginger was trying her best not to grin.

"Not like that!" Olivia protested. Her cheeks were flaming at the thought.

"That must have been awkward." Ginger was still trying to fight her smile. "I'd offer a place, but we basically live in a storeroom."

"It's fine," she said quickly, eager to change the subject. She'd definitely made a mistake coming here. How could she not expect Ginger to want to talk about Devon and the fact that the two of them were currently joined at the hip after ignoring each other's existence for years?

"He's matured a lot since dropping out of school," Ginger said quietly. "Don't let his joking demeanor fool you."

Olivia's guard went up. "He can't fool me."

"According to Jill it sounds like you need him to win the election to save the valerian."

Olivia sighed. Nothing was a secret in Blueberry Springs.

"Anything I can do to help? Maybe marry him off to someone so he looks less aloof and like a fancy-free bachelor? I had a jilted bride returning her gown the other day. She might be game." Ginger took a sip of her coffee, mischievousness making the corners of her lips curve upward.

I'll bet the two of you are married by the end of the month.

"Wait…" Olivia paused, focusing on something Ginger had said. "He dropped out of college?" Devon had had only had a few months left until graduation when they'd broken up.

"After you two…you know." Ginger gave a small

shoulder lift. "One day he was gone. Packed his bags and…" She made a whooshing sound.

But a degree was required for his current position as the town's property manager. How did he get the job if he hadn't completed his final semester?

And why had he left? Had he been more affected by their breakup and the miscarriage than he'd let on?

Why did that possibility feel as though it changed everything, when she knew it truly didn't? There had to be another reason why he'd left.

Ginger was chatting, laughing here and there, and Olivia smiled where it felt right. But she needed space and time to think, to breathe.

Her phone buzzed with an incoming call and she excused herself to take it. It was Vintra. He was just about at the meadow's parking lot. Not good. She needed to be out there in case the protesters returned and gave him grief. Plus they needed Devon out there with them. But before she could tell him to hold off, their connection cut out. She tried to call him back, with no luck.

"The cell service in this town is so frustrating," Olivia complained as she tried to contact him again.

"Tell me about it," Ginger commiserated. "The internet isn't much better. But we have hunky men." She smiled, leading Olivia back through the store. "You know, I always thought you'd end up designing dresses for this place."

So had Olivia. But back then she'd been a fool in love and under the spell of endless, unrealistic possibilities.

"If you ever want to change careers, I'll give you a shot," Ginger declared, her expression open and happy.

Olivia gave her friend a smile that didn't feel real. "That was just a hobby."

"Do you still sew?"

She shook her head.

"Well, nuts. I had a whole thing planned out in my mind where we'd have our careers here, with our little ones ripping around the store…oh, well." She gave Olivia a hug. "But if you do get bored while in town and still remember how to pull out a few stitches, my seamstress is tied up with a family emergency and I have a gown in desperate need of alterations. The poor bride lost ten pounds."

"I have plenty on the go, but thank you for thinking of me."

Ginger studied Olivia for a second, then in a flash threw her arms around her for another hug. "You guys can win this."

"Huh? Sorry?"

"The election. All he needs is a wife, and his

image will improve. That'll help him win and you can get whatever you need for your product line."

"A wife?" Olivia's voice choked with disbelief. Ginger wasn't kidding this time.

"You're one of the best PR people on the planet. Tell me there isn't a more expedient, surefire way to make Devon look like someone capable of running the town. Right now he screams carefree, daredevil bachelor. I was joking earlier, but honestly, there's nothing that would make him look more dull, steady and reliable than being married." Her grin grew. "Unless you're a newlywed like me, of course. Then things are pretty exciting. Steamy, too."

"How would Devon marrying someone in less than a week make him look stable and not whimsical, immature or carefree?"

"No, no," Ginger laughed. "You're thinking too far ahead. For now he only needs someone from his past to step up as his fiancée."

CHAPTER 5

*D*evon, still waiting to hear from Olivia and Vintra, stood outside his brother's latest business purchase—Benny's restaurant. Ethan had owned it for about a year and was already looking to sell it. However, Devon didn't think it was merely because of the current tax issue. It was more that his brother's web design company was taking off and he was burning both ends of the candle, running both places as well as Mandy's old catering company, which Ethan had also bought out a while back. There seemed to be something about Mattsons biting off more than they could chew when it came to life and jobs.

Devon adjusted his clipboard, looking up the street. The Sunday morning foot traffic was greater than usual due to the music festival and he was catching quite a few people to sign his petitions. One to stop the dam, another to convince the town to release funds to replace the roof on the seniors' continuing care wing. The center was attached to the hospital but under the authority of the town, and Barry Lunn believed a bucket of tar would fix the fact that the roof was currently threatening to fall in on Blueberry Springs's aging population. Not cool. Barry also seemed to think the dam would create jobs, but seeing the deal Barry had hashed out? There would be one new job. One.

The sun began to warm Devon as it reflected off the restaurant's main bank of windows and he pushed up his shirtsleeves. In the distance the horizon was fringed with dark clouds, suggesting rainfall after lunch. He hoped Vintra would hurry up and arrive before then.

Bored, he waited for more people to walk by. So, so bored.

His mind wandered, curious as to the errands Olivia had scooted off to take care of. He'd bet anything she was working with her lawyers over the phone. Little did she know John Abcott was already modifying a boilerplate agreement from the town's files and would have it ready by ten. Yes, that was right. One hour from now. Why? Because John was a good guy who was feeling on top of his game thanks to some running tips Devon had shared with him just that morning.

Uh-huh. Devon was connected. Not bad for a small-town dude.

He rubbed his eyes. He hadn't slept well last night and needed to stay focused. Fighting with Olivia wouldn't win him the election. Fulfilling his campaign promises ahead of time would. Getting a roof on the center. Stopping the dam. Getting a deal with Carrington. Those were the things that mattered. He would make a difference right here in his cotton shirt and jeans. He was a good fit for the job—despite what Olivia thought about his appearance. People liked him and that was what mattered. Right?

Devon smiled and snagged another group walking by, his little speech about why they should sign his petitions rolling off his tongue.

He thanked them for signing before stopping Mary Alice and her sister, Liz—two of the town's biggest gossips and two of the biggest holdouts. If he got them on side it would definitely help his campaign. People listened to the sisters, who had some serious social sway.

"Hi, ladies. Want to add your signatures to my petition? I'll take off my shirt if you do." He flexed a biceps for them, his playful shtick feeling tired even to him.

"Hon, you're too young for us and that dam is good business," Mary Alice said kindly.

Liz nodded. She'd done an article for the paper last week stating how the dam would create jobs and help with taxes. All misinformation thanks to Mayor Lunn.

"Once it's built you know it only needs one person to come check on it every few days? It won't create new jobs."

"When it's being built it will," Liz retorted, patting her tight gray curls. "And Barry said the power company will provide the town with royalties that will reduce our taxes."

"Unfortunately, that's not in the current proposed contract." Because the one they were quoting was the one Barry had tossed out when the power company had started playing hardball with numbers. Small compromises that were standard in negotiations and would have had little impact on the company's bottom line, but would have helped Blueberry Springs tremendously. But the negotiations—which Devon performed fairly frequently as part of his job—had made Barry nervous, and he'd removed Devon from the project and undersold Blueberry Springs, setting the town back hundreds of thousands of dollars and making the power company negotiators grin in delight.

That was when Devon had thrown his hat in the ring for the mayoral election.

"Building the dam won't create local jobs because we don't have qualified workers in town," Devon said easily. He had the facts on his side with this one and Liz was a smart lady. She'd put two and two together.

Liz tipped up her chin. "The workers that come here will stay in hotels and eat in our restaurants. Barry has it all sorted out, Devon. Maybe you should talk to him. He's currently being a good son and taking his mother to Betty's salon. She runs one out of her home now, you know."

He caught the dig. He and his mother weren't close, but he didn't think suddenly taking her to the salon would win him any votes.

He shook his head at the ludicrousness of it all and continued the argument. "Under Lunn's proposed deal the slated contractor will bring his own mobile accommodations and dining car to help reduce employment costs. This dam will—"

"Nicola!" Spotting her pregnant niece, Liz turned away, elbowing Devon aside.

In frustration, he clutched his clipboard by his side. What was it about Barry that made everyone believe him? It was starting to feel as though it was just Devon and the crazy protesters who understood the full impact of this dam.

You don't convey the right image. People don't take you seriously.

Man, the doubts in his head were starting to sound a lot like Olivia. He checked his phone for a message from her. All he had was one from Logan saying he was still tailing Olivia and that she'd gone to see Ginger and was now heading out again. Did that mean Vintra had arrived? And if he had, why hadn't Olivia called him to come meet up?

Nicola Samuels-Haber gave her aunts hugs the best she could, being over eight months pregnant with twins, before turning to Devon and giving him a squeeze, too. "Who was the pretty city lady you had out in the meadow yesterday?"

"They'll be married by the end of the month, I predict," Mary Alice boasted, finger raised in the air. Nicola's eyes sparkled with intrigue.

"Her? At my side through thick and thin?" Devon nearly laughed. "I might as well rub myself all over with raw meat and go lie down outside a bear's cave."

Mary Alice laughed. "Sounds like true love to me."

"Mary Alice, I'm winning that bet," Liz replied. "Devon will never settle down."

"Who is she?" Nicola asked.

"She's in charge of public relations for Carrington Cosmetics," Liz informed her before

Devon could speak. "Maybe she'll relate with this member of the public, huh?" She elbowed Devon, while sharing a conspiratorial wink with her sister.

"Don't you ladies have some matchmaking to do with people who are actually interested in that sort of stuff?" He turned to Nicola and gestured down the street, where her music festival was set to start filling the town with noise again within an hour or two. "And shouldn't you be resting?" Since she moved to here to take over the town planner position a year and a half ago, she'd barely stopped moving. She'd ditched the 'boring' parts of her job, creating a new duty for herself as the town's social convenor, creating new festivals and events to keep the residents occupied and spending money. But most of all, staying in town instead of moving to the city.

Which was great. Except for the employment issue. It was hard to stay in a town where there were few jobs.

Mary Alice added for Nicola's benefit, "They used to date."

"You and the PR lady?" Nicola asked, eyes on Devon.

Devon glared at Mary Alice. Nobody in town had known about Olivia and their past other than their mutual friend Ginger. Nobody. Not even Nicola—although she'd once figured out some of the more private details about his past love life. But she still didn't know who exactly that woman had been—well, until now.

Sure, friends and family had known he'd been serious about someone in college the Christmas before he'd returned home for good. But with the tragedy that had brought him home before completing his degree—Ethan's paralyzing car accident—everyone had had a bigger focus than what had happened to Devon's recent girlfriend. Nobody had questioned his moods, and in a lot of ways, it had been easier that way. Leaving his abruptly failing marks and all that related to Olivia behind like it had never happened.

And that's where it needed to stay. In the past. Behind him.

"Oh! The baby kicked. I hope it didn't get its sibling in the eye." Nicola giggled, grabbing Devon's hand and pressing it against her moving midriff. Whoa! That was a strong kick with a little foot right *there*. Right under his palm, like the kid was telling him not to touch its mother. Devon yanked his hand back in alarm.

Nicola gave him a look, taking his discomfort the wrong way. He wasn't sure what it was exactly about her knowing glance, but it smarted. The babies weren't about him and his own failed past, but he could tell that was exactly what Nicola was thinking.

The good thing was that he trusted her never to whisper his secrets to a soul. Plus even she didn't how many nights he'd spent awake, wondering if, had he done something differently, Olivia would have been able to carry their baby to term. If he'd caused her less stress? If he'd insisted he be there by her side instead of letting her shove him out of her life? If he would have noticed something was wrong and gotten her to the hospital in time?

If, if, if.

"Oh, another good one," Nicola said.

"Whoa there, don't have your offspring on Main Street, please," he teased, as her belly continued to move as though filled with alien life forms. "You ever see the movie *Alien*? Because I think we're about to have a reenactment here."

Nicola frowned and gave him a playful smack.

"Oh, Devon," Liz said with exaggerated impatience. She pulled on her sister's elbow and the two of them continued down the street, Devon's petitions still unsigned.

"You know…" Nicola's eyes shone with humor. "…if you and that pretty woman—"

Devon didn't want to hear it. He began singing the Ray Orbison song "Pretty Woman," trying not to think about how Olivia's nightie had just popped up in his mind like a freaking jack-in-the-box. You thought you were okay, that it was going to stay in the box, and then BOOM! There it was, scaring the crap out of you again.

Except it wasn't scary. Not at all. And that one little garment was going to be the subject of many, many fantasies where he'd end up hating himself afterward.

"If you *did* start dating that would look really good during the election. It's not a half-bad idea. Your image could use the boost of having a proper, spiffy woman on your arm."

He stopped singing. "Spiffy?"

"A relationship speaks to a certain stability you don't normally broadcast. Add in your possible deal and you'll look like the man to bring progress to Blueberry Springs."

"Is there really something wrong with my image?" He pretended to inspect his reflection in the window behind them. "Because last I checked, we are most definitely *not* getting together and my image is *fine*."

If he kept talking to people today he was going to need to go for another jog in order to clear his head.

"You know, that's not a bad idea," a voice from behind them stated. Barry Lunn. Great. That made this conversation better. "Working on your image. Although a week is a very short period of time and that woman seems a *bit* out of your league."

"Funny," Devon said, giving Nicola a look that said "Thanks, see what you've done now?"

"I'd hate to see you waste money on a makeover that won't be enough to win you my job," Barry added, hoisting his khakis.

"Maybe she's not here to give me a makeover," Devon said, then noticed how Barry stilled, considering the implications of his words.

Then it was gone. He was back to affable Barry as he smiled at Nicola. "You're looking radiant. How are those babies doing?"

Nicola smiled back at Barry, giving Devon a little "See? Some people have manners" kind of look. She was obviously pleased that someone was asking about her alien life forms. But wasn't she supposed to just spew that pregnancy stuff if it was important when they met up, like the good friend she was?

"Just fine, thanks," she said. "A bit of heartburn, but only twenty-four days to go!"

"Antacids helped my wife when she was pregnant. Have you found them to be effective?"

Nicola plucked a jumbo-sized container of them from her purse and waved it at him. "Total lifesavers."

"That's a good girl," he said, his tone slightly patronizing.

Nicola, big, tough, independent woman that she was, ate it up. No threats to crunch his nuts with her fist or anything. Seriously? What was happening?

"You have charm, Barry," Devon said with a reluctant sigh.

The man smoothed a hand over his bald spot and said with a shrug, "The townsfolk like what they know and they know me. A good man who takes care of his family. No offense, old boy."

"Oh, none taken," he said lightly. "But I think you'll be a little surprised come next Monday."

Barry laughed good-naturedly, proving himself to be completely affable and harmless. It was easy to see why people thought he was okay. Even though Devon knew he wasn't.

"I like you, Devon. You never say die. You might be a tad misguided, but it'll serve you well in life." He gave Devon a pat on the back. "Why don't you come over for a beer tonight? We'll shoot some pool and I'll give you some tips on running for mayor—for next time."

"I'm busy, but thanks." Devon's head felt as if it was about to explode.

"Then here it is, no sugarcoating." Barry lowered his voice, adjusting the collar of his button-down shirt. "You're a great guy and the town likes you just fine, but you're not quite the right fit for mayor. You're everyone's friend, you make them laugh, you help them out. I'd let you marry my daughter if I had one. But you're just not quite..."

Enough. He wasn't enough.

Barry gave up on finding the right word and clapped a hand on Devon's shoulder, giving it a squeeze. "It's a tough spot to be in." Another shoulder squeeze. "Maybe next time, kid."

Devon, furious with the man's assessment, turned to Nicola, expecting her to leap to his defense. Instead she gave a small smile of agreement.

He closed his eyes.

How come everything kept pointing to Olivia being right?

OLIVIA WAS IN THE MEADOW, feeling anxious for not managing to get hold of Devon to let him know that Vintra had arrived. In her eagerness to catch up with her lead scientist, she'd found herself out of cellular range before she could leave a full message, telling Devon they were meeting. She'd started to, but the call had disconnected and she had no idea if his voice mail had saved it or not.

She was tempted to drive back into town to try

again, but was afraid the protesters might show up and harass Vintra. If she was here she could at least try and talk some sense into them, explaining that Carrington was on their side.

She leaned against her car, donning a wide-brimmed sunhat from the Cayenne's trunk while watching Vintra zigzag through the rolling grasses and flowers as he collected plant samples. Every once in a while he'd open a tube, do some sort of smearing thing on a clipboard or shake a canister. He was completely in his element, his joy obvious, and she wondered if she ever looked like that while working on a PR issue. Somehow, she doubted it. But it was a stable, fitting career for her, the more creative member of the family.

She reached down to brush a few specks of gravel dust from the pink bow on her left shoe, then realized the right was dusty, too. She fussed a bit before straightening, then tucked her hair into a low bun. It was hot, the air strangely still, and she found herself wishing for a breeze as she neatly folded her suit jacket, setting it on the hood of her car.

A young family walked by, smiling and sharing hellos. Olivia watched them hike toward a mountain path that undoubtedly ended at a scenic aquamarine lake, their preschool-aged daughter skipping along, stopping occasionally to point out an insect or an interesting rock. Her older brother, about ten, regarded his sister with a seriousness that left an odd lump in Olivia's throat.

Their own child would have turned ten this year.

She knew she was torturing herself, wondering what their child might have been like. If it had been a girl, would she have been graceful like Olivia's sister Emma? Or if a boy, would he find himself drawn toward being devilishly free like Devon? Who would their child have resembled the most?

Olivia closed her eyes and rolled her neck.

Being around Devon brought out too many things she'd rather keep buried.

Once the family was gone, she tottered to the edge of the gravel lot and cupped her hands around her mouth, calling to Vintra, "How's it going?"

If she was lucky, she'd be able to leave town tonight.

Vintra was too far away to hear her, but she noticed the picturesque, wispy wedding-veil-lace clouds above him were dissolving as larger clouds began to form. She sighed and went back to her car, wondering if she dared zip into town to call Devon.

If Ginger was right and all he needed was a fiancée to pull his image out of the wringer, maybe Jill could step into the role. Just until after the election. They'd once dated, so nobody would find it odd for them to suddenly take up again. Plus Jill was charming and sweet and would make a steady, calm presence at his side.

However, the idea of Jill as a fake fiancée made Olivia uncomfortable, and she tapped her long pink nails against her car. Why the issue? Was it because Jill was too sweet for a PR ruse, and would likely give it all away in a tearful confession before the election? She wasn't a hardened Carrington. They knew what they wanted and went for it with relentless precision.

At least that's what her father always said. Personally, Olivia rarely found herself pursuing anything long into the night like he and her sister often did, unless it was bingeing on episodes of reality fashion shows. Those sucked her in like nobody's business, but that probably didn't fall under her father's umbrella of pursuit of world domination or getting ahead.

Maybe there was another way to help Devon, kind of like a makeover show. That could be fun. She closed her eyes, letting her imagination run. What would Devon as a mayor look like? Sound like?

Well, first of all, he needed a better haircut. That would yank him up the absolutely-stunning scale from a seven and a half to a nine, just like that.

Add a few sharp pieces to his wardrobe to give him a subtle, but much needed overhaul. Garments selected with more care than a running event free T-shirt.

A briefcase he couldn't sling over his shoulder, wrinkling his shirt. She still needed to track one down. Maybe add in a tie lacking a cartoon character. A nice deep blue to bring out his laughing eyes.

Slacks that hung off those narrow hips and tight butt. Paired with a belt. Fine Italian leather with shoes to match. He'd get votes simply for looking so hot and grown-up.

"You smiling?" Vintra asked, depositing a bucketful of testing materials beside his Toyota.

"Enjoying the sun," she said quickly, adjusting the brim of her hat.

"Uh-huh," he said, his voice full of disbelief.

Olivia cleared her throat before asking pleasantly, "Do you need a hat?" The sun had been beating down on his thick black hair and he had to be warm.

"Not yours," he said with a smile.

"Oh, come on. It would look so cute on you."

He laughed at her teasing and reached out to pet Mr. Right, but the dog hopped back into

Olivia's car. "Did I tell you Emma was talking about coming out to see you?"

"Really?" That was odd.

Something had to be up. Although having Emma out here to help would be nice. She was a details gal. She was also a typical younger sibling where the family's rules rarely applied to her, but she managed to skirt that issue by having the three *P*s down pat. Proper, polite, pretty. Exactly what the Carringtons expected from their daughters. But because Emma had smarts, she knew how to balance letting her moxie shine full and bright while still toeing the line to keep Mom and Dad happy. In other words, she had the potential to really stir up emotions between Olivia and Devon, while acting completely innocent.

Probably best to keep her out of town.

"I like what I'm finding so far," Vintra said. "It is a different strain."

"Really? For sure?" Hope buoyed inside her.

"Yup." He picked up a few more bins and buckets, as well as a shovel, and headed back into the meadow.

"Don't make that shovel obvious to the hikers!" she called after him. Or protesters. Definitely not to protesters. She glanced around. The parking lot was full of cars, but no people.

She relaxed a tad and lifted her phone,

checking for a signal. None. She probably had an email from her lawyers by now. Beyond her phone she noticed someone sitting in a black vehicle on the other side of the lot, with several cars between them. From his profile the man looked a lot like Logan Stone.

She stepped closer to take a better look and her cell rang, making her jump. She froze so she wouldn't lose the signal, not even daring to check caller ID as she slowly lifted the phone to her ear.

"Hello, Olivia Carrington," she said crisply.

"Princess, how are things going? Is Vintra there yet?" The connection was tinny, with a slight delay that created an echo in the line, making her father sound light years away. "The lawyers said you requested access rights and first right of refusal? I tried to call you."

"The cell service is horrible here."

"I told you not to buy that phone. There are better ones on the market."

"I don't think it's the—"

"And run all agreements by me first. My money, my company," he said, repeating a mantra he'd said nearly a thousand times. She'd once asked her late grandma to cross-stitch that on a throw pillow for her father. Her grandma had thought it was hilarious, but hadn't managed to find the time to complete it before she became ill. "I approved it, but next time I won't. I demand to be kept in the loop. On everything."

"Yes, Daddy. I'm sorry." It was *her* pet project and he'd said he was giving her full rein. Sure, he'd been looking over her shoulder the entire time, but she hadn't expected him to get twisted up about a simple agreement protecting them, which would cost nothing but a few hundred in lawyers' fees. Her monthly mani-pedis probably cost more. "Vintra's here."

"Will you be back in time for tonight's supper?"

Olivia was surprised by her knee-jerk reaction to say no. The idea of dressing up and having meaningless chitchat felt stifling right now, and so far from where she wanted to be at the moment, even though she craved some distance from Devon. She hedged, saying, "It depends on the results." A breeze picked up and Olivia held on to her floppy hat, reveling in the cool air against her skin.

"Well, tell Vintra to hurry it up, I want my daughter back for dinner. Luke needs to talk to you."

She sucked in a slow breath. Luke. She'd forgotten to call him back. How had she managed that? It was like she was in a whole different world out here, barely connected to anything back in her real life.

Was that the Devon Effect impacting her once again?

"Tell him I'm fine."

Her father said something she didn't catch. She moved her head slightly, hoping it would improve the reception.

"Hello? Are you still there?"

"I *said* I didn't send you off to complete your business degree at Harvard so you could ignore your job helping the company with its image. I can't see any reason why you need to stay for testing. You're in PR, not product development, and this retreat needs you."

"I think it would be wise for me to be here," she said weakly. Yesterday's little flare-up with the protesters seemed like a one-off, but it had managed to make a few news articles, which had been collected by her assistant in her morning task of rounding up any mention of Carrington's in the media. She was guessing the tidbit hadn't made it as far as her father yet or he'd be demanding she return to the retreat immediately.

Which was ridiculous. She was in her thirties. She'd proved herself. She should be allowed to feel as though she was truly in charge.

Her father was uncharacteristically silent.

"Are you still there? Because, Daddy, if Vintra's tests come back positive we could be in the running

135

for something really major for Carrington. We could change lives." She could actually back their products without that gnawing feeling in her gut as though she was lying to the world whenever she said Carrington Cosmetics couldn't be safer. Because their products could. Almost all products could.

"Change lives?" he asked.

"Change our market share, Daddy."

She could put her mark on a creation. Feel like she'd made a difference, even if it was a teeny one. Saving one woman from getting sick from their cosmetics would make it all worthwhile. Save one life. How many people could claim that?

"Our market share could be improved by a union between Carrington Cosmetics and Cohen Body Bliss," he said pointedly. "Try to be back for supper."

"Yes, Daddy." The line crackled.

"Pardon me?"

"Yes, Dad—"

"Give me the number where you're staying in case I need to get hold of you."

Olivia froze, then thought better of it and took a few steps back to where she'd been standing earlier, while saying, "Sorry, Daddy. I can't hear you. Are you still there?"

Nope. Lost him.

She should feel guilty about that.

Her father had always been protective, but had become overtly so after her breakup with Devon, taking charge of her life in a lot of ways. She could only imagine how bothered he'd be if he knew she'd stayed with Devon last night. In fact, if he knew just how big of a part Devon was playing in the deal she was potentially making…well, he wouldn't be very happy about that, either.

Clouds rolled overhead, feeling refreshing after the heat of the sun, and she put her sunhat in the car and stretched. People were hurrying back from their hikes as though late for something important. The music festival perhaps?

Vintra waved at her from far across the meadow, then cupped his hands around his mouth as he hollered something she couldn't make out. She closed the car doors, ensuring the windows were cracked enough for Mr. Right, and grumbling, maneuvered herself in her high heels to the edge of the lot to holler back. The wind had picked up, taking their words with it.

She gave up as he continued to beckon to her, and began the delicate process of tiptoeing across the soft ground in her heels. Cold air swept down from the mountains with surprising speed. She'd been too hot in her suit jacket a few minutes ago and now was wishing she hadn't left it on the hood of her car.

When she was within earshot of Vintra he asked, "Do we have permission to remove a plant? Like, can I dig up a few, roots and all?"

She lifted her phone to the sky, looking for a signal. None, of course.

"He didn't protest when I brought it up." She had no way of confirming permission with Devon, but they were under a time crunch. Surely he'd understand if they went ahead. "Go for it. I mentioned five to him, so that should be okay, and I'll take any heat if we dug in the wrong spot or something."

She felt a twinge of guilt about going ahead, but what else could she do?

Vintra stood, stretching his back. "This meadow is crazy populated with these flowers. You say it's going to be destroyed?"

She nodded.

He shook his head regretfully. "If we had more time we could harvest half the seeds to start in greenhouses, leaving the rest here for repopulation. Although splitting the plants and taking roots would be best."

"The proposed dam is going to sweep all this away before any seeds are ready. But maybe we could split the plants?" And put them where, exactly? She needed more time. She needed Devon to win the election, needed to preserve the meadow.

Maybe she could create a blend between the now Devon and a more mature Devon, so he'd look more like a real candidate. Did a mature Devon include a wife-to-be? Ginger's idea seemed crazy, but it could actually work. Nobody wanted a reckless bachelor in charge of their town. But a man settling down was a different matter.

"I want to do a lot more tests. Soil, DNA..." Vintra said. "There's got to be a reason this strain hasn't grown rampant across the continent."

"We're going to need a lot of these plants every year. Any ideas on how to guarantee supply?"

He leaned against his shovel. "Maybe set up a covered structure in a meadow like this one to work on some in the wild. Then test seeds in a climate-controlled greenhouse closer to the factories."

That would still make them dependent on Blueberry Springs. Everything kept bringing her back, tying her to Devon's hometown.

Not fair.

Vintra squatted beside a thick bunch of plants.

"I'll ask the lawyers to add a possible plant splitting clause to the agreement, assuming I ever get cell service again." She checked her phone once more. Nothing. She added the clause to her mental to-do list, along with returning Luke's call.

Vintra handed her a bucket and a shovel. "Looks like a rain shower's coming. Better get digging so we don't get drenched."

She glanced at her shoes with the pretty little toe bows, and with a shrug of resignation, tucked her phone away and ruined another pair of perfectly good heels.

OLIVIA WAS SOAKED through from the rain, muddy from head to toe, her shoes destroyed, her legs tired from struggling through the muck in her inappropriate footwear. If her sister saw her now she'd howl with laughter.

But what could she do? While out in the middle of the meadow the skies had opened up, turning the earth under her and Vintra into an instant quagmire. Olivia had fallen more than once on her way back to the car, the mud sucking at her feet with each step like a hungry monster.

All she wanted was a cup of creamy coffee and a hot shower. And fresh clothes. She glanced back to see how Vintra was doing. It looked as if he'd finished up and was on his way back to the almost-empty lot. In fact, there were only four cars left. Hers, Vintra's, the one she'd thought she'd seen Logan in earlier and a black sedan, idling behind her Cayenne.

Trouble, in other words. Was it her father coming to "rescue" her? Or was it something worse?

A man stepped from the sedan and raised an umbrella. He wore khakis and a button-down shirt. Mr. Right began barking inside her car, throwing himself against the glass.

Strike one for the man. Her dog despised him already.

"Barry Lunn," the man said, as she approached Vintra's car with two buckets containing valerian plants. "Mayor of Blueberry Springs." He put out his hand to shake hers, but seeing they were muddy, dropped his. He was full of smiles. Too many smiles.

"Pleasure to meet you. I'm Olivia Carrington with Carrington Cosmetics. It's a pleasure to be in Blueberry Springs. Such a pretty town you have here."

Barry Lunn smiled, oozing smarm and smugness. No wonder Devon didn't like him—and not just because he seemed to lack the manners to share his umbrella, something Devon would have done.

"You're working with Devon Mattson," Barry asked. "Is that correct?"

"He's brought me here, yes," she said, hoisting the plants into the Toyota's open trunk before slamming it closed. "I think Carrington and Blueberry Springs could become prosperous partners."

"You found what you came for then?" He seemed intrigued, but in a way that made her not trust him, and she wasn't sure why.

"Possibly. We're not sure yet," she said honestly. Vintra was 98 percent certain, but she'd rather hold her cards close to her chest for now.

Rain was dripping off her nose and she shivered from the chill. She moved to her own car, hoping to find an umbrella, since it would likely be too rude to do what she really wanted, which was to blow Barry off and destroy her fine leather seats with her wet self, pumping up the car's heat until she felt human again.

She wiped her hands on her dress and opened the door.

"Oh, where are my manners?" Barry asked, invading her personal space as he tried to share his umbrella at long last.

"It's fine. I have one." Olivia found her own umbrella, noting that the seats of her car were now wet from the windows she'd left cracked for her dog. She struggled to keep him in the car while closing the door again.

"Devon gave you permission to dig in the meadow?" Barry looked at her pointedly and she opened her umbrella toward him, forcing him back, before primly placing the shelter over her head. She felt better already.

"Yes, we're testing a few plants." She turned slightly, then, as if on second thought, added, "I'm sorry, did you need something or were you just coming to say hello?"

Barry gave her a smile she was certain he meant to be disarming. It likely worked on most people. People who didn't grow up around fakeness and hadn't developed a radar for it. It was one of the things she liked most about Ginger and Devon— they never did "fake." It wasn't even a possibility for them.

"Did Devon tell you a dam will be bulldozing, then flooding this meadow next week?" Barry's tone was light and she could tell he was trying to get her on his side, assuming Devon hadn't been straight-up with her.

Divide and conquer. It made her want to team up with Devon all the more.

"Yes, it's come to my attention. I was hoping to speak with you about that."

"The dam is already slated. Everything is in place and awaiting final approval."

"I understand." She paused, letting the silence grow between them, hoping he'd come up with a compromise that would suit them both. Because if he could do that, she'd have two eggs in her basket. Devon winning. Barry helping.

He gave a small shrug as if to say "What can I do?"

He was going to be a tough sell, that was for sure. But how could he not see that it was in his best interests to work with Carrington? What harm would it do to have another corporation helping Blueberry Springs with taxes and infrastructure costs?

"As mayor, I'm sure you're interested in working with companies that could help increase employment and tax revenue." She kept her tone light, inquiring and sweet, trying to worm her way into his good graces. "Carrington is a very—"

"Our town is doing fine, thank you. I hope Devon hasn't misled you into thinking we're in trouble." His tone was meant to be disarming, but all she heard was condescension.

She'd seen the business closing signs, tax sales and more. This wasn't a town that was thriving and she had a pretty good idea why.

Time for a different approach, figure out why

he was so set against Carrington. Was it her? Was it Devon? She guessed it was the latter, his direct competition for the mayoral seat.

"I like Devon's campaign platform. He really seems to care a lot about the town," Olivia murmured.

"Unfortunately, he's not the forerunner, and right now the town is chock-full of commitments to other companies. I'm sorry he's wasted your time, but there's no room for your business in Blueberry Springs. Maybe another year," Barry said, his voice low as though he was confiding, as though he actually cared enough to let her down easy. He tried to reach around her to open her car door for her.

She held her ground, anger starting a slow burn. "You know, I think he could take this election. He gives people hope. They know he's on their side and is willing to do whatever it takes to help."

Barry's kind expression grew hard.

Yeah, he was not someone she wanted to work with. At all.

Time to find out what he really thought, so she knew what they were up against.

She smiled innocently. "I'll bet if I gave him a few PR tips he could do really well. He does care about this town and that's one thing you can't dress up or fake."

"He's nothing but a kid. A bleeding heart."

"It's one of the things I like best about him, actually." And it was true. Despite all the things about him that drove her mad, he'd once been the most supportive, caring person in her life aside from her grandmother.

A car drove around Barry's, so slowly that Olivia glanced over. Logan, looking somber, was sizing them up. He stopped his vehicle and Barry moved to his own. As he bent to get in, he delivered his parting shot. "Your company isn't needed in Blueberry Springs, Miss Carrington."

He slammed the door and started his car, impatiently waving Logan's out of the way.

Olivia stood in the rain, hands clenched around her umbrella handle. There was no way she was ever going to work with Barry Lunn. And that meant she had only one hope—Devon Mattson as mayor, a man who didn't trust her.

CHAPTER 6

*D*evon did a double take from his spot under the barbershop's awning, where he was waiting out the rain. Olivia Carrington was hustling into Mandy's café looking like a wet dog. A wet, muddy dog and not at all like a put-together princess.

In fact, she looked like someone who'd been caught out in the rain somewhere, such as a meadow while digging up samples. Samples he was supposed to preapprove. And yes, he was okay with it, but he'd wanted to be there. Wanted to see the lay of the land with Olivia's scientist at her side, and make sure she didn't overstep her bounds or make a deal with someone else. Someone like Barry Lunn. Not that he thought Barry would be able to offer her anything with the dam coming through, but he wouldn't put it past the mayor to interfere, since it was obvious Devon was playing hardball in terms of opposing the dam now.

Curious, Devon held a clipboard over his head and raced through the puddles and the brisk rain. He slid into the café moments after Olivia and the man he assumed to be Vintra Badami.

"Find what you needed?" he asked.

Olivia whirled, her expression one of guilt.

Her hair, which she'd tangled into a loose bun at some point, was drenched, sending rivulets down her face. Her dress, which had been crisp and formfitting this morning, was now sagging and smeared with mud. Her feet completed the scraggly look with their mottled appearance, pink from the cold and brown from mud, with one of the bows missing from her sexy shoes. The only thing relatively clean and dry was her overpriced designer purse.

"Get chased by a bear?" he asked. Visions of her running from the local wildlife didn't leave him feeling as amused as he thought it would.

"There was no cell signal in the meadow."

She knew that from yesterday. "I thought we were working together."

Her chin tipped up. Her eyes filled with anger and determination. "We are."

"Then why did you go out there without calling me first?"

"I tried to leave a message."

"I didn't get one." He checked his phone to be sure. Yup. No messages from Olivia. Just from Logan, who said he'd seen Olivia speaking with Barry out in the meadow.

"What were you doing out there?" he asked.

"Getting samples. You said we could dig up five."

"Why did you meet with Barry?"

Olivia's eyes narrowed. "Are you spying on me?"

"Is there a reason why I should be?"

She glared at him. "You don't trust me, do you?"

"Is there a reason why I should believe you think we're a team, and have my back and not just your own? That you're not using me?"

"I am not using you any more than you're using me," she said hotly.

This was mutual—business. And not at all what he was referring to. She had used their relationship, his love, to make her parents hot and bothered over her dating a man who wasn't from their world. Devon had thought that what he and Olivia had was real, but when reality had come calling, she'd backed out, telling him that if he loved her he'd leave her alone. Forever. She hadn't even considered his marriage proposal or the possibility of them being a family. She'd withdrawn to the shelter provided by her parents, shutting Devon out, making him fear she'd keep their own child from him.

"I'm trying to do what's best for all of us," Olivia said with heat, "and you refuse to look at all the factors. You prefer to live in a dream world where everything just falls into place. That's not life, Devon. You have to make plans."

"I have plans. You just don't like them because sometimes they involved stepping into the unknown and trusting in something that's not quantifiable." He edged closer. "Like love. Not that you know what that is."

She gasped and swung back her hand as though she wanted to slap him. Vintra was watching them with a curious expression, and she slowly lowered her arm and straightened, her cool business demeanor falling into place over her anger.

"This is business, Devon. Nothing personal. Please remember that."

"That shouldn't be a problem." He made a point of giving her a cool, hard look, forcing himself to hold his breath so he wouldn't inhale her electrifying scent. "Maybe you should sign this before we go any further." He pulled the three-page document John had created for him from behind his petitions. It was slightly damp, but still legible. He tried not to act too smug as he presented the agreement.

Olivia looked surprised, adding to his feeling of satisfaction. That's right, he was the real deal even if he didn't dress like a Ken doll.

"That's wonderful," she said.

She smiled sweetly.

Uh-oh.

He handed her a pen.

She ignored the offer and tapped her phone's screen a few times. "I have one, as well."

Her lawyers worked Sundays, too? Poor little indentured slaves. Why wasn't Devon surprised?

She flipped the screen in his direction, her smile still sticky sweet. She had a confidence, a verve that heated his blood even as she challenged him, their anger at the ready like rattlesnakes preparing to strike. There was still so much emotion arcing between them that he found himself wanting to test it between the sheets, see where the raw energy took them.

She tipped her head to the side, still acting innocent. "And I added a few extra things since our last conversation. I hope you don't mind."

She was a royal pain in the butt, issuing a challenge with her eyes for him to try and one-up her. It made him want to kiss her, devour her.

Irrational. He'd never wanted to do that while playing hardball negotiating other town contracts before.

Because Olivia still has a hold on you, dummy. Despite the pain of the past, she'd hooked him hard and never let go. And like a fish on the line, he didn't know how to free himself.

"My document is longer?" he suggested hopefully, giving her a heated smile that used to melt her.

"Oh, Devon," she said, using a soft tone, her cheeks pinking. She was flirty, playing along. His body's heat level nudged toward the red zone. "It's not how big it is, it's how you use it." She handed him a stylus so he could sign her contract.

Her innuendo nearly knocked him over, he was so surprised. He eased closer, near enough that he caught the faint scent of her perfume mixed with rain. It was one he was certain would invade his mind long after she'd left. "Was that an innuendo, Miss Carrington?"

She smiled. Actually smiled. For real. She looked at him through lowered lashes, sucking in her cheeks as she fought it. She gave him a tiny, slightly hoity-toity shoulder lift that sent his blood pressure skyrocketing as it reassigned his body's energy somewhere below the belt.

He'd always loved their games.

He immediately stepped back.

No, he remembered that Olivia. The one who was playful and fun.

She was sexy. Really sexy.

And she had the power to break his heart, which nobody was ever doing again.

Ever.

Like she'd said, this was business. Nothing more.

The East Indian fellow beside Olivia spoke up. "Are you Devon?"

He nodded, half relieved and half annoyed by the interruption.

"I'm Vintra." He shook Devon's hand with enthusiasm. "I think we found exactly what we're looking for."

Olivia gave her scientist a dark look. So much for them playing it cool.

Devon grinned. He loved it when minions screwed up. "That's fantastic. Let's talk. But first, you two look cold. Let's get my sister to fill you with hot coffee—I'll wait in line if you want to get cleaned up in the washrooms. Just down that hall." He watched Olivia and Vintra go, still amazed at how muddy The Face of Carrington Cosmetics was. Even her perfect manicure was hidden under a layer of mud. Not at all like the woman he'd expected to see.

And it was unexpectedly sexy. She seemed so real. Fun. Carefree.

Not stuck up and perfect.

He reminded himself that she was simply excited about this line of cosmetics and finding the magical ingredient that pulled it all together. He found himself hoping the valerian would be exactly what she needed—not for the sake of Blueberry Springs, but for her.

Devon joined the line of customers waiting for snacks and drinks. It seemed half the tourists at the outdoor concert had come in for shelter, which meant Nicola must be freaking out over this little organizational blip. The good thing about mountain weather was that what blew in quickly often left just as fast, and they'd likely be out enjoying music again within the half hour. He sent Nicola a text saying as much, in case the transplanted city gal hadn't learned that mountain weather nuance yet.

No need for her to have her babies early due to preventable stress.

Devon turned, trying to locate Logan, who was still tailing Olivia. He scanned the café, then the street, from his vantage point. Logan had found a spot at the curb with his black car and was watching from there, the rain still pouring down.

They shared a nod before Devon turned back to the line.

It was nice having him tail Olivia, not just for her protection, but for the heads-up on what she was doing when he wasn't around.

Impatient with the lineup, Devon let himself behind the counter, certain his sister wouldn't mind him helping himself as he often did when the café was busy. He worked around her as well as Logan's daughter Annabelle who had Down syndrome and a definite knack for keeping things organized behind the counter despite Mandy's assistant—a guy with a management degree who couldn't find a job in his field—who frequently mixed up their system.

Times were tight, jobs scarce. Another thing Barry didn't seem eager to help fix.

Devon started a new pot of regular roast after he emptied it into cups for his guests, gently teasing Annabelle—who loved stripes—that polka dots were the best. She rolled her eyes at him with a smile, then proceeded to ignore him so she could straighten out the mixed up cutlery bin. Devon poured Mandy a lemonade when he heard the order, making himself useful until he saw Olivia return from washing up.

He paid for the coffee, leaving an extra ten dollars in the register even though he knew it drove his sister nuts having her till over when she tried to reconcile her accounts at the end of the day.

Smiling to himself, he carried brownies and coffee to the table Olivia was holding down. She was shaking from the cold and gnawing on her bottom lip—a sure sign something was on her mind.

"Here, drink this." He passed her one of the coffees, after dumping sugar and cream in it. Yes, he remembered how she took her coffee, and earlier had made a point of pretending that something like that hadn't been worth remembering. But now it felt less important to make that point and more important to show her he cared—was on her side so they could get along.

"Where did Vintra go?" He looked toward the washrooms, on the lookout for the man.

"A hotel room opened up so he went over to take it," she said.

"But what about you? You're soaked through." What kind of man took a room before the lady was accounted for? Make that a cold, wet woman who was your boss?

Olivia gulped her coffee and winced.

"I told him to take it. He has more tests he wants to run and needs a dry place to do that. Plus it's best if the samples are fresh. I'm sure another single will open up soon." She still had mud stuck in the crevices surrounding her nails, and her pink polish was chipped, he noted, as she cradled the cup as though wishing she could climb inside its warmth.

Devon looked outside at the sheets of rain, not wanting to reconsider his evaluation and assumptions about who Olivia had become. She was still a princess who would choose her family and their wishes over anyone else. Or at least him.

He sipped his coffee and tried to decide what to do with his cold, wet...whatever she was. Possible business associate? With the rain, another room might open up, but not before she got chilled to the bone.

"You need dry clothes and we need somewhere we can hash out which agreement we're going to sign." He pushed his chair back, collecting the three plates with Mandy's delicious whiskey-and-gumdrop brownies, and headed to the counter with them. He grabbed a bag, dumping the treats inside. Returning to the table, he collected Olivia, stopping when he saw protesters gather in the rain outside the café, voices raised.

They had to be kidding him. Was someone tipping them off every time he went somewhere with Olivia? A group of bored protesters picking on Olivia was the last thing he needed.

"Give me your keys," he said to Olivia. Her car was surely closer than his.

She folded her arms across her chest, glowering at him and his demand. "No."

"I *need* your keys."

She followed his gaze, her brow furrowing. From across the café Devon could see his sister frowning, wiping her hands on her ever-present apron as she came around the counter.

He cursed under his breath and grabbed Olivia's purse, opening it to free her car keys. Why did she refuse to listen to him?

Logan reached the café's doors, giving Devon a curt nod. It was go time.

Devon swiftly ushered a rigid Olivia past the big man, who acted like a human wall between them and the people shouting about her raping the land and digging up their meadow's flowers. Cameras flashed as she planted her feet and opened her mouth to set the protesters straight, and Devon all but picked her up, knowing that yelling at the protesters in front of the media would only make it worse. He needed the town to like her, needed her to help his case against Barry, not send Devon's campaign down in flames for being associated with someone who yelled at protesters.

"You have to let me fix this," Olivia said, struggling in his grip. "Just trust me."

"You're in my town now, Olivia. My rules. That means you're the one who has to trust *me*."

———

"THE PROTESTERS WEREN'T *in* the meadow!" Olivia argued, as Devon drove them back to his house in her little Cayenne, darting around corners like he was behind the wheel of one of his race cars. She should know—he'd taught her how to drive one. Those had been the most exhilarating days of her entire life and she'd never felt so alive. So out of character.

She trusted him to keep them safe as he drove, but knew his aggressive driving probably wasn't conveying the image they currently needed. Plus Mr. Right was sliding around in the back seat and getting excited. "And can you slow down? This isn't the movies. There are no bad guys chasing us."

Devon glanced in the rearview mirror and slowed the car while pushing a hand through his hair.

He needed a haircut. She shivered and aimed one of the car's heat vents at her torso.

"You should have seen that coming," he muttered.

She honestly didn't know how she could have

prevented that flare-up. It was almost as though the protesters were on the lookout for her now.

"I didn't do anything wrong," she said.

"Did you call them up? Is having them chase you around town some sort of publicity stunt?"

"No! And why are you so intent on making me a bad guy at every turn? Why do you keep assuming the worst of me?"

He'd asked her to trust him, but how could she when he didn't trust *her*?

"Why did you come to Carrington if you have so little trust in me and my integrity?"

He cut her a look.

"When have you ever proved I could rely on you? You pushed me away when we should have been a family, Olivia." His voice was low, shaky. "We should have supported each other, stood together, and you shut me out. You told me that if I loved you, I needed to leave you alone. Alone, Olivia. Who says that to someone they love, the father of their child?" He slammed the steering wheel hard enough that she worried the airbag would deploy.

"Devon…" She swallowed hard over the regrets, Mr. Right's little nose nudging at her elbow from his spot in the back seat. "I was scared."

"No, you didn't trust me. Didn't trust our love."

He shook his head as though frustrated with himself for voicing his hurt.

"I'm sorry, Devon." She focused on breathing, on not breaking apart.

"Are you? For which part? For giving me my walking papers and saying sayonara?" He gave an angry salute. "Or for letting me know that I'd never be enough for you? For our—"

"Stop! Okay?" She was shaking. Reminders from the past were storming around her, buffeting against her walls. She'd been so scared. She'd been twenty and trying to do the right thing. She'd been trying not to ruin Devon's life, his dreams. Trying not to humiliate and embarrass her family. Trying not to give up her own future, her life. How could she support a baby? How could she run off with a man she'd known only a few months? In the end, it didn't matter. She'd failed at all of it, not even being able to bring the baby safely into the world.

She'd regretted it all for so long, and the last thing she needed was him heaping his own hurt on top of her suffocating stack.

"You—"

"No." She held up a hand. "I don't need you marching in here and telling me all the ways I failed, pointing out all my imperfections. I'm perfectly aware of each and every way I've failed to live up to everyone's expectations, yours included."

The car filled with bitter silence.

Olivia lowered her voice, trying to control her emotions, hoping to patch up today's disaster so they could at least hang on to a business relationship. "In the meadow I stayed with Vintra in case the protesters came back. We couldn't both leave so I could make sure you'd received my message and reaffirm your consent. You'd already implied it. We're still under a time crunch and I did the best I could, Devon. Please believe me when I say I didn't mean to upset you or lead you to think I was doing things behind your back."

"Why were you talking to Barry?"

"Why were you spying on me?"

Devon's jaw tightened and he gripped the steering wheel harder.

"I don't believe it," she muttered. So much for rebuilding trust.

"Look me in the eye and tell me you haven't been considering working with Barry as a backup plan."

"He is the mayor, Devon. He's also a conceited, arrogant man who has no desire to make room for Carrington in Blueberry Springs. Which means that if you want to stop the dam and I want this valerian, we're stuck together."

She added gently, "It also means you need to

stop ushering me away like I'm a member of the royal family whenever protesters come along."

"I'm protecting you, preventing it from escalating." His brow was furrowed, his intention obviously kind and well-meaning.

"It makes me look guilty, and you by association. That's hardly what either of us needs." The muscle in his jaw bunched tighter as she continued, "Devon, I can handle myself. And if we can show the protesters we're on the same side, they could help us."

"It's not that easy, Olivia."

"Maybe it is."

Inside her purse, her phone rang. She ignored it. She'd bet anything it was her father wanting—no, *demanding*—to know what was going on in Blueberry Springs. She'd seen the cameras and hated to think what they'd captured and already distributed. Her with the earth's blood on her hands as she ran away in guilt. Well, that might be a little dramatic, but that was about how it felt at the moment.

Devon was silent for a long time. Finally, he said, "I can't see how this is going to work."

"Me neither." She sighed, feeling as though they'd crossed a bridge, had identified that they were up against steep odds, but were now at least on the same page. The let's-make-a-plan page.

"Maybe," he began carefully, "you need to go home."

She suppressed the chill that shuddered through her. "I what?" He was kicking her out of Blueberry Springs?

No, no, no.

Devon pulled up to his garage, silently getting out to open its overhead door, then drove the car in, hiding it inside as he closed them in the darkness. He opened her car door when she remained still, shocked by his level proposition.

He was rejecting her.

She'd screwed up and that was it. He was sending her back to where he thought she wanted to be—with her parents.

"I'll never be perfect, Devon, but throwing away the possibility of a deal is ridiculous."

"Maybe." He held out his hand to help her out of the car, his expression grim. "Come on, let's get you warmed up."

He looked like he might be serious. If he was, then she was about to lose everything.

She had to do something. She'd come too far, was too close to having it.

She clung to Devon's hand after she was free of the car, forcing him to look at her in the garage's dim light. "I'm trained for this." *Please trust me.*

"I have a lot at stake here, Olivia. And I don't

know if you got this or not, but this is my home. My people. My family."

"I have a lot at stake, too."

"Yeah, making more money," he said, turning to the door that led into the house. "Hardly the same thing."

Wordlessly, he disappeared inside, Mr. Right scrambling after him, barking a hello to Copter. Stung by Devon's impression of her intentions, Olivia followed, stopping in the entry. If she went any farther she'd leave a trail of mud. She heard the back door open and close as he let the dogs into the backyard, then the sound of him running a bath before he returned with what looked like a handmade blanket.

She shook her head. Yeah, she was cold, but so what? She'd warm up again. Probably even before she died. If she let him drape the exquisite afghan, likely knit by his grandmother or someone equally dear, over her she'd ruin it.

When she didn't accept the offering, Devon placed it over her shoulders despite her protest.

"You're cold."

"Not cold enough to ruin a handmade blanket."

He pulled the afghan tight under her chin, meeting her eyes. Her shivering stopped. "See? Immediate problem solved." His voice was low, patient, completely sexy.

"You're such a man."

"You used to like that about me."

His tone was lighter now, his solemn mood from earlier hidden. She wasn't sure if it was a good sign or not.

"Devon, we can do this. We can beat Barry."

"I'm running you a bath."

"Very thoughtful, but you're avoiding me."

"I'm thinking."

She knew he could be like her on things that mattered a great deal: stubborn. She needed to strike now, not once the cement around his mind had time to harden into concrete, making it immovable.

Her phone rang again as Devon went to shut off the bath water. She wrenched open her bag and answered with a curt, "What?"

"Ovvy?" It was Emma, using her childhood name. Her voice was small, which meant things were not good.

Olivia's problems faded away as she focused on her sister. She had the feeling this was not about her and the protesters making the news. It was something much worse.

"What? What is it?" And why was she miles and miles away from her right now? Yes, Emma was in her late twenties—almost thirty—but Olivia was, and always would be, her big sister, and would always feel the need to be at her side when she ran into trouble.

"You know how Grammy had that thing with her bone marrow?"

Olivia's legs lost the power to hold her up and she sagged to the floor, grateful that Devon was in the other room. "Yes," she whispered.

"The doctors called me with some test results."

"No," she whispered, her heart slamming in her rib cage.

"They...they think everything might be okay, that it's not bone cancer or anything scarier than a bone cyst or a lump, but I'm still scared. They found toxins like in Grammy. Our cosmetics are supposed to be safe, Ovvy, and I haven't used anything but Carrington."

Olivia shut her eyes, knowing this changed everything. Every. Thing.

The injustice of it, the unfairness, made her want to throw a rock through the front window of the family's office headquarters back in South Carolina, as well as scream and yell about why they hadn't made a change sooner. How could they care more about their bottom line than the health and safety of women—their own daughter included? Olivia knew it wasn't that simple, but it felt that way.

This was going to devastate their father. Absolutely. He'd feel as though he'd done this to his baby girl. "Do Mom and—"

"Don't tell anyone. Not a soul."

"I swear I won't." Both sisters knew that if anyone outside the company discovered that their cosmetics had made one of their own family members sick it would become a PR nightmare—one Olivia was nowhere near equipped to handle. Scandals like this could ruin a company, their family, her sister. "I love you, Emmy."

"Don't lose the valerian, Ovvy. Please. Women need it."

Olivia looked up as Devon returned to the entry where she was still on the floor. "I know, Emmy. I won't."

She stood up. There was still time to figure this out.

"I promise."

DEVON DIDN'T KNOW what Olivia's phone call had been about, but there was a set look in her expression that hadn't been there before he'd gone to check on the tub.

He didn't know what to expect from her any longer.

She'd gone from proper businesswoman to a

mess. She'd ruined not only her shoes and her manicure, but the dress, too. He was pretty certain its label said dry clean only, not wash in rainwater and mountain mud like you were a little kid. Earlier, it had been slightly endearing seeing her appearance less than perfect, but now her whole look from top to bottom said woman-dangling-at-the-end-of-her-rope. He didn't think it was due to their arguing or even their past, but rather, something else. Something current and vital.

He slowed as he approached her. When he'd suggested she go home, he'd been serious. She was convinced they could win, but he couldn't see how. Not when they kept butting heads and bringing up the past, unable to trust each other.

But looking at her now…he got the distinct feeling she wasn't going anywhere. She was prepared to dig in.

Olivia stepped forward. "We need to win this, Devon. If you don't become mayor, the dam goes through and you lose…" She twisted a hand through the air as though trying to sum up his world. "And I lose…" She clenched her fist as though pulling on something, her face tight with what resembled grief. "I lose what's important to me."

"There isn't enough time to pull this off."

"Then we need to move faster."

She kicked off her heels and stepped forward again, sliding slightly with the mud that had built up on the bottoms of her feet. Devon reached out, steadying her as the blanket fell from her shoulders. The way she clung to him, that special fizz that always seemed to permeate his bones whenever they touched, grounded him, made him think maybe she was right. Maybe they could be partners again.

He was a sucker.

"Devon, you need this. *I* need this." Her voice was shaking and he knew it wasn't just the cold. Miss Cool and Aloof had been impacted by something during that call and it had changed everything for her. "You need to win that election at all costs."

"At all costs? You sound like the country's safety is at risk, Ms. President," he said lightly.

Devon may have been willing to unearth his ex-girlfriend after a decade of avoidance, but it didn't mean he was desperate enough to forsake who he was or what he stood for.

"We need to figure out how to turn this around and then do it. Immediately."

When he remained quiet Olivia let out a shudder, her whole demeanor deflating. He lifted the blanket from the floor, carefully wrapping it around her again. But when he saw her face, his soul cracked open.

She was crying. Bravely trying to hold it in, be strong.

He stood awkwardly, unsure what to do.

He'd seen her cry only once before, and he'd been walking out the door, her begging him to understand.

Slowly he dragged a hand down his face. *He'd walked out the door*. In the car, she'd said she'd been scared when she'd found out she was pregnant. He'd been shocked, for sure; scared too. But only for a moment, because he knew he had Olivia. And if he had her, he had everything that mattered.

However, she hadn't felt the same way. She hadn't felt secure in the idea that he'd be there for her, that she could hold on to him and he'd find a way to keep them both safe. He'd assumed at the time that what he'd offered—himself, his love, a small town and a good job—was an insult to her upbringing. And maybe that was true in part, as it would have been a big change for a woman who'd grown up in a mansion. But he'd walked right out that door. Said things he couldn't take back, then left when she'd told him to, granting her wish to deal with it all alone.

Maybe he should have stayed. Maybe her words had actually been less about him and more about what she'd said in the car today—that she'd felt as though she'd failed.

But to him she hadn't. She'd created something out of their love. A life. Something to be joyful of.

And yet Olivia seemed to have felt the pregnancy was a personal shortcoming.

I'm perfectly aware of each and every way I've failed to live up to everyone's expectations.

If only she'd known how much he'd loved her, how much he'd wanted to bring her home to Blueberry Springs, show her off, have a family and be the luckiest man on Planet Earth. Where she'd seen failure, he'd seen nothing but opportunity.

He reached out to her, tenderly wiping a tear from her cheek.

"Emma has what Grammy had and it's because of cosmetic toxins and it's all my fault for not finding a cure—a solution—a stabilizing agent sooner."

"What?" She was barely making sense.

She swiped at her eyes with the back of her hand, no careful dabbing to protect her mascara. She was real, raw, and it terrified him. "I know it's not my fault, but it feels like it is." She grabbed his shirt in desperation. "I need this valerian. I need this for the products. I can't allow more women to get sick. I just can't." Her grip on his shirt lessened, her desperation replaced with resolve as she took one step back, composing herself through the tears. "So I either work with you or I go around you. Do you understand?"

Her tears were still falling, streaming down her cheeks. Despite it all, he could see her resolve. Her strength.

Her mind was made up.

He'd seen that look once before and knew not to disregard it. Especially where her family was involved. And Emma was her kid sister. He knew what that was like. That protective feeling, the need to shelter a younger sibling from the slings and arrows of life. It was a big burden, but it was worth it. And sometimes, more important than anything else.

Devon couldn't abandon her. Not when her sister needed her the most. He couldn't right a wrong from the past, but he could prevent himself from making another. He would stand by Olivia. He wouldn't leave her to face the fear alone.

He pulled her into his arms, hugging her close. "How are we going to make this work?"

"I know a good PR manager," she said hopefully.

He took her gently by the shoulders, holding her at arm's length, studying her. Did he trust her to help with his campaign? To work some magic on their mutual cases?

But at all costs?

"I don't want to compromise my values, who I am," he stated.

"I promise you won't have to."

"Partners then?"

"You might have to get married," she said with a wan smile.

"Strangely enough, that's not the first time I've heard that today." He directed her toward the bath-room. At the door, he removed the blanket from her shoulders, catching a hint of her perfume. It was new, but so wholly Olivia it brought back memories from college.

He didn't know what he was doing, keeping her around. It was probably the stupidest thing he could possibly do—inviting in a whole new world of guaranteed pain. And yet…it felt right.

His fingers found the top of her zipper and Devon braced himself for the peep of her lavender lace undergarment.

Olivia jumped forward, spinning. "What are you doing?"

He laughed, raising his hands in the air as though under arrest. "This is my cue to leave. Good luck getting out of that thing." He turned, but she caught him.

"Just…just close your eyes," she said with a sigh. "I really don't want to be stuck in this stupid dress for days just because I can't reach the zipper. Mud is not my color."

"Was that a joke?"

"Yeah, that was a joke."

"Good." His smile felt genuine. "Then we can definitely work together."

She turned, revealing the back of her dress and what felt like so much more. Her trust. Trust to help her save her family. Trust to help her with a product line that seemed equated with her identity.

Trust.

From Olivia.

The very idea darn near broke him.

CHAPTER 7

Olivia bit back a smile as she took in Devon's discomfort. After her amazing, rehumanizing bath—hot water had never felt so luxurious—she'd dressed him up like an adult and instructed him on how to behave like a proper, respectable candidate. There was no time like the present if they were going to work together so they may as well make the most of their waning weekend hours to do a little campaigning.

He'd bickered. Said people knew what he stood for. The wardrobe change was all too much, too fake. Blah, blah, blah. Argue, argue, argue.

Yeah, he didn't do fake. She hadn't been asking him to. Just shed a light on his finer qualities, of which he had several.

If Emma hadn't needed her, Olivia probably

would have told Devon to take a flying leap for all the grief he'd given her. Instead, she'd swallowed her frustration and summoned a level of patience most often found in saints. And it had paid off. She'd worn him down until he'd placed some well-earned faith in her abilities, and was currently looking very professional in his suit, his "sign my petition" spiel polished.

The plan? He was going to ask the senior citizens of Blueberry Springs for signatures on his petitions and she was going to watch how he operated, then come up with a strategy on how to maximize his best qualities.

Easy.

She'd been trained for this kind of stuff.

The only hiccup was that she obviously wasn't going to make it back to the retreat tonight. She'd missed golfing with her father last night and was about to cancel tonight's dinner with the family as well. If she didn't play her cards right, her father could quite possibly send a helicopter to come claim her. But she would worry about that later.

Right now she needed Devon to win her the rights to a field of valerian.

"You know what?" he said from the doorway to the continuing care area, where elderly patients with medical needs resided. "People can either take me or leave me." He loosened his tie—the only one he owned that was devoid of a cartoon character. "I'm not changing for them or pretending to be someone I'm not. If they like me, they like me as I stand."

"Do you want to win?"

He glared at her as he weighed his options, before marching into the room, clipboard in hand, his tie loose but still not completely discarded.

Uh-huh. She'd thought so.

"Nothing like having your ex-girlfriend rake your personality and image over the coals to feel good about yourself," he muttered when she caught up with him.

"Don't be a baby. You're still you. Only less obnoxious."

He turned, head tipped the side, feigning boredom. "Did you just insult me?"

"Oh," she said innocently, enjoying that they were able to engage in some lighthearted banter. "I thought you were trying to come off that way. So sorry."

He let out a light snort, but she caught the hint of amusement dancing in his eyes. "You're a real pain in the butt, you know that?"

She smiled sweetly.

Devon cracked his neck and rolled his shoulders. "All right, Miss PR. Do your thing."

"I am doing my thing. I'm watching you flail about and avoid acting like a real candidate."

"I'm not flailing and I *am* a real candidate," he grumbled.

She pretended to make a note on her clipboard.

"You want to see me strut my stuff? Is that it?" he asked, leaning closer. He smelled amazing. "Do you?" he challenged, his voice low. Her body tightened in something that felt an awful lot like anticipation. If, say, she was actually attracted to the man. Which she wasn't. She was much too mature to fall for a guy like him. Again.

"Strut away, mighty peacock," she challenged.

He turned and strutted to the nearest table, his feet doing some strange kick thing that had the older ladies amused. Olivia sighed. Was he intentionally trying to do the opposite of what she'd asked? *Highlight your trustworthy, leadership qualities, underplay your goofy, immature side.*

Apparently that was a difficult thing for him.

The women's expressions turned to concern as their amusement over his entrance faded, and Olivia straightened, on the lookout. What had he done? What had he said? She eased closer to catch what Devon was saying.

"No, no. No funeral," he declared, loosening his tie. "Sorry to concern you. Just dressed up because, as you know, I'm running for mayor." He struck a pose, and Olivia sighed and looked at the ceiling, summoning her strength.

The table of women relaxed and Devon shot Olivia a glance as if to say, "Told you the monkey suit was too much."

Okay, so maybe she'd overestimated a tad. It didn't mean she was completely off base. He had to look the part and a suit was better than what he usually wore, even if his hair was a bit too long and brushed the top of his shirt collar.

She focused on the group, using their reactions as she would a feedback panel. He was receiving genuine smiles and lots of hellos, which was good. People in their golden years didn't often put up with crap or act insincerely. But that didn't mean they were taking him seriously. In fact, one of the women was stroking the sleeve of his suit jacket, easing closer.

Oh, dear.

Olivia cleared her throat and subtly swung her clipboard, cuing Devon to move into his pitch for signatures. He waved her away, laughing at something someone said and joking about taking off his shirt to flex for them.

He was his own worst enemy. Rapport and laughter didn't mean support for his campaign. Didn't he understand that? He needed to leverage what he had to get signatures. He helped people.

They counted on him. Deliver that message loud and clear. Tell them what he wanted them to do, what he needed from them. Then move on. Chop, chop. Work the room.

It was time to step in and help, but she'd ambitiously overdressed in the last remaining outfit in her overnight bag—a pantsuit. She needed to loosen up a bit before she stepped in, and she also needed to have her bags overnighted to Blueberry Springs so she'd have something fresh to wear come morning. Olivia stepped from the room, sent a message to her sister asking her to pack her suitcases for her, then arranged for a courier to pick them up from the retreat's hotel.

Satisfied she had things under control, she patted her bun before carefully letting her hair down. She unbuttoned her suit jacket before opting to remove it completely. She had to be careful she didn't appear to be trying too hard before these men and women donned in comfortable attire—sweatshirts with kittens sitting in flowered meadows, and pants with elastic waistbands.

Tomorrow, when she had her suitcases, she would aim for something a bit more down-home and casual. Still professional, but maybe a little less…precise.

Quietly, Olivia joined Devon, standing beside him. She gave the group a big smile. "Hi, I'm Olivia

Carrington, Devon's friend. Did he mention that he wants to help the residents here with a new roof?"

The table of women perked up, one murmuring, "Oh, what a dear you are, Devon. Always so thoughtful."

"So helpful," another added.

"But as you may have heard," Olivia said, "the current mayor, Barry Lunn, doesn't agree that you need a new roof."

"He says tar would patch it up," one of the ladies said, then pressed her mouth in a determined line.

"Been saying that for months and is there still water leaking into my room? Yes, there is," another muttered, taking a sip of deep red juice. "The sound of it dripping in a rainstorm makes me have to pee all night long. It's a form of torture, I tell you."

"Devon believes the roof needs replacing," Olivia stated, trying to keep the ladies on track, "and as mayor, he would do that. Immediately after coming into power."

"Really?" The women were eyeing Devon.

"You deserve a roof that will keep you dry and safe," he said.

"And my sherry stash!" the woman with the juice said, lifting her plastic cup in a silent toast. "The day the roof fell in would be the day I needed it the most." She grinned at Olivia and downed the rest of the liquid. "Doctors recommend several servings of fruit a day, and that should take care of at least one of 'em."

Devon laughed and gave the woman's hand an affectionate squeeze. "We'll keep your stash safe, Gran. I promise. All I need are your signatures today and your vote on election day."

"Then consider it done." Gran, pen poised over the petition, asked, "Can we sign more than once?"

Devon shook his head.

She snorted and frowned. "Since when do you care for rules?"

"Reggie can sign," Devon said.

"Reggie's my boyfriend," Gran said to Olivia, leaning closer as though sharing a naughty secret. "Oh, and be a dear?" She shoved a piece of construction paper covered in cotton balls her way. "This thing looks like a three-year-old made it. Toss it out, would you?"

Olivia accepted the craft. "It's…"

"It's trash. Put it where it belongs." She turned to Devon, demanding, "When is Beth going to quit popping out babies and come back and run these activities? She at least had us make crafts that were interesting and less juvenile."

Devon said quietly to Olivia, "Her granddaughter usually runs these activities, but is on maternity leave."

"Baby number four," Gran said. "Oz can't keep it in his pants, apparently."

Devon chuckled. "Give them a break. They're crazy in love."

Olivia vaguely recalled that feeling. It generally overrode anything in the "better judgment" department.

"He's a very good dancer, you know. Even if he did break my hip that one time."

Olivia gave Devon an inquiring look. "Long story," he muttered out the side of his mouth.

She was getting sucked in. They needed to move faster, spread the message, then leave.

But everyone, including Devon, was so relaxed, so chatty and at home. It reminded her of when she used to volunteer at an old folks' center. The regulars had taught her several sewing techniques to help with her costumes for a drama production. Half the time she'd forget to sew, absorbed by their life stories instead.

It would be so nice to just sit and chat without an agenda. Chill out, relax, have fun, laugh.

But that wasn't why she was here. Women like Emma needed valerian.

"Shall we get Reggie to sign?" she asked.

"Reggie Max!" Gran leaned back in her chair

and hollered, "Get your butt over here and sign this petition. And bring your bridge buddies, too."

A man across the room grumbled but complied, putting down the playing cards he'd been shuffling and bringing several friends over to Gran's table. Not bad. But Devon needed to move faster. Seeming to understand the issue, he moved to the next table, trying out Olivia's technique of "help me help you."

He'd always been a fast learner. And darn if he didn't look handsome, so patient when he had to repeat himself louder so someone hard of hearing didn't miss out on what he was saying. He was a good man and Olivia found herself hoping he won even if Carrington ended up having to search elsewhere for the illusive magical ingredient.

"When are you two getting married?" Gran asked, sliding the clipboard back to Olivia after the men finished adding their names.

"Sorry?" She blinked at the older woman.

"You and Devon. He's a dear."

"We're just friends."

"We can fix that," Gran replied with a mischievous wink.

"Day after tomorrow," Devon teased, leaning back in his chair to collect the clipboard. "Didn't invite you because it's an open bar."

"Oh, you," Gran said with a laugh. "The jeweler in town is having a sale, I hear."

"No jeweler required. Livvy's not my type and vice versa." Devon's face darkened and he moved back to his new table.

Olivia swallowed as Gran's eyebrows lifted. Then she dropped an elbow on the table to lean closer. "Is that so?"

He'd asked her to marry him once. A very long time ago.

She'd said no.

Of course she'd said no! It hadn't even been a real proposal. It had been a knee-jerk act of desperation, him scrambling for a way to deal with the very adult reality of becoming parents. They'd been young, newly in love. Not ready for a lifelong commitment and big responsibilities. She'd been grateful her mom and dad had been there, steady, calm, plan in hand, giving her time and space to think while pulling herself back together again, even though it had meant stepping back from Devon.

He hadn't understood, though, and had taken it all as a rejection and stormed off, thinking she was permanently choosing her old life and family over him, their love.

She supposed in a way she had been. But he'd

been so quick to assume the worst it still hurt after all these years.

"Daredevil racer," Gran said, with a hint of excitement lacing her voice. "Sexy man beast who never dates anyone longer than about three seconds? Not your type? So very boring of you, dear."

Olivia smiled, not feeling it. That had been the very thing that had attracted her to Devon in the first place. And then she'd discovered so much more than she'd expected. It seemed as though she was still discovering.

"You still race?" Olivia asked Devon.

Devon mumbled something she couldn't quite catch as he stood. He'd already collected a table of signatures. He was a quick study and she felt a surge of pride.

This could be good. Great, even.

Devon chuckled at Gran. "And did you say 'sexy man beast'?" He leaned over her table, planting a kiss on the top of her head. "I like it. I might get that put on a pin for my lapel."

"Don't you dare," Olivia said, even though she knew he was joking—or at least she hoped so. But he was a total dear, kissing his grandmother. The two had a rapport that made Olivia envious. Grammy, her mom's mom, used to joke around—the only one in Olivia's family with a sense of humor other than

Emma. Their only remaining grandparent—their paternal grandmother—would never tolerate that kind of oddball behavior. Visits were a very somber affair, with constant judgment in regards to manners.

Gran informed Olivia, "He can't beat his sister Mandy around the racetrack any longer."

"Really? Tell me more," she said, giving Devon a wicked smile.

"Hey, now..." he said mildly. "I'm right here if you plan to slaughter me with inaccuracies."

"You're lucky you two are so close," Olivia said. "You must have such fun at family events."

"Oh, we're not related," Devon said in surprise.

"Then why do you call her Gran?"

"Everyone does," Gran said matter-of-factly.

"I actually can't remember your real name," Devon said, studying the older lady.

"Me, neither," she said with a wise look full of mischief.

"Gran is...let's see... My sister's ex-boyfriend's wife's grandmother." He shrugged and gave Gran's shoulder an affectionate squeeze that made Olivia's heart tighten. "So that makes her mine, too."

"Well, that's sappy," Gran said. "You still on for strip poker Wednesday night? I'll bring the sherry."

Devon, say no. You're running for mayor! Say no!

Devon caught Olivia's expression and let out a laugh, his whole face brightening.

"Sure, Gran. I'll be sure to go commando so you'll have a chance of seeing something good this time."

Gran laughed in turn, and Olivia honestly didn't know if she should believe the two of them. She really, really hoped they were joking, because if they weren't there was absolutely no hope she'd ever make Devon into proper mayoral material— even if he did have a way of making her smile.

So Devon had a campaign manager. Or a public relations rep. Whatever title it was that Olivia had claimed for herself. And she was good, too. He'd seen the changes in how people perceived his run for mayor when he'd done that light campaigning at the old folk's home. Everything Olivia had told him to do—except wear the suit, of course—had been right on target.

He yawned and pushed away from his kitchen counter where the two of them had just finished hashing out their land agreement and a tentative PR and campaign plan.

It had been strangely easy. No arguing.

Everything was secured. He felt hopeful. Truly hopeful.

Still, staying on guard for the two hours they'd

worked after getting signatures at the home had tied up his mind. He'd felt it was his duty to look at everything they'd discussed and planned from all angles, so he and the town wouldn't be taken by a surprise loophole.

It was almost eight-thirty and he was ready to unwind after their long, productive day. And he had just the ticket—one pass for tonight's sold-out music festival concert with Vapid Magpie, a band he'd been longing to see for what felt like forever.

But what was he supposed to do? Ditch Olivia? Even if he'd had a ticket for her, she'd likely consider Vapid Magpie unsophisticated shouting.

There were still no vacancies in town, which meant he had to remain the pleasant host.

"Is Ginger home tonight?" he asked. "She might be keen for some catching up with you."

"You have a hot date?" Olivia asked lightly.

The doorbell rang and Devon bolted from his spot, Copter barking loudly, waking Awesome Dog. The two followed him to the door.

It was Trish, Devon's stepmom. Copter tried to lick her hand, then lay down beside Devon when she pulled her hand out of reach. Awesome Dog preferred to hook his bottom jaw over his top one and watch Trish from afar.

"Uh, hi, Trish."

Trish leaned to her left, trying to peek into the

house. "I hear you have a woman staying with you. That pretty one from the city."

Devon wondered how he could get rid of his stepmom without hurting her feelings.

The bangles on her arm jangled as she waved at Olivia, who'd come up behind him. He sighed and stepped aside, introducing them to each other.

His stepmother's eyes lit up. "Oh, you are so beautiful!" She added in a low aside, "What a fantastic catch, Devon."

At least she hadn't told him Olivia was out of his league. How many times had he heard that in the past forty-eight hours? Yes, she lived in an entirely different world. One with rare paintings on the walls, not framed running bibs and ribbons that werc only there thanks to a decorator friend. Real marble, not plastic flooring made to imitate. Not that it mattered. He already knew she didn't want to be part of his world.

At least not beyond raping the land here, as the protesters so aptly put it.

But Trish? She thought Devon was up to snuff, which was an unexpectedly nice compliment.

"Welcome to Blueberry Springs!" Trish pushed past him. "I love the length of your nails. Is the nude look in?" Olivia had removed her chipped polish after her meadow mud incident, and Trish was comparing her racer-red nails to Olivia's.

"Did you need something, Trish?" Devon asked.

"Oh, I just wanted to say hi." She smiled and eyed Olivia's ring finger. "Are you staying here? With Devon? And you're single?"

"Trish," he said patiently. "This is a business thing. Nothing more. Everything is booked, with the festival, and even though she's Ginger's old roommate, I'm the only one with space."

"I can't believe they live in that mess!" Trish stated, placing a hand over her enhanced cleavage. "Someone ought to put them on a TV show that can fix them. They're like hoarders. If she was my daughter—"

"Don't meddle," Devon said automatically.

Trish patted her hair. "Well. I was just *saying.*"

His stepmom meant well and she did try to be helpful. It wasn't her fault that she'd been thrust into motherhood when his father had presented her with a houseful of teenagers. She'd had to sprint to catch up with her new role and had slightly overshot aspects of it, as she was only eight years older than Devon, who'd been thirteen at the time.

"My husband—Devon's father—is always looking out for Devon's baby sister, but Devon won't let us do that for him." She patted his shoulder, beaming at Olivia, who'd remained silent so far. "He's a big boy and wants his independence."

"I'm thirty-two."

"Your father and I like to look out for the ones we love," Trish explained. She turned back to Olivia. "I heard you've already changed a few minds about this boy's ability to run this town."

"I *have* the ability to run this town." And he was not a *boy.* He was a man. A man who had come home from school one semester shy of completing his degree because the family had needed a stabilizing presence after Ethan's accident. He'd spent the next few years struggling to buoy the family's spirits, and taking night classes in the city to complete his degree. He was pretty certain that excluded him from being referred to as a boy.

"You're very good at your job and you'd be a fine mayor, Devon. It's what I tell all my friends," Trish said gently. "What are you doing tonight?" she asked Olivia. "Devon's going to see Sappy Bagpipes—"

"Vapid Magpie," Devon corrected, shoving his hands deep in his pockets. He was surprised Trish was keeping tabs on him.

"—and the girls and I are playing cards. Why don't you come join us? There's no need for you to be alone."

The "girls" were Mary Alice, Liz and a few other of the top dozen gossips in town. Devon shook his head, hoping Olivia would take his cue.

"That sounds lovely," Olivia said pleasantly, and he died inside. She would never make it out unscathed.

"Please, no," Devon muttered under his breath, and his stepmom shot him a look before focusing on his ex-girlfriend. Trish was giving Olivia a thoughtful look and Devon was certain she was slowly piecing together their past.

"She has a ticket," Devon said quickly. Nicola had organized the event; surely she could wrangle another ticket or let Olivia slip in the back.

Olivia's eyes lit up. "I love Vapid Magpie."

Devon tried not to act surprised.

"So aggressive and angsty." She hooked her arm through Devon's with a smile. Her chest was pressed against him, distracting him, her smile dazzling and genuine. It felt right having her on his arm, her mood light and joyful. "And your son is going to be a fabulous mayor, Trish."

And that was why he loved Olivia.

That girl could pick up his hints like nobody else.

Not that it was love-love. It was just an expression, really. Just friendly, friend-type stuff. The kind that didn't involve thoughts about certain lacy items worn to bed under his roof.

Yup. He was going to have to exhaust himself at the festival so he crashed as soon as his head hit the pillow, or he'd be up all night, his brain filled with fantasies that involved the two of them and that little nightie of hers.

Nope. His mind was going down that dirty road again. It seemed like every interchange in his brain looped around to head back in that direction once the vision of her nightie fed in.

Trish's eyes seemed to be stuck on their entwined arms, her gaze drifting up to take in Devon's expression, then Olivia's tousled curls, her tasteful pearl earrings.

No. No-o-o. She was somehow linking things that shouldn't be linked. Ever. She was as bad as Mary Alice.

"You know, Devon dated someone in uni—"

"Hey, look at the time!" Devon said suddenly, causing Copter to bark and leap to his feet. "Sorry, Trish. We've got to run or we're totally going to miss the concert."

OLIVIA GRABBED DEVON'S ELBOW, allowing him to lead her through the throng of dancers moving to Vapid Magpie's latest hit. They were in the center of town, at an outdoor stage set up near a large oak tree where a fluffy gray cat was currently yowling, her little kitty voice half drowned out by the music.

"Look!" She pointed to the feline and Devon gave a smile of recognition.

"Fluffy. She'll be up there until someone rescues her."

"The poor thing."

Devon shrugged and pulled Olivia farther into the warm mass of people scattered across the soft grass.

"Will someone go get it?"

"Oz usually does."

"Who's he?"

"The husband of Gran's granddaughter."

"He's a firefighter?"

"Nah, the cat just likes his attention." Devon came to a stop, hollering his approval for the band as the song ended. He looked happy, free.

How was it that in the middle of all their worries and battles he could just let it all go? They'd been civil for a few hours, but how was his stomach not a tangled nest of concerns and what-ifs?

Well, he was Devon. That's who he was.

She sighed. Maybe, instead of fretting over their differences, she should learn to take a bit of it for herself here and there. It wouldn't kill her to let loose a little, would it?

Not fall for Devon like the last time she'd let

herself go, but just…enjoy the ride and get off before it got too nutso.

"How did Nicola get these guys to come here?" she asked, in the momentary quiet before the next song began. The band had recently broken out and was in high demand. Blueberry Springs was a small town out in the middle of nowhere. The two did not fit.

"She's got skills." He grinned, and for the first time since hearing about Devon's ex-girlfriend Olivia thought she might have competition for his affection.

Whoa. Stop that thought train.

She was not competing with anyone for his affection. She'd been down that path and had no interest in being lured there again despite how surprisingly fun this afternoon had turned out to be. They'd worked well together—like they had in their college classes—and she'd seen a new, more mature side of Devon. But that didn't mean she was in love with him.

A man in camouflage clothing appeared close to them and Olivia stumbled against Devon, his arms going around her like a natural shield as he caught her. She'd seen the guy around town, watching her.

"Hey, Pete," Devon said, releasing Olivia. She immediately missed his warmth, the feeling of safety and comfort that always seemed to come with his embraces. "This is Olivia. Olivia, this is Peter Lunn. He's Barry's son."

"Nice to meet you."

He nodded, but didn't reply, the crowd pulling him back in again.

She turned to Devon. "You have him spying on me, too?" She hugged her arms, feeling exposed.

"Nope." Devon leaned closer, speaking into her ear as the music throbbed, "He got kicked in the head by a horse when he was a teen. He's barely spoken since."

"That's awful." Just another quirky piece of Blueberry Springs history. But why did he keep watching her? It made her uncomfortable. "And what about Logan? Why is he spying on me?" She'd seen him parked near the concert, talking with someone who gave him a wristband, letting him in. He was around here somewhere, too.

"He's not spying."

"Well, whatever it's called in Blueberry Springs —what is he doing?"

"He's in security."

"And?" She gave him a pointed look and waited.

Devon didn't want to answer, she could see that. But when his blue eyes flashed to hers, she saw him give in. "He's following us. Making sure the protesters don't...I don't know. He's just making sure we stay safe."

Olivia didn't know how to react. He'd hired Logan, her best friend's husband, to tail her because he was worried? Logan had chased Barry off in the meadow with his presence, and he'd also helped them escape from the protesters outside the café earlier. But it all felt unnecessary.

Her father was overprotective. He was also controlling and domineering.

Devon wasn't. In fact, his little stint of protectiveness actually felt kind of...sweet. It made her feel... No, she wasn't digging into that can of worms. There were too many warm fuzzies ready to come out, thanks to his unrequested chivalrous act.

No. It wasn't chivalrous. He didn't trust her to make decisions that impacted the both of them. It was him trying to take control, keep her from talking to the protesters and making things worse. He didn't trust her to have a plan that would take care of their mutual best interests. She had to remember that.

But it *was* a little bit sweet.

"You're protecting me?" she confirmed, realizing Devon was watching her worriedly.

And see? He was worried how she'd react. How could that not change the way she felt?

No, he didn't want her to blow up, shut him

out, send him off to the hills on his own. That was all.

Their eyes met for a long second and Olivia's body warmed as the two of them drifted closer. She could feel the heat of his body, the firmness of his muscles as her hands landed against his chest. Her head tipped back, lining up with his. Her lashes drifted lower, her mouth opening slightly. Someone jostled Devon, breaking the spell.

They jumped back from each other, and Devon began to dance like he was trying to shake something out of his system. Olivia joined him. That had been close. Too close. Kissing would complicate things. Really complicate things, because she was pretty certain that once she started kissing Devon Mattson there would be no stopping.

She allowed the music to take over, send her mind into hibernation as the beat flowed through her, waking up muscles that hadn't danced in years. As she let herself go, she moved faster, falling into sync with Devon's moves. He laughed, shaking his body, sending any remaining tension that lingered between them into the darkening mountains surrounding the small town. Her smile grew, real and big. It was like they were free again, their pasts irrelevant.

She was doing it, letting it all go, and she was not one bit in love with the man she was dancing with, the man she'd somehow linked fingers with so they wouldn't get separated in the moving throng.

"I forgot what it's like," she shouted as dancers nudged them, sending them into each other more often than not. It wasn't a hardship being pushed against Devon, but it was awakening parts of her she needed to keep in sleep mode.

"What?"

"I forgot…" She shook her head. She'd forgotten how free it could feel, being around him. How her guard wasn't just let down, but was given its walking papers. It was like…like she was safe to finally breathe.

Dangerous. That's what it was.

She needed to remember why she was here— for Emma. For Grammy.

Nothing else.

She untangled her fingers from his, pretending she had to adjust the ponytail she'd put in earlier.

She could have fun, but she needed to stay focused.

She continued to dance, but the feeling of being lost in the music was gone.

Several songs later, a man limped over and handed them two red cups of beer. Devon accepted them, passing one to Olivia. She shook her head. Never accept an open drink from a stranger.

"Olivia," Devon said, hauling her closer with an arm around her shoulder as he hollered over the music, "This is my brother Either."

"Sorry? What was that?" she asked. Either? There were some strange names out there, but nuh-huh.

Devon grinned like a brother ribbing his sibling. "Either or, Ethan snores," he sang.

"Pleasure to meet you," she said, her own voice loud enough to carry over the music. "I can't believe you survived growing up with this guy."

Ethan laughed, revealing a white scar along his chin when he tipped back his head. "He might try to convince you he's a great man..." His brother leaned closer. "...quitting school to come help out when I was paralyzed. But really, he came back because—"

"Either, shut it."

"He was a big, crusty—" Devon gave him a brotherly shove, causing him to switch gears slightly. "I had to live with him for months. After a while I didn't know who was commiserating with whom."

Olivia was struggling to keep up with the conversation. Ginger had mentioned something about Devon dropping out, but not why. Now she knew. But commiserating? Had Devon been as broken-hearted as she had?

Devon and Ethan were communicating silently now, Ethan frowning, looking serious, Devon stern.

Finally, Ethan gave a harrumph and moved off.

Devon held the beer toward her. She accepted the drink, taking a sip.

"That was nice of him," she said into Devon's ear. "Kind of like your stepmom. She obviously cares about you a ton."

Devon looked uncomfortable. He downed his drink as dancers moved around them. "Yeah, they're okay."

"So what was that about college?"

"I came home early to help."

"You dropped out?"

"I finished my last five courses through a local college."

"He said you two were commiserating—"

"He's a grump. Don't believe a word he says." Devon's expression was closed off, telling her the conversation was over.

She laid a hand on his arm, knowing he was trying to hide how much their breakup and losing the baby had meant to him. "I'm sorry things didn't work out differently for us."

He met her eye, giving a short nod.

A new song began and Olivia tried to find her earlier mood of being free, but it was gone. She felt watched. Cold. She wanted to go home, take off her heels, which kept sinking into the soft grass, and just...breathe.

Devon tossed his empty cup over his shoulder and smiled, back to his unaffected self.

"You littered!"

He shrugged. "I'm on the cleanup crew. Wanna help?"

She could practically see her breath as the sun set over the mountaintops. She'd freeze her butt off if she came out here again late at night to pick up cups that people could have simply placed in the trash receptacles.

She shook her head just as someone bumped into her arm from behind, sending her cup flying through the air, beer arcing beneath the strobe lights.

"Oops!" Devon laughed. "Looks like you get to help, litterbug."

CHAPTER 8

Monday morning Devon sat in the barber's chair with Olivia and his barber, George, standing behind him. Olivia's suitcases had arrived from her hotel that morning and she was dressed much more casually than she had been for the past few days. Her hair was loose, the ends of her curls brushing her breasts whenever she moved, distracting him every time he looked her way. It didn't help that she was wearing a fuzzy, short-sleeved sweater that hugged every curve and caused his body to forget that those curves belonged to a woman his heart had long ago marked with a giant Danger sign.

She looked good, relaxed, confident. It was oddly attractive.

In a purely platonic way, of course.

Because honestly, he'd have to be blind not to notice that she was still exceedingly pretty—especially when she smiled like she had while dancing last night. She'd crashed into him several times, thanks to other dancers. Which was cool. He didn't mind having her supple curves pressed against him.

Not that Olivia was smiling right now, deep in business mode. But she was still pretty, her face an endearing mask of concentration like it had when she'd be working on her costume project in college. It made him wonder if she liked her PR job as much as the career she'd dreamed about, but had ultimately abandoned—fashion design.

"You were good at designing dresses, you know," he said.

Olivia blinked and looked up from the magazine page she'd been showing Devon's barber. Creating gowns had been a big part of who she was, and he wondered if their breakup had caused her to remove that dream from her life, just like he'd removed everything associated with her from his.

She tapped the page, indicating the look she wanted George to recreate on Devon. "This one."

All right. So she didn't want to talk about it.

He yawned, exhausted. They'd been up late picking up trash after the concert, and he hadn't been able to unwind afterward. He'd actually expected the high princess of Carrington to waltz home to bed, but she'd stuck around, helping. He wasn't sure how it made him feel, but it had definitely melted some of his reserve toward her princess side. That and seeing her all muddy from the meadow yesterday. Yeah, it probably wasn't a good thing. But when had any kind of warning from his brain stopped him from doing dangerous "not good" things? Pretty much never.

But things were okay. This morning they'd signed the final version of the Carrington-Blueberry Springs agreement, so if he messed up, the town would at least be a little bit protected.

Well, no. There were still ways everything could go south. She could declare that she hadn't found what she wanted, and walk away. The agreement gave her exclusive rights for a year, which meant he wouldn't be able to pull in anyone else to try and save the town from the dam.

Which meant he needed to put his easily persuaded libido on ice.

George and Olivia were arguing over the proposed haircut, and Devon shifted uncomfortably, reminding himself that he wasn't changing for her. It was for the town.

And it was just a haircut. It didn't mean he was becoming a fake. But a haircut for a man was basically a makeover.

No, not a makeover. "Reframing him." That was what she'd called it. And he'd seen the power of that strategy yesterday when she'd managed to sway everyone in the continuing care wing to sign his petition in less than twenty minutes.

Every last one of them.

Help me help you.

It was brilliant.

She was brilliant.

"That's almost the same haircut I've been giving him since he was knee-high to a grasshopper," George protested.

"It's different," Olivia insisted. "Here." She reached for his sheers, adjusting the length guard. She went to place it against the back of Devon's head, but his barber intervened.

Whew. There was confidence and then there was overconfidence.

"He's paying me to do that job," George said, "and I don't think it's best for you to try your hand at this today if he has to be in front of cameras later."

Right. The press conference Olivia had called. That woman got things done, that was for certain. And she saw things, too. She'd picked up what Ethan had been laying out for her last night. He'd figured out that Olivia was the one Devon had been brooding over when he'd returned to Blueberry Springs, and his dodo-head brother had, for some reason, thought she should know. And then she'd apologized to Devon, bringing up all those feelings again. Feelings that were like a tumbling waterfall, never seeming to stop when she was around.

Olivia began fussing with Devon's hair. "I want it longer here, shorter here. Definitely shorter everywhere. It's much too shaggy." She slid her fingers into the strands at the top of his head, grabbing a chunk of it. The move sent shivers down Devon's spine, as a woman hadn't pulled on his hair in a very long time. Even just platonically.

George met Devon's eyes in the mirror. "You sure about this?"

Devon shrugged. "Is my head lumpy?"

"You have a nicely shaped head," the man assured him.

"In that case, give it a go, and if it sucks, shave my skull."

"You will not!" Olivia scolded, standing between Devon and the barber as though they were about to go straight to plan B without trying A first. "It's going to look fine."

"It's true. I can make everything look good," Devon said, pretending to buff his nails on his chest.

"I said fine, not drool-worthy, you conceited man."

Devon grinned. She was definitely relaxing, letting her guard down, becoming someone he could enjoy spending time with again.

Danger!

Man, but he missed her. Missed this fun version of the best girlfriend he'd ever had—even though she'd torn his still-beating heart straight out of his chest.

George went to work, his scissors snipping madly, Olivia at his side, supervising and holding up the magazine every once in a while. She was critically watching every cut, frequently referring back to the image at hand.

Devon watched the hair fall from his head, fairly confident that Olivia knew what she was doing with her "makeover." Funny how quickly he'd come to believe in her, trust her. Well, with his appearance anyway.

"If all else fails I'll at least save some money on shampoo," he said.

"You're not as funny as you think you are," Olivia said, barely looking away from George's work.

"Funnier?"

"Nope." She sent him the smile he'd always felt was reserved just for him.

Wow. He probably needed to shake off that feeling.

But man, he longed for it, even though it brought a familiar pang of loss to the surface.

George spun him around, putting Devon's back to the mirror to finish up, before plunking his scissors and comb into a jar of blue liquid. He squirted some sort of gel or mousse or something onto his hands before running them through Devon's hair, shaping it. Devon tried to lean away. George was supposed to just trim and let him be. Not style it. That's why he went to a barber and not a salon. He was a man. He didn't want to give up his man card in exchange for a haircut.

"Sorry, son," the barber said, catching his expression. "We have to complete the look."

"Please tell me I don't look like a hipster."

George chuckled. "I wouldn't let her do something to you that would have you run out of town."

"Again, you guys are not as funny as you think." There was amusement in Olivia's voice, though. That was good. She probably liked the results.

Finally, George was done. He stepped back to take in the effect. "Yes," he said thoughtfully. "I think that will do just fine."

Devon raised his eyebrows at Olivia. She had the same pensive look on her face before breaking into a smile, her cheeks pink. "You look very handsome, Devon."

"I didn't need a haircut for that to happen."

"He's always been a looker," George said, flipping the hair cape off him. "And has the confidence to match." He spun Devon around to face the mirror, giving him a playful smack across the back of his head. He held up a hand mirror behind him, angling the chair so he could check himself out.

Devon smoothed a hand over his head. The sensation was foreign. There was definitely a lot less hair.

"Do you like it?" Olivia asked. She sounded as though she was holding her breath.

"Yeah, it'll do," he said eventually. It was an incredible difference. His cheekbones looked like they'd been sculpted, his face more angular. He was striking. "But I think there's a problem."

"What?" Olivia began scrutinizing his haircut with concern.

"We're going to have to hire someone to beat the ladies off of me."

Her body relaxed and she shot out a hip while giving him a saucy look. "Seriously, Devon? How big is that ego of yours?"

"I thought women were more interested in things like shoe size or hand size?"

Behind him, his barber choked on a laugh.

"Incorrigible," Olivia said with a sigh. "Come on. We have a press conference in thirty minutes and I have a new outfit waiting for you downtown."

"I'm like a Ken doll," Devon muttered, getting another chuckle out of his barber as he paid for the trim. "Thanks, George. You did good."

"If you're Ken, does that make me Barbie?" Olivia piped up. Their eyes connected and the air around them crackled with an intensity he'd never once experienced with anyone else. Olivia Carrington being playful, flirtatious.

Man, did he ever love it.

"Sure, Barbie." He glanced at her chest—it was quite nice in her curve-hugging top—and she swatted at him.

"Careful, careful. Watch the hair. It's new."

"Because if I'm Barbie and you're my Ken, then it means—"

"I don't have any balls."

Olivia sent him a look. "I wasn't going to say that."

He gave her a soft smile. "It's okay. I think your makeover will probably be worth giving up my manhood."

OLIVIA STOOD in the doorway near the front of the town's meeting room and looked out at the people who had gathered for the press conference. Disappointed pretty much summed up how she felt. One man in the front row held microphones for what looks like every news station in the closest city, Dakota, which she supposed wasn't so bad. There was also Liz Moss-Brady, a local reporter—and gossip—who was chatting on her phone and obviously just putting in time. A few other people were sitting in chairs, looking around as though they expected treats for showing up.

In about three minutes she'd haul Devon out from the adjoining room and hope the reporters got a few sound bites that would push his name forward, get the town and surrounding areas to wake up and take notice.

Near the back of the room, the door was wide open. Logan glanced inside, scanning the room, giving Olivia a small nod before crossing his arms, taking up a post just outside. Through the doorway she could see one black military-grade boot and his shoulder. Total bodyguard.

She shook her head. A bodyguard was still kind of sweet.

A few people shifted as someone else entered. "Are there cookies?"

Olivia shook her head slowly.

"Oh." The man's shoulders fell and he left the room.

Cookies. Next time bring cookies.

And where was Vintra? He'd promised to be here, promised not to get sucked in to his experiments and forget to come. He was supposed to explain the science and the sustainable, greener side of her product line, as well as Blueberry Springs's part in that. Then she'd chip in with how Devon had put it all together.

Dazzle dazzle. Looky here!

She sighed and checked the time. She hoped Mr. Right wasn't destroying the guest room at Devon's. She usually kenneled the dog if she had to leave him at home for any length of time, as he had destructive tendencies that seemed to kick in around the three hour mark of his supposed "abandonment."

Another person came in, looked around and left. Olivia sighed. What was she going to do if they failed to put Devon in the mayor's seat? How would she face Emma?

Ginger appeared in the doorway, jumping up to give Logan a quick kiss before hurrying into the room. She gave Olivia a big hug. "Hey! I thought I'd come out and show some support."

"There's hardly anyone here," Olivia whispered. "Is that normal for Blueberry Springs?"

"Um, I'm actually not sure if we've ever had a proper press conference before."

Ginger peeked into the adjoining room, where Devon was waiting for his cue. She said with a sly smile, "I like his new haircut. Very dreamy."

"He's not dreamy."

"And that outfit." Ginger fanned herself. "If he had an accent and I wasn't married, I would be all over that."

"Ginger…" Olivia warned, an unwanted spike of possessiveness flaring inside her.

"You can't send him out like that."

"What? Why not?"

He looked professional, and the way he paused, listening, helping, *seeing* a person? He was perfect. She glanced into the room to confirm her assessment, her heart slamming hard against her ribs as Devon looked up in question, his eyes so blue, his shoulders so strong, those cheekbones so—

Ginger giggled and dragged Olivia from the doorway so they were out of Devon's sight. "He looks like bait. Like…like a playboy ready to ride. Alpha CEO about to conquer every fainting woman with damp panties in his path. You know?"

Olivia leaned away. "Your hormones are completely out of control. He's not…" The word *sexy* came to mind. He *was* sexy. Sex on a plate. Every inch of him lickable.

Wow. Okay, so her own hormones might be a bit out of whack, too.

"He's hot. Do you not see what you've created?"

She did see. That was the problem. He looked exactly like the kind of guy she could go for, the kind she could bring home and have her parents go gaga over. Yeah. That amazing. Even more amazing than Luke.

She should really call the poor man back, she thought distractedly.

Later, later. There was time.

"You need to hitch him up to someone," Ginger continued. "Otherwise he's too perfect. There are too many possibilities, endless directions he could go with this new and improved version of himself. Especially since he's a known flirt."

"I went too far?" Olivia sneaked another peek at the man in question.

"Honey, he's dreamy. Perfect. Amazing. Hot. Sexy. Scumpdiddlyicious."

"Not a real word."

"Well, if it isn't, add it to the dictionary and put his picture beside it, because that's what you've created. Marry him off. Now." She gave Olivia a look and took a seat in the front row, crossing her legs.

Olivia tried to act cavalier, even though her heart thudded extra hard.

A wife.

For Devon.

Why on earth could she see herself in that role?

Olivia could be doing a song and dance up in front of the reporters and nothing would help. Vintra had explained the green aspects of their plans, because the local valerian was indeed exactly what they needed.

She had it. She just had to bring it home and convince these people to vote for Devon.

With enthusiasm, Olivia had talked about Carrington Cosmetics, a small family company that cared about their customers, the land.

People yawned.

She brought out Devon. Heads had snapped his way in interest and she turned the mic over to him with a whispered, "No joking around."

"The town thinks I'm not good enough to be mayor," he said, and Olivia froze. "But do you see a town that has jobs? One that supports green initiatives such as organic, all-natural cosmetic lines? One that preserves its identity and values nature?" He gripped the podium, his tone somber and quiet. "We're dying here. This town grew, but we didn't have the jobs to keep our new citizens here, and our internet connection isn't fast enough for people to telecommute with reliability. We expanded subdivisions, but we didn't create jobs, didn't financially support improving our infrastructure. So we taxed our local businesses higher to make up for our lack of foresight. And now those businesses are closing. What will happen to our neighbors? Our families? We're a dying town that will soon to be in the shadow of a million ton dam." He made eye contact with everyone in the room. "You ever see that movie? The one where the dam cracks, then breaks?"

Olivia shivered as he waited, letting his words sink in before saying, "Help me help you. Help me help Blueberry Springs."

Nothing.

Liz had gone back to her phone after the buzz of interest in Devon's new look. The man in the front row was yawning so hard Olivia could hear his jaw popping.

"Is that it, Devon?" Liz asked, standing.

"No, that's not it," Olivia snapped, her patience gone. He was a good man! He was doing everything right. Why did they refuse to see that?

"Well, unless you two are getting married, I'm done," Liz declared, picking up her giant purse. "As nice as you are, Devon, I can't see you taking the mayoral seat. I'm sorry."

Olivia swallowed, desperation flooding her. Emma and other women like her were going to lose if the reporter walked out of the room.

Ginger locked her gaze with Olivia's, giving her a slow nod.

"Then you're not done, Liz," Olivia said clearly. She looked at Devon. He always made her feel real, special, a part of something. Taking the fake leap with him, even if just for a week? It wouldn't be so difficult to pull off. They had enough history to make it look convincing.

But it was deceptive. Wrong.

And she'd get hurt. Open old wounds, then scrape glass across them.

But she could do that for Emma, her sister. Her family, her blood. She could do it for women like Grammy.

Liz turned in her chair to face Olivia, her expression dry, unimpressed.

Ginger pointedly cleared her throat.

There was only one way to save this.

It was now or never.

Olivia should probably choose never.

But before she could pull her brain back to home base to revise the words it was currently sending to her mouth, it completed its mission.

"Devon and I are getting married."

DEVON CHOKED.

His brain stopped working.

Was he still awake?

Because…him? Getting married? To Olivia?

Oh, no. Just…no.

He had to be dreaming. A total nightmare.

Liz, who had been only half present during the press conference, sat on the edge of the nearest chair, her clever gaze taking in everything that was happening up at the lectern. "You look shocked, Devon."

Olivia reached over and squeezed his hand, her fingers digging into his in desperation, her eyes silently begging him to play along. How did his ex-girlfriend think this was okay? That he'd go along with such a crazy stunt? That he'd *want* to playact being in love with her? Her. The woman who had thrown him out of her life, then slammed and locked the door after him.

It didn't matter why she'd done it—she'd done it.

Sure, the past twenty-four hours together had been all right, and they'd managed to play nice and had almost kissed at the concert, but this… There was no backtracking, no "oh, she just misspoke" without looking like a huge fool and completely wrecking what little credence he'd built up in his campaign.

He replied honestly, "I didn't expect her to say that."

Liz cocked her head to the side, no doubt picking up on nuances in his body language that he was unable to hide.

It was all a lie. A great big lie. He'd fallen that far in his quest to help the town. Did that make him a true political candidate now? He was a liar, chock-full of deceit, in bed with large corporations.

Olivia took over the mic. Her hands were shaking like leaves in a hurricane and she gripped the lectern, her knuckles whitening. She gave a sheepish, sweet smile to the audience. "We had planned to tell our families first."

Family.

His family was going to be excited. Shocked. Surprised. Happy. Freaking over-the-moon.

Lied to.

By him.

Olivia was fielding questions about their en-gagement and proposal with a fluidity that made him wonder how often she misrepresented the truth. No, *misrepresented* was too kind, too soft. She was obliterating the truth, bulldozing it, burying it, marking its location with a little white cross.

She'd seemed so sweet, so much like the old Olivia that he'd forgotten that she was a business-woman out to get what she wanted at all costs, and would go right over him if he stood in her way.

He needed to get out of here. He couldn't pretend that this woman who had shattered his heart was someone he was going to allow in once again. He couldn't stand in front of the town and pretend she wasn't a shark, that she was harmless.

She'd broken his heart. That was a pretty big thing in his world.

The small group of reporters were all smiling, laughing, eating it up. Devon's stomach rolled.

"Devon, tell us more about how you and Carrington are going to create a greener, more prosperous Blueberry Springs." It was one of the reporters, eager for a sound bite.

Devon blinked. Were they for real? Did they not understand how ridiculous it was that they wanted to hear him repeat what he'd said earlier, like it mattered now that he was engaged to Miss Business? How did that make him a different person than he'd been two minutes ago?

Olivia clasped his hand again, her smile too tight, her eyes locking on his with a desperation that broke through his shock.

He hated himself right now. Hated that he

wanted to seize this opportunity to help her, help himself and the town.

His mouth hovered in front of the mic. From down the hall he heard loud voices, and the main door to the conference room closed.

He answered questions on autopilot, feeling uneasy about the increasing noise level outside the room, which was now turning heads. Someone had sent in the protesters.

It was time to go. He politely thanked everyone and tried to act casual as he hustled Olivia offstage. His grip on her arm was tight as he steered them into the connected meeting room. He immediately texted Logan, who was likely very busy on the other side of the wall.

"I am so sorry," Olivia was saying over and over again, her breath coming fast and hard enough that he thought she might be in danger of hyperventilating.

Devon sent the text and paced, hands in his hair. It was too short. He wasn't himself any longer. Wasn't in control of his life, his destiny. It felt as if he'd sold a piece of his soul. Or maybe Olivia had simply carved it off and eaten it again.

"Devon?" she pleaded.

"You just forge ahead with whatever you want, don't you? What you think is best, without taking into consideration what I might want, how I might feel… None of it matters as long as you get your way."

She took a step back, blinking. She opened her mouth to argue, her eyes wet. She looked decimated, and he knew deep down that she hadn't meant to blurt it out, that she wouldn't choose this farce. But she'd also created a sizable mess, putting him in an impossible position.

Man, that was messed up. How could he actually feel bad for her? But he did. It didn't help his anger, though.

"I have to *lie* to my family, Olivia, to voters. To everyone."

"I know. I'm sorry." Her head was bowed, her fingers tangled together.

"That's not who I am. I have never *once* lied to my family. Not even when I broke curfew as a teenager. And now I have to act as though I love you, and I don't."

That was one mistake he'd promised to never make again.

She was blinking furiously, her voice shaking as she repeated, "I know. I'm so sorry."

"What are we going to do? It's a mess out there." They couldn't take it back; they had to go forward with it. They had to trust each other.

The first time he'd trusted her, she'd taken his

heart. This time she could take his family, his town, his very identity.

But they were in it together now, as thick as thieves, and if they were going to make it out the other side without being decimated, they had to be honest with each other and trust each other like they never had before. They had to put all their hurt aside and become a real team.

Someone rapped lightly on the outer door—different from the one that connected to the meeting room. Devon cracked it open. It was Ginger, and the sound of protesters was suddenly overwhelming. He could hear Barry Lunn hollering above the din, "I'm sure they'll treat those rare plants with care. And besides, she doesn't really need them— she says their products are already perfectly safe and that they haven't harmed a single person. Her whole family wears Carrington."

Someone put a muzzle on that man. He was definitely not helping, and Devon wondered if that was Barry's intent. Redirect attention away from him and the dam, while setting his opponent up for something that surely wasn't good.

Devon dragged a hand down his face, focusing on Ginger, who was repeating something.

"Logan says use the back exits." She pointed down the emergency exit hallway before disappearing down it herself.

"Right. Okay." Devon glanced at Olivia. For once she wasn't trying to go talk sense into the protesters, but was waiting for his cue. He turned to her, speaking quietly. "I may have left you when you needed me the most, and you may have pushed me away, but if we're going to get through this we have to put that all in the past and stick together through thick and thin. If we don't, we both go down."

She nodded slowly, eyes cast to the side, unable to look at him.

"We stand back to back. I swear on my white horse I won't leave you. In return you promise not to shut me out."

She lifted her face, determination radiating off her as she straightened her shoulders. "Throw me in the loony bin if I ever marry for money or social standing."

He smiled. He'd quoted a conversation from the past and she'd quoted it right back. The promise was that if she gave in to her parents' expectations about her future, her life, then he was to come rescue her on his white horse.

He hadn't. But there was always time to correct the mistakes of the past.

CHAPTER 9

*W*hat had become of her life? Olivia had been in town for approximately forty-eight hours and was now fake-engaged to man she hadn't spoken to in a decade. She had angry protesters popping up around town, a security detail on her case, and she'd discovered her sister was sick, thanks to the very company that had given them everything they had.

And to top it all, her news feed had gone insane with mentions, and none of them were positive. The press was calling her a litterbug who didn't care about the earth. Accompanying photo—the beer cup being knocked out of her hand at the Vapid Magpie concert, only it looked like she was throwing it. Another of her as a big muddy mess, with a predictable headline about her company

raping the earth. Another of her at the press conference saying she was marrying Devon—that
headline essentially hinting that she'd created a
puppet so she could take over the town.

It was bad. She'd been searching for hours to
find a clear way out of it all—that magic pin to de-
flate the balloon of trouble so everyone could see
beyond it. See the truth, which was that Devon
would be good for the town. But all she'd found
was a headache that grew with each hour and each
new article.

Mr. Right jumped onto Devon's couch, curling
up beside her as the sound of a smokejumper's helicopter grew near. She rubbed her temples, trying
to pull herself together. She could feel the threads
letting go, unraveling, taking her with them. She
sniffed once, twice, then before she knew it, was
engulfed in Devon's strong arms as the dogs
crowded around.

He should have thrown her on the first bus out
of here, but instead he was being supportive and
kind. In the town building he'd said the sweetest
things, promising to be there for her. She didn't
know why, but those words had nearly broken her
apart. He was such a good man and she'd been a
complete fool pushing him away all those years
ago. Yes, she'd been overwhelmed, but she'd also
been dumb.

And now, with one moment of blurtacious behavior, she'd set them both up for enormous consequences. Her father would be angry, Luke hurt and upset. That she could handle. But Devon's family would likely be overjoyed that he'd found someone, then mad at her when they broke up the fake engagement. Add in the disaster that would occur if the town realized their mayoral hopeful was a liar—because of her.

She'd really put Devon in a bad spot.

"It'll all work out," he said. "We're a team, remember?"

"But your family's going to invite us over for supper and ask when we're going to have b-b-b—"

How was she going to get through this? She couldn't even say the word *baby*.

"Shh." Devon placed a finger over her lips, silencing her. "We can dodge the tricky stuff, and besides, I offered to marry you once. We'll be naturals." His tone was light, his effort to soothe her so much more than she deserved.

"I'm sorry, Devon."

"Don't be. Asking you to run away with me meant turning your back on your family, and that wasn't a fair thing."

"I wish I'd had the courage to say yes."

He was silent, his arms tightening around her.

She leaned back so she could see his face. "Can you forgive me someday for being so…awful?"

He kissed the top of her head. "You gave up a lot, you know, trying to do the right thing."

"That doesn't make it okay."

"Maybe not, but I think I have a better understanding now of why you did what you did."

There was a knock at the front door, sending the dogs barking. Devon got up, peeking through the peephole. He cursed under his breath. "We've got company."

The last thing she wanted to do with her puffy eyes was play pretty hostess.

"What in tarnation is going on in Blueberry Springs?"

Olivia jumped at the sound of her father's voice.

Devon stood between her and her dad, who was already looming in the doorway, his face red. Olivia's whole world stilled. There was nothing but the sound of Mr. Right's insanity freakout he reserved for her father.

"First, I hear there are protesters," her father boomed. "Then I see a picture of you looking like an unfit mess. Then one of you throwing alcohol around in a mosh pit last night. You've skipped three days of our company's retreat, ordered your sister to send your suitcases here and now you're *engaged*? To him!" He jabbed a finger in Devon's direction. Copter barked a low warning, moving between Devon and her dad. "Olivia Dawn, I demand answers, right this instant! And get this mangy mutt out of my face."

Devon rescued Mr. Right, tucking the squirming dog under his arm.

Olivia looked out the window. She could see Logan on the front step, arms crossed, looking unimpressed. She followed his gaze to the soccer field at the end of the road. There was a helicopter surrounded by curious kids.

"Daddy, this is a residential street." So much for the small-family-company image she'd been trying to cultivate around town. Not that, according to her news feeds, she was doing a very good job of it, but this definitely didn't help.

"Answers, Olivia," her father demanded.

Behind him, Luke stood tall, his eyes burning into Devon.

Oh.

Olivia sat, suddenly spent. Copter came over and tried to nudge her hand over his head.

Luke.

She hadn't called him back.

"I'm sorry."

"You're engaged?" Luke asked, his expression pained. "To him?"

Luke had an inkling of how drastically bro-

kenhearted she'd been after the breakup with Devon. Not the full extent, of course, and definitely
nothing about the baby, but enough to know all
of this was...sudden and somewhat out of
character.

"I can explain," she said weakly.

"You'd better," her father said.

"Sir, if I might," Devon said, his voice clear and
strong. He looked like a knight, ready to
defend her.

She'd never loved a man more.

Her father whirled on Devon. "You've caused
enough trouble for one lifetime. You don't get to
come back for more!"

"Daddy! It wasn't his fault."

"You need to let your daughter live the life she
was meant to," Devon said. "She's a grown woman
capable of making her own choices, but as soon as
she starts believing in herself, carving out a niche,
you come storming in to take over."

"Is this what 'believing in herself' looks like?
Because to me it looks like ruining the company I
spent thirty years building."

"Daddy!"

Luke opened his mouth to speak, but thought
better of it.

"Princess, we're going."

"No."

Her father blinked once. "I'm sorry?" His voice was quiet. Scary quiet.

Logan Stone filled the doorway, his brow furrowed. He looked ready to toss the first man who ticked her off.

"Daddy, Emma's sick."

Oh, no.

She really hadn't meant to say that. Luke's expression turned to one of concern and he took a step forward, while her father's anger simply increased.

"No," her father said. "This is about you and the mess you've created with your pet project. It is no more, you hear me? You're lucky I don't fire you."

Mr. Right squirmed in Devon's arms and barked at her father.

"Women need this product. And we have it, Daddy. We just need Devon to win the election and we'll have a whole meadow of valerian."

Her father turned his shrewd eyes to Devon. "That's what this is about? You needed my daughter to win an election?"

"Not exactly, sir, but we are working together."

"Daddy, this isn't about Devon. It's about the plants."

"Then find them elsewhere. You're not to go near this man again."

Olivia took Devon's hand, standing united with

him, unable to meet Luke's eye. "I'm an adult and I can choose who I want to marry." Devon gave her hand a supportive squeeze.

Her father was slowly taking in every detail about Devon's appearance, sizing him up.

Luke stepped forward, facing Devon. "You left her, pal. Broke her heart. You don't deserve a second chance. You don't know what she wants, you don't know her best."

"And you know everything about her?" Devon retorted, his eyes a deep well of emotion. "Every. Thing?"

Luke's eyes narrowed before he slid his gaze to Olivia, trying to decide whether Devon was bluffing. "Are you sure about him? About this?"

"Yes." She spoke quickly. "This isn't about the past." She moved to Luke, touching his hand. "You've always been my friend and I—"

Luke placed a finger over her lips, silencing her. "Olivia, hush. Get your closure. You know I'll be here when you need me." His gaze flicked to Devon, who put down a squirming Mr. Right, who then grabbed the cuff of Luke's pants, growling and trying to drag him toward the door.

"You're being foolish," her father said.

He was probably right. She had two men who didn't love her fighting over her, when all she was trying to do was help the company.

"I want to show you something. Come sit." Olivia sank down on the couch and pulled out the projections the marketing department had put together. Devon had printed it off for her, and it was the one bright ray of hope she'd had in her afternoon. Her father didn't move. "If you want to see the extent of my foolishness and why I insist on staying here, come sit," she commanded, her voice firm.

Her father's face softened slightly as though he was reevaluating her. He glanced at Devon, who gestured to the couch with a shrug. He'd calmed the dogs, and both were sitting at his feet now, although Mr. Right still gave out the occasional low growl.

When Luke went to join them on the couch, Olivia held up her hand. "I'm sorry, Luke," she said softly, "but this is..."

He looked disappointed, hurt, but he nodded once, ever the supportive friend. "I understand." He gave Olivia one last, lingering look, then headed outside. He returned a moment later. Devon, who had been heading to the kitchen to give Olivia and her father privacy, turned. The two men locked eyes. "Treat her right. She deserves the best."

Devon nodded.

"No. I mean it. If I hear..." Luke let out a long

breath, composing himself. "Just treat her right and there won't be any problems."

Olivia could tell Devon was holding his tongue as Luke left. His eyes met hers, his expression unreadable, before he left her alone with her father.

Olivia took a moment to pull her heart back into her chest. Any woman would be lucky to win the love of either man. So very lucky.

With her father by her side, she showed him the projections. He remained silent until she got to the end.

"Who put this together?" he asked, flipping the pages.

"The marketing department."

Her father tossed the bundle onto the coffee table. Then he turned slightly, studying her. She felt nervous, underdressed. Too casual.

"I'm worried about you."

"What? Why?" She picked up the printouts. They were solid, conservative at best. There was nothing to worry about.

"I'm concerned about last time." He lifted his gaze to the wall that separated them from Devon.

Oh.

"I've never seen anyone as devastated as you were."

The two of them had never talked about her and Devon after her father had transferred her to

Harvard and away from her ex-boyfriend and any memories associated with him.

"Promise me you'll be careful. Don't let him break you again."

"It takes two to break a heart, Daddy, and I did more than my share last time."

Her father stood with a hearty sigh. "I'm giving you two days to fix this. If things get worse before then, I'm pulling the plug on the project."

"You can't, Daddy. This is it! It's important."

"I know, but this whole thing could take us down." His tone was gentle, almost pleading. "Please understand that I have to protect Carrington above all else."

"But Emma and I *are* Carrington."

He gave her a sad look of understanding. "I know."

———

DEVON STOOD IN THE DOORWAY, watching Olivia. Her father had just left and she hadn't chased after him. Instead, she'd stood up to him, spoken her mind, given her sales pitch. But most of all, she'd stayed.

She'd chosen him, Devon.

And that felt pretty spectacular.

The most gorgeous and absolutely sexiest

woman he'd ever laid his sights upon had chosen him, their plan. Over her father's demands.

And yeah, yeah, yeah, he knew it wasn't quite that big. She was choosing her project, but it still felt like she was choosing him, too, and he wanted to revel in that win for a moment.

He sat down beside her. "You all right?"

She gave a nod and accepted the glass of wine he'd poured for her, then took a hearty sip.

"So?"

"I have two days to fix the PR mess or he's pulling the plug." She gave a small smile and a shaky laugh. "I've never stood up for myself with him before." She looked down, her expression turning somber. "I have a big mess to clean up."

"I'll help."

She laughed and the sound warmed him from the inside out like nothing had over the past decade. He'd missed that. "You're part of the big mess, you know." She leaned in, bumping her shoulder against his, setting her glass on the nearby coffee table.

She was taking this disaster quite well…which meant she'd either cracked or, dare he think it again, that it was an all-new world, one where she might actually choose him?

Then again, maybe she was simply choosing between the corporation and her sister. Because this was about business. Nothing personal.

He really needed to remember that.

"Am I really part of the mess?" He peered deep into her eyes for the truth.

She looked away with a sigh. "No, not really. But I'm afraid I'm going to fail, that I'm going to mess everything up again." She dropped her head in her hands, her loose curls creating a curtain around her face. He knew she wasn't freaking out, just thinking.

Nevertheless, anxiety squeezed him tight. "We'll figure it out. And you know what? I'll set you up with Jen Kulak. She's a local guide, and if anyone can find you more valerian, it's her. Okay? I'll make sure you won't lose even if I do."

Olivia had tipped her head up to look at him, scrutinizing him in a way that left him feeling bared before her.

"What?" he asked.

"Why are you being so nice?"

"I'm a nice guy. Didn't you notice? Or were you too busy staring at my chest?"

Her lips hooked up into a small, sly smile. "It's a good chest."

"I work out," he said, flexing subtly.

"Careful or you might rip your shirt."

"It's happened before. Women find it sexy, though."

She picked up her glass and stretched. "I'm bagged. I know it's early, but I'm going to call it a night."

"Olivia?"

She turned.

"You're doing the right thing...for your sister, for the company, for everyone."

She paused, her smile soft, her eyes moist. "Thanks."

He wanted to add that he was sorry if it was making things harder for her and Luke. But then again, the man had barely fought for her. He'd stepped away with honor. Who needed honor? If you loved a woman and thought you had a chance, you fought for her.

Devon caught Olivia's hand, giving it a brief, reassuring squeeze. "This is going to happen for you. I promise."

She gave another faint smile, then headed to her room. Devon sat for a long while, soaking up the silence. Two days to clean up the mess.

He walked past Olivia's room, wondering what he was going to do with himself. He'd let the dogs out already, but it was too early for sleep and his mind was stuck in hyperdrive. The way the press had all of a sudden slaughtered Olivia, the protesters showing up in the town offices right when he and Olivia had launched their A game...he had a feeling the timing wasn't at all coincidental, and that this was all due to Barry Lunn and some well-timed tip-offs to the media and collection of protesters.

He texted Logan to see if his suspicion seemed off target, and got an immediate reply. Logan already had a friend, Zach Forrester, secretly investigating Barry. It made Devon uncomfortable, but at the same time, if their current mayor could stoop that low...then wasn't it Devon's responsibility to find out, so he could protect his hometown? His family?

Plus, according to Logan, things were escalating. He'd found Olivia's Porsche, which they'd left outside the town offices, papered by the protesters. The entire car had been covered with glued-on flyers protesting corporate greed, toxins, environmental issues, and pretty much anything else ever protested in the free world. He only hoped his brother-in-law Frankie, who owned a custom body shop, could save the paint job before Olivia saw her car again.

Logan signed off, reminding Devon to lock his doors. The man would be sleeping in his car, watching the house, and had already taken the liberty of adding a few surveillance cameras and motion detectors.

Things were getting serious and Devon joked that Logan should add tracers to their cars, as well. He had a feeling when Logan didn't reply that there would be tracking devices on their cars come morning. But if that helped keep Olivia protected, then it was well worth it.

Devon paced the hallway outside their bedrooms, trying to figure out how to get a step ahead of Barry. A big step. An election-winning step. Because with Olivia standing up for herself in front of her father? Well, she needed a win. And those protesters needed to see that she couldn't be cowed.

"Devon?" It was Olivia calling him through her closed bedroom door.

He let himself into her room and froze. She was in that nightie created for every male fantasy, sitting on the futon, her back to him. Surely there was a different nightgown in her suitcase that she could wear instead of this piece of temptation?

"Yeah?" he asked, his voice cracking. Nice going, body. Way to make him sound like a man.

"Do you trust me?" She looked at him over her shoulder, her brow furrowed with sorrow.

He was at her side before he could think better of it, her hand in his.

243

"Of course. You have a solid plan. And I think having a sit-down with the leader of the protest group will solve a lot." But so would running Barry out of town, if that had been his style.

"No." Olivia pressed her bare knee into the side of his leg, the short nightie riding so high he could almost see her panties. Not that he was looking. Much. That was a lot of creamy inner thigh, though. Enough to distract any man, prevent him from looking his woman in the eye.

Not his woman. Roger that. But a few right moves and she could be.

How horrible was he? She was in a tricky place right now, vulnerable. He needed to be a gentleman. Look up.

Man, she had beautiful cleavage. So round and—

"My eyes are up here, Devon."

"Your nightie is enough to give any man—sorry." Not appropriate. Had to be nice, adultish and all that. Prove himself. No jokes.

"I meant, do you trust me?"

Two days ago the answer would have been a heartfelt "no way." But since then he'd…what? Changed his mind?

She pulled away as he pondered the question.

"I care, Olivia," he said, grabbing her hand. "I care what you think. I care that you're scared, hurt and frustrated right now. When I let you give me a makeover, I let you in. I couldn't do that if I didn't trust you. Yeah, you're not perfect, but that's what I like best about you. You do your best to get back up when you've been knocked down, and oddly enough, I think you might actually have my best interests at heart."

Her lips were on his before he could register the fact that her exquisite, barely clad body was wrapping itself around his, pushing him back against the bed with a familiarity that broke through his ability to resist. He couldn't keep his hands to himself, his fingers slipping under her garment, up over her rib cage before he forced them back down to her waist. She kissed him with tongue and body, leaving him shaking with pent-up desire he wasn't sure he should release.

Her hands were petting his chest, untucking his shirt, smoothing their way over his abs, cupping his face. Everywhere. Desperate. Cool and familiar. She panted and gasped, spurring him on, and there were too many sweet memories of her letting go as they worked their way to nirvana, too much still simmering between them despite everything that had separated them, hurt them. He could practically taste the lethal doses of desire and attraction, but there was also a hint of something else. Something bitter, and much more devastating on a soul level.

He couldn't afford to lose this game. Not a second time. He wasn't strong enough.

He rolled her off him and stood, locking his hands behind his head as he sucked in a deep breath. His new position was worse. Now he could see her in all her sexy, tempting glory, stretched out on the bed, reminding him of how utterly intoxicating and consuming she could be. Her thighs seemed as though they went on forever. Except he knew exactly where they ended and exactly what that spot tasted like.

Seeing her in this sexy little number meant to drive a man wild with its teasing, seductive innocence, her lips plump from their bruising kisses—it did things to his mind that he had no right to act on, and might never again. And yet he'd never met a woman as curvaceous, clever and charming, and Olivia…she just got under his skin in a way that made everything in his life wholly about her.

Never again. She was like one of those traps you saw in movies where the forest floor suddenly dropped out, sending you into an inescapable hole.

She bit her bottom lip.

Man, that drove him nuts.

Olivia had given him the green light. She was inviting him in. Choosing him.

And he was standing on the opposite side of the room like a scared fool.

She sat up, turning her back to him once more, apologizing over her shoulder, her eyes cast down. Her massive curls brushed her bare skin and he wasn't sure if she knew the effect, but it made him want to sweep those locks off the nape of her neck and trail kisses down to her shoulder blades. He still remembered all the ways to make her tremble and call out his name, fingernails dug deep into his back.

But the one thing he couldn't remember was why they couldn't have that again. Why he was resisting.

"WHAT WOULD you do if you were me?" Devon asked Olivia.

"Right now?" She didn't want to answer that.

His words about liking her because she wasn't perfect had been like a balm on a burn. She'd thrown herself at him, kissed him like she was starving for affection, for his body, her need so great…so embarrassing. And he'd rejected her.

He trusted her title, her job, but not *her,* because she continued to fail him, fail herself as she put them in impossible positions.

She cut her eyes away from his body, so tempting, so *right*. Straightened her back, trying to act unaffected by the fact that only moments ago she'd been panting, kissing him, wishing his hands would go higher or lower. Not play it safe, but give in to that something that burned between them. Blast away the confusion of their day and just *connect*. Give life to that something that had flashed between them, scorching her with a crazy need for him.

But that wasn't what he wanted. It was about business. She should have remembered that. Sex would make it personal, take them down a one-way road. And make it harder to go back to Luke and all that awaited her with him. But somehow, right now, that didn't seem to matter. She wanted more than Luke could ever give her.

She wanted Devon. He was what mattered. He was the one who made her feel real, and she wanted every morsel he'd allow her to claim.

She cleared her throat, focusing on their PR issue. "First, I'd rally friends and family for support, and demonstrate all the ways you are, in fact, not a puppet."

"Not as a PR person. As…you."

"What?" She looked up.

He licked his lips and swallowed. "I meant…if you were me, right here, right now." His body language was quiet, as if he was waiting for a cue. Which way? Yes or no? "What would you do?"

Oh. *Oh.* He meant…here in the bedroom.

He knew that whatever they did would change things, and he cared enough to make sure she didn't think this was going to be a mistake. He needed to know that she wanted this—whatever it was—for all the right reasons.

He cared.

Wow, that was sexy.

And it gutted her, reminding her of what a rock he'd been for her in school, the support, the ability to read her, see her, set her free.

She stood, guiding his hand to her waist, standing close, sharing heat. "I would start by doing this." She gave him a soft kiss, her palms light against his shoulders. "And this." She wrapped her arms around his neck, kissing him longer, slower. "And if you were in my shoes, what would you do?"

"I'd probably lick my chest," he said honestly, giving her a wicked smile.

He still knew her so well.

———

OLIVIA DIDN'T KNOW what had overcome her. She watched Devon sleep, his naked body curled against hers. She'd seen him try to be a gentleman, try to back away from the inevitable. They'd ended up in bed anyway, taking their time as they revisited some of their favorite places.

Even though he felt different than he had years ago, his body more honed, less erratic in its power, he'd been the same. He still contained the same perfect blend of gentleness and strength. As they'd moved together she'd felt the connection. The old one. The one where she felt unchained, as if nothing was holding her down any longer. It forged with the new, bringing up a well of feelings.

She'd forgotten how light, how happy she could feel. How easy a smile could feel, how his returned one could open her heart, her entire being.

He was amazing.

And he was her fiancé.

She rolled onto her back.

Fiancé.

It wasn't real. Wasn't true, but it was certainly a problem. And not just because she was lying to everyone in this little town he was striving to win over. They were lying to the people he'd known since forever, people who trusted him.

The biggest thing would be to minimize any potential damage by preventing anyone from seeing their deception.

In the bedroom, it turned out, she could fake

her way through an engagement. But kissing Devon in the light of day? Holding his hand? Smiling and making doe eyes in public? Putting herself out there and revisiting old emotions? And all those little gestures…they somehow felt much more intimate than what they'd done last night. The tender touches and looks that new lovers shared were going to be difficult—difficult because what if her heart started to believe they were real?

She sneaked a peek at Devon, his body limp in slumber, a small smile curving his lips.

The town needed him.

"Good morning," he said, his voice deep and sleepy.

"Hey," she said softly. He hadn't moved back to his own bed in the night even though the futon was small, not quite a queen. She wasn't sure what that meant, exactly.

"I haven't slept like that in forever."

She'd forgotten how sexy he was with his five o'clock shadow and raspy voice. She needed to be careful, not kid herself that he was actually hers.

"Vibrating with masculine power, as always, I see," she teased.

He grinned, flexing his biceps. Mr. Right wiggled his body up the covers, then laid his nose on Devon's arm. What a sucker her dog was.

"Face it, Devon Mattson." She sat up and

smoothed the sheet over her, feeling awkward for her nudity. She needed her clothes. "You're nothing more than man candy."

He chuckled. "I thought you were working on improving that."

"One day at a time."

"So? What's on the docket today, Livvy?"

She paused, letting the nickname sink in. Livvy. He used to call her that when they were dating, and hearing it again made her feel warm inside.

Dangerous.

Endearments and nicknames were definitely on the danger list. Those were the things that were going to trip her up, hurt her. But him calling her Livvy wasn't the big one—it was Liv. If he called her Liv it meant he cared and was feeling tenderly toward her. And that, for her, would surely mean game over.

"Mostly damage control," she said, tugging the sheet a little higher before stretching.

Devon caught the bedding with his toes, helping it drift lower. She curled forward, snatching it up again. "Devon!"

"It's not like I haven't seen it before." He stretched a hand to her hip, where she had a tattoo of a butterfly. "Except this." His head ducked under the sheet, his lips touching its wings despite her attempts to squirm away. Last night was one thing, a good thing…but she didn't want to get into a cozy habit of acting like they were truly fiancé and fiancée, and had rights to pleasuring each other.

"I got that after my grandma passed away." She finally managed to wiggle out of his grip.

His eyes met hers and he eased back to his own side of the bed, his knee sticking out from the covers, revealing a long scar she'd noticed last night. She flicked her gaze to it.

"That's also new."

"I was putting a metal Christmas star on a roof."

"Always helping others, hey, Boy Scout?"

He smiled. "Some things don't change. Like your affection for Porsches."

"If you find something you like, why not stick with it?"

"Why indeed?"

Their eyes met and she found that connection, that ability to share words with one simple look, reengaged. She'd missed that more than she'd realized, his familiarity warming her.

They'd once been best friends. They'd once been great at playing off each other, letting life and all its seriousness fall behind as it became about just the two of them. And even though she knew this moment was fleeting, she couldn't help but wish it could last forever.

Fiancée. Why did that sound so good rolling around in his head? That word should be sending him running to the hills. And it wasn't.

Maybe because it was all fake.

That, and he was basking in the glow of having been spectacularly taken advantage of by a woman who knew her way around his body like she owned it, commanding it with her every move.

Oh, yeah. It was definitely that.

This fake relationship thing was going to be awesome.

"So…engaged, huh?" he confirmed, sitting up as she began searching for clothes, the sheet tucked around her.

"Is there a better plan, or way out of it?" She wasn't looking at him.

Back to business. Pleasure time over.

He understood that. They'd had flares of connection all night and then again this morning, and it brought with it a flood of memories. All pleasant, but with a not-so-fun ending.

"I have to go in to work, but I think there's something we need to take care of first."

"What?"

"I have something for you."

She gave him a look out of the corner of her eye. "Should I be nervous?"

He waggled his eyebrows. "Not in the least."

He slipped on his pair of boxers and zipped into his bedroom. He opened his closet door, reaching high inside. He'd forgotten about the box. Almost. But not quite. Kind of like his feelings for Olivia. He'd deep-sixed those, but they seemed to be bubbling up anyway—unwanted, unnecessary. He reminded himself it was just the sex doing that, unearthing things, stirring up the past. It wasn't real, it was just a form of therapy—bringing them up so they could be placed properly on the funeral pyre this time, giving them both closure so they could move on and find the right person to complete their lives.

He rejoined Olivia with a shoebox and lifted the lid. There was an odd assortment of mementos from their relationship that had managed to find their way back to Blueberry Springs, and among them was a ring box.

"I bought this when…"

Her large brown eyes expanded, welling with tears.

Yeah. Exactly.

He swallowed hard, forcing his voice to be light. "I thought maybe this could become part of our ruse."

He opened the box and held it out. The ring, which had diminished in his mind over the years, connected to such pain, shone bright, feeling suddenly ever so large and full of potential and hope.

OLIVIA COULD BARELY BREATHE from the effort of holding back tears. Devon had bought her an engagement ring. All those years ago, when he'd asked her to marry him, he'd been completely serious.

And the mementos in the box... So many of them. He'd kept them through the heartbreak, through everything. Why? What did it mean?

She held back a sob, her whole chest burning from the effort of holding it in.

It really had been so very real. For both of them.

What if she'd said yes? What if she'd taken the insanely risky leap? What if they'd run off together? Would they still have lost it all? Or would it have turned out okay—even the baby—because they'd held on to love?

She managed to inhale, then exhale, a torrent of tears breaking free despite her attempt to fight them.

"Oh, Devon," she whispered, her fingertips brushing her lips.

This felt real.

A fake engagement that felt as though it had been brought out of the ashes of their past, rekindling the hope she'd once had, giving life and meaning to last night's resurfaced feelings.

"Just for the ruse," he whispered again, his voice choked with an emotion she didn't dare look up to confirm.

She curled her legs under her, leaning forward. But instead of taking the ring, she kissed him for believing in her when she hadn't. For choosing hope. For trusting and loving her. For keeping the ring. But most of all, for trying.

His mouth opened in surprise as their lips connected, her tongue tangling with his. His arms went around her waist, slowly bringing her closer, angling her down onto the bed alongside him. He brushed the hair from her cheek with such tenderness her tears started again.

She should stop this. Before things went the wrong way, got too deep, felt too real.

But it felt so right—like nothing she'd ever experienced with anyone else, and she didn't ever want the feeling to end, because she still cared ever so deeply for Devon Mattson.

CHAPTER 10

*D*evon had gone in to work and Olivia was currently trying not to admire her new ring while hiking through the forest with local guide Jen Kulak. The day was bright, her hope like a bubble in her chest, ready to expand to the point of lifting her feet off the ground.

She was happy. *Happy.*

She hadn't felt this way in a very long time.

It's not real, she reminded herself. But that didn't mean she couldn't allow herself to savor it, roll the treat around in her mouth, tasting and exploring it in wonder.

It wouldn't last. She knew that. But right now it was wonderful and perfect. Just like last night had been.

Smiling, she hustled after Jen, a new mom who

was chatting up a storm, while taking on the trail like a mountain goat, scampering up the inclines even with the added weight of a chubby baby strapped to her chest.

"What a view," Olivia said halfway up, turning to look out over the forest, hands on her hips as she struggled for breath. There was no view. Just trees. Lots and lots of trees. Although on this particular hill, about twenty minutes into the hike, all plant life was short, waist height or less. That was odd. Clear-cutting? Fire? Mudslide?

Jen came back down the trail to stand beside her.

"How are the new hikers?" She looked down at Olivia's tan-and-blue hiking shoes. "Any rubbing?"

"No, they're great, actually." Olivia wiggled her toes. When Jen had picked her up at Devon's that morning, she'd taken one look at Olivia's outfit, driven her to the sporting goods store she ran her excursions out of, and outfitted her from head to toe.

And Olivia had to admit, the clothing was all great and very comfortable. Even the brand-new footwear was surprisingly comfy. Most of her heels needed days of breaking in before she could trust spending hours in them. Unlike these shoes. She could practically live in them.

"Good. I thought so." Jen began walking again,

slower this time. "I love the forest. Did I tell you I once thought I'd burned this part of it down? Oh, man. The whole town was full of smoke and there was a voluntary evacuation." She had a purple streak in her blond hair and part of it had escaped her ponytail. She brushed it out of her eyes and laughed. "But it turned out to be arson, not me. That's how I met my fiancé, Rob."

Jen became unusually quiet and Olivia looked at the ring on her own finger. *Fiancé.*

The word and the ring felt foreign, yet right. She couldn't imagine how much Devon, a student at the time, must have spent on the ring. That was likely the real reason he'd saved it all these years. Not out of hope or anything else. He'd probably planned to give it to the first woman who came along and declared herself his fiancée.

That thought hardly sat well.

"You okay?" she asked Jen, focusing on the woman's frown and silence, instead of her own muddled thoughts.

"Yeah, yup," Jen replied with false cheer. "He was the fire investigator sent to check me out, if you can believe it. Totally doomed relationship situation, but it somehow worked out in the end."

Olivia twisted her ring, wondering how she and Devon were going to end their relationship and when. Maybe she could just go home and avoid a public breakup. They could eventually let the word out that they'd been unable to do the long-distance thing.

She'd miss him, though. She liked feeling as though someone had her back. Joking with her, lightening the mood, accepting her, flaws and all.

"When are you and Devon getting married?"

Olivia's head snapped up. Wedding. Right.

She took a deep breath to steady herself.

"We haven't chosen a date," she said carefully. "The election is keeping him pretty busy right now."

"I never thought I'd get married," Jen said soberly. "I promised myself I wouldn't...but after having Finn..." She gestured to the sleeping baby strapped to her. "It just felt like the next logical step. We were already living together and it was good. So, you know?"

Olivia nodded as if she understood, but there was something in Jen's eyes that looked an awful lot like fear.

Jen started laughing as she turned to head back up the path that wound its way through the shrubbery. "I tumbled down this hill once. Oh, man. That's when I realized I was falling in love with Rob. You can't slide down a mountain with just anyone without realizing you have feelings for them."

Olivia tried to figure that one out as Jen continued, "I guess I'm just saying you never know what's going to bond two people together."

"Right." That she could understand. Like her and Devon. First they'd bonded over a hellish management class, and now over a fake engagement and a mutual need for a stinky flower she hoped to find more of on this hike.

"So you two used to date?" Jen asked.

"We were pretty serious in school."

"What happened?"

Olivia shrugged. "Life, I guess." Literally.

"Was he your first serious guy?"

"Yeah," she said softly.

"Those ones always leave a funny hole, don't they?"

"Yeah, they do," she agreed, not wanting to dig into all of that. "Are we almost there?"

"Just over the top of this rise."

Olivia had wanted Vintra to join them, but he'd protested, saying he needed to finish up the tests in his little hotel room, which he'd managed to score for another night, keeping them in Blueberry Springs for at least another day.

And the clock was ticking for Olivia to fix things so her father didn't turn off the lights.

But she had a plan. As always. She would collect the valerian for Vintra, meet with the protesters' leader at one. Help Devon with his campaign, as well as write a few press releases for both of them.

They reached the top of the incline, and before them stretched an area that had been burned and was now filled with small trees and plants trying to outdo each other in the cleared space. And lots of white flowers glowing in the sunshine.

"Ta-da," Jen said lightly.

Olivia inspected one of the closest plants. It was the valerian strain she was looking for. "This is it. Thank you." She stood, stretching, mentally counting how many plants filled the clearing. At least two hundred. Not enough, but it was a decent backup plan, and they could mine a few seeds and roots before the area became overgrown again, choking out the valerian.

Jen's son woke up, his perfect mouth puckering before a large, toothless yawn overtook half his face.

"He's adorable," Olivia said.

Jen smiled. "We named him after the movie star Finian Alexander. His new wife has ties to Blueberry Springs."

"It's a nice name."

Olivia stepped off the path to inspect the valerian and Jen released her baby from the gadget that had him strapped to her. "Can you hold him for a second? I need to use the bushes. Childbirth is torture on the bladder."

Olivia accepted the baby, blinking at him in surprise.

She stood, bouncing him on her hip while chatting, careful to keep her back to Jen, who was searching for a bush.

"Do you like hiking? Hmm?" she asked Finn. The boy reached up, placing a hand on her cheek, his eyes so large, wide and trusting. "I'm Olivia." She shook his tiny hand and he rewarded her with a gummy smile that made her heart tug. She inhaled his scent, holding him close while looking out over the field of valerian. "I'm going to create a product that will keep all the women in your life safe, okay, Finn? I'm looking out for them."

"Hey, thanks," Jen said, returning to them and reaching for her child. "So? It's the right valerian?"

Olivia nodded and they set to work selecting a small plant to take to Vintra.

"Devon's helped me out with a ton of stuff, and it's nice to be able to help out his fiancée," Jen commented.

Olivia nodded, absorbing the reference. She was going to have to get used to being called Devon's fiancée, and the little blood rush that followed.

She packed up her bag and they headed back down the mountain.

Jen's brow was furrowed again and Olivia wondered what was on her mind.

"When are you getting married?" she asked.

Jen inhaled sharply. "This weekend."

"Wow. That's exciting."

Jen smoothed her child's hair, quietly taking extra care with her steps down the trail.

Olivia pictured something small, outdoors, casual, but full of love. "An intimate affair?"

"Yeah. I don't really have a lot of family to fill my side of the church, so we're doing something outdoors. But it's supposed to rain and the music festival has everything booked up and I lost weight and my dress is floppy and horrible. I wanted to elope, but everyone in town just kind of started inviting themselves and planning it all." Jen sat heavily on a boulder and sighed. Olivia winced, worrying about the woman's tailbone.

"That sounds stressful," she said, sitting beside her. They were in the shade, the rock cold under them.

Jen tightened her ponytail with a ruthless yank. "I can handle it." The way her brow furrowed told Olivia otherwise. "I mean...Rob. It's not like if we're married anything's going to change. And so what if there's a party? It's nice that people want to celebrate with us, right? Yeah, it's totally fine. Good. Great." She stood up, heading down the trail again.

Olivia had the feeling the woman would break out into a run if she was alone.

"Can I help?" Olivia asked, catching up.

"It's just jitters."

Jen had saved her bacon, giving her a viable backup plan for the valerian. Olivia wanted to help her, wanted to fix things for her. Be the kind of woman Devon deserved. "What about your dress?"

"I'm still losing baby weight." She rested a hand on top of Finn's powder blue sunhat. "It's too big and Ginger's seamstress is out of town until next week." She muttered under her breath, "I knew we should have eloped."

Ah, Jen was Ginger's bride in a pinch, the owner of the gown Ginger had asked Olivia to alter. A few days ago she'd been afraid to allow her old dreams back into her life, but now she was confident she could face a minor alteration without losing track of herself or her current goals.

"Maybe I can help. I used to sew."

Jen frowned doubtfully, taking in Olivia's crisp new hiking outfit. Yeah, she looked a poser. Someone who bought all the right stuff to look the part, not someone who could actually create something with her hands.

"I'm only a few classes away from a minor in fashion design," she said. "I designed and created wedding gowns from scratch for a drama production."

Jen was considering her and Olivia held her breath. Her little résumé didn't sound too bad, actually. But as Devon had mentioned, she'd given up her dreams and now here she was.

"I'm pretty sure I still remember how to take in a dress," Olivia added. "Ginger can vouch for me."

"You know, she's the second Ginger I know?" Jen was relaxing now, her assessment of Olivia seemingly over. "Are you sure you don't mind trying?"

"What's the worst that can happen? You still don't have a dress and we have to beg Ginger to find something super last minute?"

Jen turned to face her, suddenly engulfing her in a hug, little Finn sandwiched between them. Olivia smiled, feeling more like herself than she had in eons.

DEVON PUSHED his papers into the new leather briefcase Olivia had found for him and stretched. It felt foreign and grown-up, but it was nice. Surprisingly soft and definitely professional. He checked his watch. He'd grab a quick lunch, then join her for her meeting with the protesters' leader, Muriel Rossis. Logan had promised to continue tailing her today, as well as be present for the meeting.

Devon paused, absently tapping his desk. Last night with Olivia had opened up the past. Their anger and hurt had been put deeper into storage, its power waning. Olivia seemed to be slipping into his life as if she'd never left.

He'd been able to successfully push it all away until he'd seen her face when he'd given her the ring that morning. She'd looked so…honored. Delighted. Like the piece of jewelry represented much more than a discarded relic that had been lying around in his room. It had been almost as though it had settled a long-standing turmoil inside her.

Devon tugged at his tie. The whole thing had felt…it had…

Man, he couldn't breathe in here. He opened his office window and gulped in the fresh mountain air.

He ran a hand through his hair, grumbling at its shortness. He needed this week to be over. There were too many things to worry about, too many things to keep an eye on—including his heart.

"Hey!" Don, an older man on staff who had bounced in and out of retirement a few times, paused in his doorway. "I hear congratulations are in order."

Devon turned from the window. "Right. Are you and your wife coming to the candidate dinner on the weekend?" It was an event he was dreading. Speeches. Boring, boring, boring. It was like painting walls white, then watching them dry so you could put on a second coat. Pointlessly boring. Who actually changed their mind after a dinner like that? It was a big fuss for nothing.

"We haven't decided yet. Are you bringing Olivia?"

"I'm not sure. Her office is actually out of town."

The man considered his reply. "Priscilla wants to meet her. She's heard the rumors about how she's made you a changed man and wants to see for herself." He gave Devon a wink. "You know, taming the wild stallion of Blueberry Springs."

Devon let out of a bark of laughter. "Stallion, huh? I'd need to have had a lot more successful dates in my past to make that name anywhere near realistic."

Then again, if Don's wife wanted to meet the new woman in town—the one who had hooked Devon, tamed the untamable and all that—maybe the dinner *was* a good idea. He hoped Olivia was still around by then.

Don had a hint of a smile as he took in Devon's

uncharacteristically subtle, plain necktie. Self-consciously, Devon smoothed it over his chest. It was a pricey silk item Olivia had picked up along with the briefcase.

She'd informed him that the tie would bring out his eyes, and his manhood seemed to be in question because every time he looked in the mirror he saw it. Eyes brought out, shining like those of a dimwitted fool who'd become smitten by a woman who had no intention of sticking around long-term.

Then again, neither did he, and at least they both knew it this time.

"It looks good on you." Don nodded with pride. "Clothes make the man."

"Yeah."

"So wedding bells?" Don asked.

"Yup." Devon latched his briefcase, shaking his head when he discovered he was smiling. He let out a chuckle of disbelief. "Crazy, huh?"

He thought of Olivia's glimmering eyes so full of…whatever it was. Thought of her trusting smile, their session in bed. It really wasn't so bad pretending to be engaged.

Don just raised his eyebrows with a knowing grin and disappeared down the hall, calling out, "See you at Brew Babies."

"What?" Devon asked, leaning out of his office.

"For lunch. A bunch of us are meeting up in ten."

Devon checked the time. Sweet deal. An early lunch with the guys—exactly what he needed to get his head on straight and Olivia out of his mind so he could concentrate.

"Be there?" Don asked, walking backward.

"Promise no ribbing from the guys over my engagement?"

Don just laughed and Devon went back for his briefcase, knowing his sudden hookup was definitely going to be the focus of a lot of teasing. Brew Babies was only a five minute walk, but arriving a bit early would give him a chance to settle himself before the friendly firing squad let loose.

As Devon closed his window he saw Barry Lunn's son, Pete, cross the street, a ream of papers in hand. Devon peered closer. Were they from the same batch that had plastered Olivia's car? Was there truly a connection between the protesters and the current mayor, or was Devon becoming paranoid?

"Howdy, stranger."

Devon turned to see Jill Armstrong smiling in his doorway. Ex-girlfriend, fellow employee and valerian expert.

"How was your weekend?" he asked, knowing

she'd planned to do some hiking and flower investigating after meeting up with him and Olivia.

"Great. I found more flowers I needed for the creams and a healing balm."

Just another reason to save the meadow. Jill had found more than valerian there and was building her own skin care line that she hoped to expand next year. Maybe even with a firm like Carrington. Although the chances were the two weren't quite a fit unless Carrington expanded their own product line into lotions and creams. Luke Cohen's firm would be a good match—assuming the guy wasn't currently plotting Devon's demise due to scooping his woman out from under him. Not that Devon planned on keeping Olivia, but the man didn't know that.

Devon still couldn't believe how Luke had just let him have her. Olivia deserved a man who'd at least fight for her, fight for love. Devon nearly snorted in disgust, surprised by his feelings of protectiveness for her.

Wait one hot second. Olivia had taken Devon to bed. Did that mean she wasn't serious about Luke?

Aw, man. That actually made him feel a bit bad for the guy.

Which meant, again, he needed lunch with the guys to help get his head back on straight. Too much thinking. Too much worrying about other people. He had an election to win.

"The balms are coming along?" he asked Jill, realizing he'd tuned out what she'd been saying about plants.

Her eyes lit up, her passion evident. "I'm going to sell my first entire skin care line at the farmers market this weekend." She reached over and snagged his tie, flipping it over with a frown. "Where's the cartoon character?"

"There isn't one today."

She was still frowning, her expression floating somewhere between unhappy and, well...unhappy.

Devon allowed her to stroke the smooth fabric flat again, and felt mildly guilty. The relationship between him and Jill had been short-lived because, as usual, he hadn't been enough of that special, magical blend women needed from a man. She'd been a wonderful, patient girlfriend, but had ultimately deserved more than a daredevil goofball. In some ways he'd always thought they would eventually pick up where they'd once left off. Possibly make one of those if-we're-not-married-by-thirty-five-we'll-marry-each-other pledges like their friends Moe and Amy had going on.

Jill was staring at him, searching for something in his gaze. He felt like he had to make it up to her—though what, exactly, he didn't know. For being with

Olivia? For appearing to have backed out of their friendly, never-actually-verbalized marriage deal?

But things had been awkward and bumpy between them for some time now, and she had to know they weren't ever going to get back together. They just weren't right for each other.

"I like this new look," she said. "Are you growing up, Devon Mattson?" Her tone was playful and flirty as she came closer.

"Not a chance." The thought that she might find his makeover appealing left him feeling the need to retreat.

"Because to me, this all looks a little sudden. A bit…fishy."

"It's real." He cleared his throat, putting his chair between them for protection, glad the chair's back reached past crotch level. Just in case. "Olivia and I used to date years ago and we just kind of…" He shrugged, not wanting to lie, but wanting the right story to get out there.

He was becoming as bad as Olivia.

Jill stared at him for a long moment. "You never mentioned her."

He cleared his throat, feeling uncomfortable. "It was a bad breakup."

Silence stretched between them.

"Well, it's nice for you. You deserve someone…"

Her eyes settled on the tie, the new briefcase. "Someone you're willing to change for."

OLIVIA WAS CURRENTLY BEING DRAGGED away from Main Street by Ginger, who had her by the arm. Logan silently walked beside them, his forehead deeply furrowed. Olivia and Jen had dropped off the valerian for Vintra and then Jen had left Olivia at Devon's—should she start calling it their place? —so she could get changed out of her hiking clothes before finding lunch and then meeting with Muriel Rossis, the protest leader.

She was now in a pair of pale pink flats, designer jeans and a frilly blouse. Professional but casual. The day was beautiful and Olivia had planned on walking downtown to have lunch before retrieving her car from the spot she'd parked it in before yesterday's press conference. But Logan, who was still tailing her, had given her a lift, and in the end they'd wound up on foot, following Ginger to a pub for lunch.

"You'll love this place," her friend assured her, as they cut across a residential street, the small homes lining it well-kept and adorable. Flower boxes, large porches. Rosebushes. Olivia could just about imagine herself sitting in one of the porch swings, idly watching the day go past.

They rounded the corner and there was a gravel parking lot—no impossible heels on her feet today! —and a pub called Brew Babies. Even from fifteen feet away Olivia could hear the hubbub inside the busy place.

"I should warn you," Ginger said. "A couple of people wanted to meet you—the woman who finally managed to pin down Devon."

Olivia felt a shot of pride for catching Mr. Unattainable, before remembering it was just an act.

"Hey, guys!"

Olivia turned, recognizing the voice. Devon. Her fiancé.

She panicked inside. How was she supposed to act? Ginger, her old BFF, would pick up on everything. But she was also the best secret keeper in the world. However, Olivia really didn't need to pile another secret on her friend's shoulders. And then there was Logan, who seemed to notice absolutely everything and had been trained to ruthlessly identify sneaks and liars. In other words, her.

Olivia waited for Devon to catch up, then rose up onto her tiptoes to plant a kiss on his cheek. He smiled.

"What do I have to do to get one of those on the lips?"

"We're in public," she scolded gently, hoping Ginger and Logan bought the excuse.

"Smooch away, lovebirds. Doesn't bother me. I used to be Olivia's roommate, remember?" Ginger winked at them and Olivia felt her face heat. "Oh, you're so cute when you act all modest."

Ginger opened the door to the pub, ignoring a sign that said it was closed for a private gathering. As they stepped into the dimly lit room, Olivia's eyes were momentarily blinded by the change in light. She stumbled backward as voices hollered, "Surprise!"

Devon wrapped his arms around her, sheltering her from the sudden outburst. She began laughing, delighted as her eyes slowly took in the faces of several people she'd met over the past few days, plus some. Even Vintra was there.

"For us?" she asked.

Devon stiffened, his arms like a vise around her. She was certain she heard him curse under his breath.

To their right was a table laden with wrapped gifts, and he cursed again as his gaze followed hers. He muttered something about taking advantage of people's trust.

She was going to lose him. He was going to confess and the repercussions would be huge for him. She couldn't let him fail. She had to protect him.

She turned in Devon's arms, placing her hands against his shoulders. "We've got this." She straightened his tie with affection, letting a smile play at her lips.

Devon's arms, which had been around her, loosened, his hands drifting until they landed on her hips.

"You have a plan?" he asked.

"Always."

Over her shoulder she noticed Ginger and Logan sharing a look.

"Just…roll with it," she whispered to Devon.

An older man she hadn't yet met, but who looked a lot like Devon, placed a flute of champagne in her hand, another in Devon's. He smiled at her, then turned to the gathered group lifting his own flute in the air. "Cheers to the new couple! And can I just say, it's about time someone managed to rope this boy into a serious romantic commitment?" The room filled with hearty cheers. "You're obviously one of a kind, woman." He smiled at Olivia again. "Welcome to Blueberry Springs."

Breaking up was going to be so hard.

She turned to Devon. "To us and our dreams." She clinked her glass against her fiancé's. They each took a sip, eyes locked, and several people let out soft awws.

"Kiss! Kiss!" Clinking began on glasses as though it was a wedding reception.

Olivia lifted a brow, looking at Devon. "Better make it convincing, sweetie." She gave the crowd a coy glance and people hooted with laughter.

"We may as well give them what they want," he said with a shrug. He took her champagne and handed it off to Ginger, along with his own. Olivia stood uncertainly, unsure what he was up to. He grasped her, bending her backward as their lips met, giving her a deep kiss with a great amount of flourish and show. The room erupted again.

He set her back on her feet and the man who'd toasted them shook her hand. "I'm Devon's father, Cory, and this is my wife, Trish. I believe the two of you have met?"

Olivia nodded and Trish beamed at them and dabbed at her eyes.

There were more introductions, and so many hugs. Hugs from everyone. Heartfelt congratulations. Before long, Olivia felt as if she'd been introduced to the entire town, and began to lose track of names until a very pregnant woman, Nicola, was introduced. Olivia could tell from the way Devon acted that he and Nicola were close. So close that, judging from how the woman was staring at Olivia, she knew every single one of her secrets.

And maybe she did.

Olivia glanced at Devon, but he didn't seem at all worried.

"It's a pleasure to meet you at long last," Nicola said.

"Devon talked about me?" Olivia asked curiously.

"He talked about you by not talking about you," Nicola said with a small, knowing smile.

Olivia looked to Devon once more, but talk changed to their engagement, Devon's new look and whether or not he would win the election. The room was busy, full. Laughter was the most prevalent sound, drowning out the small jukebox playing in the corner. Her unconditional welcome and Devon's little affectionate touches slowly became overwhelming, and Olivia eventually found herself seeking a quiet space to breathe.

She wanted to be a part of this. To have it be real. Blueberry Springs was a good town, with a good group of people, and she only hoped that the plan she'd made with Devon not only worked, but managed to keep everyone safe from the pain that was undoubtedly coming down the line, thanks to her.

DEVON JOINED Olivia at the small table tucked near a corner of the boisterous party. She'd retreated there a few minutes ago, looking as though her energy was waning. And he could see why. Her act as the adoring fiancée, genuine as it seemed, had to have been demanding on many levels.

Over the past hour or more she'd poured everything she had into her act, remembering names, making connections, asking about people and making them feel special, liked. Acting as though she planned to stay in Blueberry Springs forever. She'd glowed, looking the part of a happy, newly engaged woman about to embark on a wonderful new life.

It had felt natural having her at his side. Comfortable. She'd said the right things, making people laugh—him included. She'd been vibrant, beautiful, and he hadn't been able to resist placing the odd affectionate kiss on the top of her head as a thanks for making it all so easy.

Easy to lie to everyone he knew and cared about.

People were calling them a power couple, were saying Devon was going to win the election.

Their plan seemed to be working, but it felt as

though something important was going to implode.

He cared too much. About everyone. About this. Even the exhausted Olivia.

"I think it's safe to say this is a tad out of control," he said quietly.

Her eyes danced as she gave him a weary smile. "Totally. But look at how much they love you—the whole town is throwing us a party. That's pretty cool, Devon. And I hope you're campaigning out there." She finished off the flute of champagne she'd been nursing. She licked her lips, intoxicatingly sexy. He'd caught himself watching her legs throughout the party, strong and long in her jeans, her ruffled blouse flowing around her generous curves. Hiding them in a way he didn't appreciate.

And she was his.

For the time being.

Alvin Lasota, a bit of a curmudgeon and old-timer, sidled up. "You really running for mayor?"

"He is," Olivia said on his behalf. "You going to vote for him?"

She had his number, just like that. Direct and straight down the pipe. Exactly the way to handle a man like Alvin. Olivia was officially the best.

Alvin gave her a once-over. "You from the city?"

"Yes."

"I figured as much." His usually frowning lips

dug deeper, similar to the furrows his tractor made in fresh soil.

Devon reluctantly made introductions, knowing Alvin was testing them. But he also knew that if Olivia could win over someone like Alvin, the town was as good as his.

"What makes you think he'd be a wise choice for running this town?" Alvin asked, and before Devon could interject with his reasons, he continued, "We've seen what he does with that little Honda car of his. What will he do with the mayor's car?"

"The mayor doesn't get a car," Devon said patiently. Olivia placed a hand on his forearm as though reminding him not to blow it.

Alvin scowled. "I hear she's living with you and you're not married."

Devon's protective side reared up as Olivia flushed with embarrassment. "You know what?" he said carefully, "I don't see how our relationship is any business of yours."

"As a man who plans on running this town, you are my business, I think—as is everything you do or don't do."

"I still don't see how my personal life impacts my ability to do the job."

"All I'm saying is that maybe I don't want to vote for someone who doesn't have his personal ducks in a row. No offense."

Devon darted a look at Olivia. No fancy shoes and briefcases were going to fix that one.

Olivia's eyes flashed as she leaned closer. "Devon is the most helpful, most honest person I have ever met. He's going to make a mighty fine mayor of your little town. And even though I'm still uncertain how he'll straighten you out, I'm pretty sure he'll find a way, as he is the most determined man I've ever met. And while you might not admire or love that about him, I do."

She leaned back, waiting for Alvin's next move.

The farmer slowly began to nod. "I like her."

"I do, too," Devon said, wrapping an arm around her shoulders and drawing her close.

She smiled at him in that special way and he felt as though the whole world was his oyster. Alvin gave them both a tip of his hat as he left them and Devon knew he had one more vote.

He let out a chuckle of disbelief. "You're amazing, you know that?"

"Keep the compliments coming, big guy. I like it."

"Did you enjoy the party?" he asked Olivia.

"Loved it." She gave his hand a squeeze, her huge smile tugging at his heart.

It was dangerous to start thinking like he was—that maybe the woman he'd once loved had never really left. That she was still in there, and maybe they could get it right this time.

He needed to remember that her sparkle wasn't from love or affection. It was due to the attention, the prestige of being engaged to a man who might one day run the town. Olivia had walked out of one self-important life and right into a new one— one of her own design.

But this wasn't his real life and anything that happened in correlation to that was nothing but practiced behavior on her part. Everything was an act and anything they built between them was being placed on an unstable foundation and would ultimately crash.

"Livvy," he said, clearing his throat as he fought to push away his emotions. "We're not engaged. We need to—"

"I know."

"They brought gifts."

Her eyes shone with excitement.

"For the engaged couple."

The smile slowly faded. "Right." She gave the pub's doorway an uncertain glance as though wishing to escape through it.

"This has gotten out of hand." So fast. So darn fast.

She swallowed hard. "There's etiquette we can fall back upon."

"I assume we're not talking about actually getting married."

They both glanced away when their eyes met.

"What do we do with the gifts?" he asked quietly.

"We aren't expected to open them here today." People had already begun to drift back to work, their lunch breaks over. Her voice was shaking slightly and he wondered if she was feeling guilty, too. "We hold on to them and return them, unused, when we break up. Send a note and a thank-you."

"What if it's monogrammed?"

"I doubt there was enough time." She was soothing him, he realized, her hand running up and down his arm. And oddly enough, it helped.

He glanced at her. Something between them was different. New.

But it was still just an act.

"You like this, don't you?" he accused. "The hoopla. Being the center of attention."

She looked down at her newly polished nails, her shiny ring. There was a hesitancy, a hint of guilt in her expression. "It is easy to get caught up in it all." She looked up suddenly. "But, Devon…?"

"What?"

"Just…don't think. Okay? This stuff is what I've been trained for, so just follow my lead and we'll be okay. We'll get through this. One day at a time." She placed a cool hand against his cheek, her expression tender. "Now kiss me."

"Livvy…"

"Smear my lipstick, otherwise the people who've been watching us fret will catch on."

And just like that, the tension in Devon's shoulders eased, because there was one thing he was good at and that was messing up Olivia's lipstick.

———

OLIVIA WAS EXHAUSTED. The party had been an amazing surprise and had caused her to fall in love with the quirky little town. She'd seen the admiration, the affection for Devon, and when she'd cracked jokes about how people had better vote for him they'd laughed and assured her that they would.

He was a good man and she was proud to be the woman at his side, helping him.

But the lying. The deceit. It tied her stomach in knots and she forced herself to focus on what was true, genuine, and to let that shine.

A few people were still in the pub despite the party wrapping up, and she made sure she chatted with them, thanked them for coming. The dutiful wife-to-be of the candidate de jour.

Please, please let him win.

"I called it!" Mary Alice said with a triumphant laugh, toasting her sister. "Married by the end of the month."

"They're only engaged," Liz retorted, giving Olivia an unimpressed look. Apparently she thought she was going to lose a bet or two.

"There's a big election going on, Mary Alice," Olivia stated. They were not marrying by the end of the month. They weren't marrying, period.

"After he wins would be a perfect time."

Olivia felt a swell of excitement. Mary Alice was on side! And her support could help turn the tide for Devon.

"You think he'll win?" she asked honestly.

"Well, who knows. But him getting engaged...I suppose it's made me realize he's done some growing up over the past few years. He's got my vote."

"He'll be good for the town," Liz added.

"He's outgrown his daredevil side, and with a woman like you to keep him in line? He'll do all right." Mary Alice hauled Devon into the conversation. "You caught yourself a good one, Devon."

"I know," he said simply, giving Olivia a smile that made her heart flutter.

"I'll admit I wasn't sure about you," Mary Alice said, sizing her up. "All sophisticated and from the city, no less." Olivia self-consciously smoothed her jeans. She'd dressed much more casually this afternoon, trying to fit in, and her outfit hadn't received a single second look. "But when I heard you were helping out Jen with her wedding dress? Now, that's just kindness. That's what we do here in Blueberry Springs."

Devon was watching Olivia with a soft look that made her feel self-conscious and seen. He just had that way about him and it turned her insides over every time.

"Well, it would be silly not to," she said. She explained to Devon, "Her dress is too big because of the weight she's lost since having Finn, and there's nobody else available to adjust it in time."

"Livvy is great with that kind of stuff," Devon said, smiling at Olivia.

Mary Alice turned her focus to Olivia. "And as for the wedding, we'll plan it for you. How's June 30?"

"This is where I bow out," Devon said, quickly backing away.

Olivia laughed and turned to Mary Alice. "You know I like veils?" she teased. "White flowers with flecks of pink in my bouquet?"

"I'm writing it down," the woman said, pretending to scribble in the air.

"How much did she put on that bet?" Olivia asked Liz.

"Enough that she wants you married by the end of the month." Liz sighed dejectedly, which made Olivia reassess her sister.

"Well, that's very soon…" Was she really going to start planning a wedding?

Olivia nearly laughed. Of course she wasn't! She was just teasing, knowing she could take Olivia along for a ride. Just as long as she wasn't kidding around about voting for Devon.

"All the best things in life fall into line quickly," Mary Alice said. "Let us know what kind of cake you'd like."

"Chocolate," Olivia replied, without thinking.

"Midnight lunch for the reception? Dance?"

"Of course." Olivia waved them out the door and shook her head. They were too much. But they made her feel welcome and accepted. As if she could become a part of this place that was full of laughter and warmth. This town felt like it could bring out the best in her, that it could become home.

Which was silly.

She'd be leaving as soon as the two of them had what they needed, and all of her feelings, which were simply an effect of being included in Devon's oversized life, even temporarily, would fade away. Fleeting. Elusive.

The pub was almost empty now and Olivia

looked around for something to help with. Nicola was pacing in front of the bar, hands on her large belly. She looked uncomfortable despite her tent-like shirt and leggings. Before Olivia could go over to see if there was something she could do, a lanky man with dark hair came up to her. He was dangling her car key. Cautiously, she took it.

"The car looks good. I left it out front." He smiled and shook her hand.

"The car?" she asked.

"Yep. Congratulations, by the way. Mandy's ecstatic she'll be having a sister-in-law soon. Too much testosterone in the family is her claim."

"She's just tired of being outvoted," Devon said, joining Olivia, his chest pressed against her shoulder, staking his claim. "This is Frankie, my sister's husband. He, uh, cleaned up your car."

"Oh, the mud?" She smiled at Frankie. That was nice. "Thank you."

"If you need any tips on how to handle the stubborn Mattsons, let me know," Frankie said with a smile and a wave, before turning to head across the room to his wife.

"Oh, I think I can handle you," Olivia said, facing Devon. "Can't I, baby?"

"That you can."

"So he cleaned my car?" she asked, changing the subject before her flirting got out of hand.

"Uh, yeah. He did." Devon was frowning at the floor and she had a feeling he was omitting something. Something that would smash the beautiful globe of happiness she'd been enjoying.

"What are you hiding?"

"The protesters stuck a bunch of posters to your car yesterday, so I had Frankie clean it up for you."

"Oh." A bitter taste filled Olivia's mouth. They'd vandalized her car? How was she going to keep that from impacting the way she reacted in the meeting with Muriel?

Yes, it was just a car, but it was the same make and model Grammy had bought her for her sixteenth birthday. Devon might be sentimental about his Honda, but she was about her car, too. And having someone disrespecting it felt personal.

She went to check her phone for the time, to see how long she had before meeting Muriel, when Nicola let out a pained moan.

Devon was at his friend's side in an instant, his tone calm. "Hey, you look like you should sit down."

The woman waved him off, her face pinched.

"Can I help with anything?" Olivia asked. Her top bet was that Nicola was in labor. "Maybe find a doctor?"

"I'm fine," she snapped.

"Whoa, easy now," Devon said. "Don't eat anyone. Leave that for the mountain lions."

He was rubbing the woman's lower back like they were...like...

No, Devon and Nicola were good friends. That was all. Olivia knew that.

Her head was seriously out of whack if she was struggling with jealousy right now. She had absolutely no right.

"It's all going to be okay," Devon said soothingly.

Olivia remembered that voice. It meant he cared deeply for...

No. No jealousy.

"We'll take care of everything," he said, trying to coax her toward the door. "Find everything you need and get you to a hospital."

"You think just because I'm pregnant I can't still be organized?" Nicola said, digging in her heels. "I'll have you know I planned this party this very morning and it was good."

Olivia found herself taking a step back even though Devon chuckled, as if Nicola's mood was harmless.

Olivia glanced around. "I think I'll just..."

Nicola's hands spread across her midriff as she winced.

"You okay?" Devon asked, his expression one of alarm.

"Cramps. Just cramps," the pregnant woman breathed. She was waving a hand like she was looking for something to sit on.

Devon swooped under her arm to support her and Olivia grabbed a nearby chair.

"I think you might be in labor," he said mildly, as he helped Nicola onto the seat. "Maybe we should take you to the hospital. Find that man of yours."

"I need to stand." Nicola struggled to her feet again, with Devon trying to help. "Walk it off," she wheezed.

"Should I call an ambulance?" Olivia asked, pulling out her phone and nearly dropping it. The woman's expression suggested she was about to pop out both babies at any moment.

"No," Nicola protested. "No. I need to stay. Todd said he'd be back in town by two. I can hang on until then."

"Nic, I've already told you, no having babies on the lawn," Devon stated. "And that also goes for the pub. Moe and Amy would not be impressed with the cleanup."

"Tell me about it," Moe grumbled, wiping down the bar behind them.

Nicola growled at Devon and he took her hand,

letting her squeeze it as the "cramp" rocked her. He winced, but otherwise didn't let on that he was basically being crushed.

He was strong, solid. Steady. Calm, caring and confident.

Any woman would be lucky to have a man like that by her side.

And it could have been Olivia.

But it hadn't been because she hadn't trusted him to take care of things, hadn't understood that the Carrington way wasn't the only way and that an out-of-wedlock pregnancy while still years away from completing her degree wasn't the end of the world.

"I have to make sure Moe gets paid," Nicola panted, scrambling for something.

Olivia found a purse that had been dropped on the floor and passed it to her.

"I know where you live, so don't worry about it," Moe said easily.

"Is Nash still here?" Devon asked. The bartender pointed down the washroom hallway and Devon nodded. Still the epitome of unfazed and in control, he directed Nicola around a table as her contraction eased up. "Olivia? Can you find Nash Leham? He should be just down that corridor."

There was a cluster of people coming and going

near the back entrance, chatting away as they dealt with decorations, gifts and such.

She had no idea which man was Nash.

"What does he look like?" she asked.

Nicola and Devon both glanced at her. "Like you," they said in tandem, taking her aback.

"Wha—excuse me?"

Devon's attention was riveted to Nicola as he said impatiently, "Just search for someone who looks like he's from your world."

CHAPTER 11

*D*evon stood in a hospital he'd been in too many times to count. The familiar, unnaturally shiny floor and the scent of the harsh hand soap brought a wash of unease. And yet today was a happy day. He was wearing a gown over his clothes and holding a tiny and impossibly perfect child. A baby girl. Every finger and toe accounted for, her miniature hands full of unexpected detail.

"She's amazing," he said to a happy, glowing Nicola, who was limp in bed after a quick, two-hour labor with Dr. Nash Leham at her side. Two babies. Boy and girl. Both healthy. "She even has fingernails."

Nicola's husband, Todd, returned to the room with more ice chips for his wife, and placed a kiss on her head. Devon offered the baby to the proud dad, but Todd was already scooping her sibling out of the nearby bassinet, offering him to Nicola. She waved him off with a feeble yawn, having already held the babies, and obviously feeling exhaustion setting in. Todd had arrived just in time for the delivery. Until then, Devon had been the one in the room holding Nicola's hand—well above the business end of things—stepping in for the man instead of her two aunts, Mary Alice and Liz, who Nicola had asked to stay in the waiting room with Olivia.

Devon should go, let the new parents be alone. But instead he walked the length of the room, marveling at the package in his arms.

All those years ago, his words expressing to Olivia what he'd wanted from their pregnancy, from their relationship, had merely felt like the unattainable, not quite real. But right now he knew just how deeply he'd meant them, even if he didn't fully understand them.

He'd wanted this. And as a result he'd kept everything to do with babies, creating a family and even falling in love again at bay, since Olivia.

He'd been denying himself for too long.

But could he let go again?

Put himself out there?

He peeked into the hall. Nicola's aunts had abandoned their station, but Olivia was still there, looking overwrought, her hands twisted and her face white. A total emotional minefield. One false move and they could both be blown to bits.

And yet he knew if he wanted to rebuild his life, find love, family and happiness, he had to start somewhere. He had to face the past, the guilt for not being present when she'd miscarried, for not trying harder to be there for her and holding on, when everything was pushing him under and away from the only woman he'd ever truly loved.

"Want to see the babies?" he asked her, a funny lump developing in his throat. *Play it cool,* he reminded himself. This wasn't about the two of them. "They're gorgeous little poopers."

Olivia hesitated, then came closer, peeking at the bundle settled in his arms.

"She already loves me," he said with a joviality he didn't feel. "Even babies know a handsome man when they see one."

Olivia didn't speak.

"Want to hold her?" He needed to leave. Now. He couldn't field the imminent emotional fallout that was mired in their past. It was zooming in like a sudden summer storm, set on decimating what was left of his shields, the only thing that protected him from laying his heart bare and torn at Olivia's feet.

He needed to heal, but this was too much.

They'd almost had this. A child of their own.

He shifted the baby closer to Olivia, desperate to relieve himself of the warm infant, but she shook her head. He turned back to the room, saying over his shoulder, "Come meet the boy so I can I teach him how to pick up chicks."

Olivia followed him in. He settled the baby in the crook of Nicola's arm, then pulled out his phone. One last act of it's-all-good before he could burn rubber, maybe tear along one of the mountain dirt tracks in his aging Honda. The thing could barely take the abuse anymore and he'd promised himself months ago that he was done racing, but the need to push the line, tempt fate, was too strong.

"I think we need a few family pictures."

Keep it light, then bow out.

Todd moved closer to his wife, holding their son, kissing Nicola on the forehead again. Devon took several candids, as well as a few posed shots. Over his shoulder, he could feel Olivia watching the new family.

"You okay?" he asked quietly, after he'd taken a requisite number of pictures.

She nodded, her chin wrinkling.

He had no doubt what she was thinking. His mind was already there, too.

"I'll send you the pictures," he said to the new parents, having to clear his throat once or twice.

Nicola nodded in agreement, admiring her babies once again as if she couldn't believe they were truly hers. She smiled at Todd, leaning closer for another kiss.

They loved each other, had overcome a crazy amount of fear to be together and had changed, finding their love to be enough.

It gave Devon hope that one day he could find what they had.

"And it's a good thing you listened to the future mayor or your kids' birth stories would have involved being born in a pub," Devon said with a chuckle, edging toward the door.

"Shut up and save the river hike. There are some rare flowers down there," Nicola muttered. He had a feeling that if she hadn't just birthed twins she'd be pulling out her whiteboard and planning the more intricate details of his campaign here and now.

"You're just saying that because it's where you and Todd discovered you loved each other." Nicola rolled her eyes in reply. "But don't worry. It's on the list. I'll pop in tomorrow, okay? Text if you two need anything. Sorry, you *four*."

"Would you like to hold one of them?" Nicola asked Olivia, as Devon moved toward the door.

She shook her head, arms crossed over her

stomach. She started backing from the room. "Congratulations. They're wonderful."

Devon caught her gaze before she fled past him, her pain and sorrow as evident as if it was his own.

He let out an involuntary, jagged shudder. Everything with Olivia just kept feeling too close to home.

OLIVIA'S FEET ate up the hospital's hallway despite her efforts to slow down, act cool and unaffected like Devon. People were pausing, watching her go by, sensing something was wrong.

"Are you all right, dear?" It was Mary Alice, hauling a mittful of helium balloons that said Congratulations and It's a Boy and It's a Girl.'

"Yes, yes. Fine. The babies—they're great," Olivia whispered, trying to find a quiet place to haul herself back together.

It had been ten years. So very long ago, but right now it felt raw and fresh like the pain was new again. Her parents had been intent on them giving their baby up for adoption, but that had never been Olivia's plan.

Devon hadn't believed she would give him their child, hadn't trusted her, just as she didn't trust herself whenever she was around him. She knew he believed she'd shut him out because his love and the life he offered wasn't enough for her, but the truth was he had always been enough. More than enough. So much so that it consumed her, caused her to lose sight of reality and start believing in fairy tales.

When she'd lost the baby she hadn't been relieved, as her parents had. Instead she'd felt like she'd failed Devon in one more way. And watching him holding Nicola's child, seeing that happy yet haunted look in his eyes, she knew just how badly she'd hurt him. He'd been a reflection of what she'd been hiding inside for so long. His pain was just as deep as her own.

She'd wanted to reach out, share the sorrow like true lovers, true friends. Heal each other.

Just look for someone who looks like he's from your world.

No matter what she'd felt today, their connection couldn't overcome the fact that they were from two different worlds and that nothing was different, nothing had changed.

"Livvy?" Olivia flinched at the nickname and the way Devon said it with such tender care. "You okay?"

His face was creased with pain, loss and grief. But he was worrying about her. Her.

She'd failed every single one of them, then

spent the past ten years striving to never let so many important people down again.

It hadn't worked.

Nothing ever worked.

And she was on the brink of failing again. Trying to straddle two worlds and feeling as though she didn't quite belong in either one.

DEVON FELT like he was losing Olivia. He hadn't realized he'd even had her, that her walls had tumbled, until now. She was throwing them up again, pushing him away. He could feel her retreating, see it in her big, scared brown eyes. Closing off.

During the party, when he'd heard she was helping out in Ginger's shop, working on a wedding dress...he'd felt as though she was choosing this life, her old dreams and self, this world. Him.

And darned if that hadn't felt like the most amazing, natural thing. And then with the babies... he'd felt his own walls dissolve.

He reached for her now, knowing he couldn't run away from their pain, couldn't leave her to deal with this on her own no matter how much he wished to. He had to pull himself together and be there for her. He snugged her body tight to his, cradling her against him, grateful for her lack of resistance.

"I'm sorry," she whispered.

"For what?"

"I would never have denied you our child." She looked up at him, her eyes pleading for forgiveness, understanding. "I was setting up a way to give you full parental rights."

"Ginger told me." Olivia's parents had been determined, but she'd apparently been trying to straddle the line between them disowning her and making sure Devon could raise their unborn child without her family's interference. It couldn't have been easy.

"I'm sorry I failed you, Devon. I'm so sorry."

"You didn't fail, Olivia." His voice was shaking. How could she blame herself for something beyond her control? And why couldn't he have been more careful with condoms? It had been his love for her that had destroyed their relationship.

"But what if I—"

He shushed her. He knew what a haunted forest the "what if" trail led into.

"You did the best you could, Livvy. I understand that. Keeping the baby would have meant giving up everything. Your dreams, your family's respect, your degree, your future. I would've only had to hire a nanny once I'd settled here in town and the baby came along. I respect that you were trying to look out for me in a tough time. I couldn't see it then, only my own pain. I'm sorry if I made it harder for you."

Olivia's tears were streaming down her face and he gently dabbed them away.

"We should have been a family," she whispered. "I should have trusted you. What if I caused it by pushing you away?"

It took Devon a second to realize what she was saying.

She was blaming herself for losing the baby.

Pain sliced through him like a sword. He held Olivia tighter, squeezing her against him as though he could wring out their sorrow. He'd once believed he'd had no more tears, no more sense of pain or loss.

He was wrong.

The healed wound reopened as though it had never closed. There was nothing he could say that could make her feel better because as irrational and wrongly placed her blame had been placed, he understood.

"And what if I caused it by being a jerk?" he asked, voice hoarse.

He didn't know if he was the one shaking or if it was Olivia as they clung to each other, choked sounds coming deep from within them both.

She'd carried this for a decade. A decade.

And so had he.

But together...together they could forgive the past. Together they had the possibility of healing.

DEVON HAD BROUGHT Olivia back to his house, and the two of them had slowly undressed each other in the late-afternoon sun, their pain so exposed, so raw. Tenderly they'd made love, becoming one once again as they let each other in, healing old wounds and each other with their bodies, with their shared grief.

Olivia had awoken in the middle of the night, still exhausted from letting go of old wounds, of releasing, of being cared for. Of being loved.

She hadn't planned to stay after meeting Nicola's babies, but then Devon had reached for her in the hospital hallway, becoming her rock in the emotional storm. And so she'd stayed, because the truth was she still loved him.

But she didn't have a clue what she was going to do about it.

She snuggled against Devon, drifting off, waking to the sound of knocking at the door, the dogs barking.

"What's going on?" Devon asked from deep in his pillow. He lifted his head, looking wiped.

She sat up, feeling lighter than she had in years. It was as though a load had been lifted. The pain was still there, but knowing she didn't have to hide it, that she didn't have to face the emotions alone any longer...that made it so much easier.

"What time is it?" Devon asked.

Olivia found his alarm clock on the floor and turned it to face her. "Nine-fifteen."

It was already Wednesday and she had to be at Ginger's store at ten to refit Jen's wedding gown for the weekend wedding.

Devon was up in a flash, hauling on clothes, not bothering to shower. "I'm late for work and I have a feeling my boss won't be happy after blowing off most of this week."

Olivia watched with disappointment as his flesh disappeared under layers of clothing. She swung her legs over the side of the bed and stretched. She had nothing on the docket for today other than the dress. Her eye caught the flash of her ring and she tried to school her smile. She'd slept with her *fiancé*. Scratch that, *made love* to her fiancé.

And it had been...amazing.

Life was good. It felt nice to be wanted and needed, to have someone who knew what she desired, then delivered it. It was even better than it had been all those years ago.

And last night, the way he'd brushed her tears away, and they'd been able to talk about their past like adults? She'd be lying to herself if she said that didn't matter, that it didn't make a difference.

This time felt different. It *was* different.

An illusion that could be punctured, perhaps, but in this moment, it felt like it would all be okay.

Except for whoever was banging at the door.

And there was something else, too. She was forgetting something.

Meet with the protesters at one! That's what it was.

She stood with a gasp, facing Devon who was tucking in his shirt. "I missed my meeting with Muriel yesterday!"

The party and then the babies… Muriel was going to think she'd been blown off and that Olivia didn't care about her or her concerns.

Devon bent to give her a quick kiss. "We'll figure something out. I'm sure she'll understand." He hurried from the room to answer the door. Olivia tossed on clothes and followed, passing the guilt-inducing stack of engagement gifts waiting just inside the front entry.

Devon opened the door. It was Logan, checking in on them. "You two okay?"

"We overslept," Olivia said sheepishly.

Logan took in their disheveled appearances, his brow lifting ever so slightly. "I guess my wife was right, you two were just busy." He checked his phone, then tapped a piece in his ear, saying, "Confirmed, Zach. Motion and door sensors online and working."

Olivia tried to hide a smile, but as soon as she glanced at Devon and found he was trying to bury his own, she broke into giggles. He planted a quick kiss on her forehead, then picked up his briefcase.

"Good luck with the dress and with Muriel."

Devon hurried out the door to work, Logan trundling down the steps alongside him, speaking in manly-man protective terms as he went.

Olivia went and sat in the kitchen for a moment, thinking. The dogs had settled together on Copter's bed, looking expectantly at her. She got up and fed them before starting a pot of coffee. She really needed to buy cream if she was going to be here any longer.

She sighed, a feeling of impending loss deflating her. So quickly, she'd gotten in so deep. Over her head with Devon.

She didn't want to leave. She wanted to stay, be a part of his life, this town. Everything.

But today was the last day to work things out with the company's PR issue or her father would be pulling the plug. She'd spent most of yesterday being with Devon, feeling all those old feelings, completely forgetting about her real life. That's what it was like being around him. She forgot who she was, where the real world was even located.

Sucking up her courage, Olivia phoned and left a message with Muriel, relieved when she didn't have to speak to the woman directly, even though it would have been better.

When Olivia was ready to head over to Ginger's shop, Logan was at the end of the driveway, waiting. He opened the passenger side door of his car when she came down the front steps. "Today you ride with me."

"Why? What happened?" Her thoughts went to her cleaned up car.

"I have a feeling."

"About?"

He simply shook his head and gestured for her to climb in, while she wondered if today was going to expand her bubble or burst it.

CHAPTER 12

Olivia paused at the threshold of Ginger's store, Veils and Vows. It felt as though within a few short days she'd stepped right back into the old dream life she'd once had. The one that had belly-flopped.

She reminded herself that it wasn't quite like her college days. She didn't have Devon, despite appearances, and she was just taking out a few stitches, tightening things up, not designing gowns.

But a small voice told her it could be like old times, only more.

Still hovering on the threshold, Olivia turned and looked out at the street behind her. It felt as though she was being watched. She spied Logan sitting in his car at the curb, waiting for her. She gave a small wave and stepped into Veils and Vows, inhaling the scent of new fabric. Most people probably didn't even notice the subtle aroma, but to Olivia it felt like home.

She moved slowly, taking in the expansive room with its racks of snow-white gowns So much tulle, satin, silk, lace, and all the special, delicate fabrics that made her heart beat a little faster. For years she'd been squelching ideas and now they flooded her mind, one after another. She reached out, smoothing her hands over the white fabrics. Short gowns, long gowns. Ruffled, sleek. Simple, complicated.

And all along the outer walls were shelves with final touch accessories. Tiaras, jeweled hair clips, beads and gems. Garters, shoes, veils. Everything a bride might need.

Sugar and spice and everything nice.

Olivia inhaled again and smiled.

She was going to help Jen Kulak shine on one of the biggest days of her life, and let her chosen dress showcase the fact that the new mom had as many curves as the average mountain trail leading into Blueberry Springs.

The bride-to-be was already there, her son happily cooing to himself in a stroller in the spacious, adjoining room that served as a fitting area. It had a large stage with various raised platforms where brides could stand while having their dresses altered, a wall of mirrors in front of it. A few tall windows allowed natural light to flood the room, with comfy furniture in front for waiting guests, and small tables littered with bridal magazines and catalogs. Shelves near the fitting rooms held more accessories, more catalogs, more shoes, as well as alteration kits. The room was a haven and Olivia felt a skip in her step as she joined Jen and Ginger.

Jen went to change into her dress, an asymmetrical gown that bared one shoulder. Ginger handed Olivia a kit. Pins, scissors, stitch rippers, thread, measuring tape—it didn't seem like much, but to Olivia it was like greeting an old friend.

This was going to be a lot of fun.

"Jen?" she called through the change room door. "Are you wearing your hair up or down?" Her straight blond hair with the purple streak was currently about shoulder length and would look good up, but Olivia worried it would look too plain.

"Up. Just a casual bun at the nape of my neck."

Classic. Simple and elegant, but a smidge plain overall. Lacking the spunk that seemed to be characteristically Jen.

"Will you wear your nose ring?"

"Yes?"

"Good. Are you wearing a veil?"

"I hadn't planned on it."

"Mind if I grab one? I have an idea." Specifically,

a short, super fun veil that would help illustrate Jen's individuality.

"Sure."

Olivia strode into the main salesroom, her eye already on the prize. The delicate veil was only about a foot long, but would add a splash to Jen's whole look. Perfect. Before she returned to the fitting area, she caught a glimpse of Peter Lunn watching through the storefront's window. She waved uncertainly. He returned the wave with a smile, heading for the door.

This town and its characters, as much as she loved it all, was taking a bit of getting used to.

Peter walked right up to her, a glossy page from a magazine in his hands. He held it up so she could see it.

It was one of the more successful ad campaigns for Carrington Cosmetics, featuring her and Emma as models, happy and free. Olivia knew why the ads had worked—because her own sparkle had finally matched her sister's. She'd just started dating Devon and had been secretly working on a minor in fashion design. At the time of the shoot she'd been happier than a debutante at an invitation only designer sale, and the camera had captured it.

Funny how after all these years she felt like that same woman again, only stronger.

Devon made the difference in her life.

Peter's grin grew wider as he pointed to her picture, and Olivia laughed. "You recognized me?"

He nodded.

"Well, thank you. I don't model for Carrington Cosmetics any longer, but my sister still does sometimes."

And Carrington wouldn't be there for any of them if she didn't get ahold of Muriel and convince the protesters to focus on what truly mattered —the dam.

Peter thrust the image at her, and Olivia asked, "You want me to sign it?"

He nodded, and she found he had a pen at the ready. She signed the picture, her gaze lingering on her younger sister. Olivia hoped things turned out okay and that their new line would prevent illnesses in women across the continent and world.

She thanked Peter, and with a renewed sense of purpose headed to find her phone so she could call Muriel again. She wasn't taking no for an answer.

She reached the woman on the eighth ring and apologized before Muriel could hang up. Olivia proposed a new meeting time for that afternoon, and the woman was oddly accommodating. So much so that it made Olivia wonder what was going on—something good, surely?

She texted Logan and Devon with the meeting

information, then returned to the fitting area. Within half an hour she had Jen's gown hugging her body and the bride in love with the spunky, short veil.

"You're a lifesaver," Jen said, tentatively hugging Olivia so pins holding her dress in place wouldn't pierce them.

"As long as Rob isn't too gobsmacked to say I do," she teased.

Jen laughed and her son, Finn, banged his rattle.

"I'll make the alterations today or tomorrow," Olivia said, sending Jen to slip out of the garment.

"I told you sewing would be old hat," Ginger declared, gloating as she did so. She was keeping Finn distracted, wiggling her fingers and giving him goofy smiles.

"I guess it's like riding a bike—at least so far," Olivia agreed.

"There's our bride-to-be!" said a woman with dark hair streaked with white, joining them. It was Wanda, Ginger's grandmother. She swept Olivia into a giant hug. "I haven't seen you since before Harvard! Such a bright one you are. So tell me, how did Devon propose? Ginger, you need to take her picture and put it on your wall." She waved a hand. "Well, when you get your bride wall started."

Olivia felt a flicker of doubt as Wanda's joy

washed over her, along with assumptions that simply weren't true.

"You are buying your dress here, of course," Wanda confirmed.

"I'm sure she'll design her own," Ginger said.

"I don't do that anymore." But if she did, she was confident about its style.

"Well, we'll see," Ginger said with a knowing smile, before backtracking. "The wall is one of the million ideas I came up with at the business retreat where I met Logan. Oh, here's Lily!" She went to greet a woman, pulling a rose-colored bridesmaid's dress off a nearby Reserved rack in the process. Over her shoulder she called, "Olivia, since you're here, do you have a moment to add a few pins for my seamstress, Ella May? She's going to be so behind when she gets back."

Olivia shrugged. She still had a few hours before meeting with Muriel, and plenty of time to stitch up Jen's dress before her big day, as well as do some PR for Carrington and Devon.

Lily was pretty, a few years under thirty, and she had that resigned look about her that said always a bridesmaid, never a bride. She was also fast, tossing on the dress as quickly and effortlessly as if it was her usual wardrobe and not the jeans and tee she'd been wearing.

Wanda came over to help with Lily as Jen joined

everyone in the big room, setting her son up under a blanket to breast-feed.

"The dress is gorgeous on you," Olivia said. The rose gown did wonderful things for the woman's complexion. "I'm Olivia Carrington."

"Lily Harper."

"Are these the shoes you're wearing?"

Lily nodded.

"She's Devon's fiancée," Wanda interjected.

Lily half turned to take a better look at Olivia. "Devon's sister and I were best friends before I moved away in high school."

Her name felt familiar in that context. "Did you send him care packages when he was in college?"

Lily beamed and clapped her hands. "I'd totally forgotten about those! We used to bake at Mandy's, and Ethan would try to sneak a few treats for himself." Lily blushed, her eyes bright with happy memories. "Is he still around?"

Olivia nodded.

"I'm just finishing chef school, which has taken me ages and ages. I can't wait until I'm a full chef and get to run my own place." She rubbed her hands together as though plotting world domination.

"It sounds like Ethan wants to sell his restaurant," Olivia offered.

"Really?"

Wanda nodded. "That's what he keeps saying. That and his catering business, too."

Olivia fiddled with the hem of Lily's dress in the ensuing quiet as Ginger and Wanda fussed about, arranging shelves. Ginger was reorganizing things and it sounded as though her grandmother simply put items back where they used to go out of habit whenever she came to help out. The two were close, though, and Olivia had no worries about them sorting it out, but listening to them bicker was amusing.

"You and Devon have known each other a long time," Lily stated.

"We've been out of touch for years."

"Seeing him again—was it like old times? The crush and feelings...did they come back?" Lily was watching Olivia like she needed the answer for herself.

"Yeah," she replied softly. "In some ways it's like time didn't even pass."

There was hubbub in the main room and soon they were joined by Mary Alice and Liz, who were eager to catch up on all that was new with Lily. The older women made themselves comfortable, helping out when Olivia needed something out of reach. They kept up a steady stream of chatter as they handed items such as veils to shopping brides, plied Jen with accessories, all while offering advice and alternatives, and spreading the news about various townspeople.

It sounded as though everyone was wondering when Devon's sister was going to get pregnant. So far, quite a few bets had been lost on that one.

"Now about your handsome groom," Liz said, her voice taking on an air of importance. "What do you have in mind, Olivia? Suit or tux?"

"He's incredibly sexy in a tux," Olivia said, her mind flipping back in time. So many memories.

With his new haircut and more chiseled features he was going to look even more deadly handsome, like a gentle James Bond. She'd be ripping those clothes off him before he even had her over the threshold on their wedding night, that was for sure. "Very debonair," she murmured, lost in the fantasy.

Mary Alice pulled a tin of mints out of her bra and sucked on one. "What's your color scheme? A blue cummerbund would look nice on him."

"Employees get a 20 percent discount on everything—even special order items. And because you won't let me pay you for the alterations, you're getting the discount," Ginger said, whipping out a massive catalog. Her eyes were shining with excitement as she began flipping pages. "I see you both in something traditional, but without the stuffiness. Subtly sexy."

Olivia backed away from Lily, ignoring the wedding planning the women were trying to do on her behalf. "All done."

Lily stepped down from the platform and turned in front of a mirror.

Liz had a phone to her ear. "If you want something before the fall, the only dates left open for the hall are late October."

"No, no. I booked June 30," said Mary Alice. "There was a cancellation."

"What?" Olivia felt things slip out of control, like too many layers of satin pressed under a speeding sewing machine. "No, I like...autumn— no, winter weddings."

She needed to set a faraway date so there'd be time to cancel and get their deposits back if the women got too serious about their planning. She'd thought they were joking yesterday, but today they seemed serious. Very serious.

"Oh, the thirtieth is coming up fast," Wanda said excitedly. She reached for a catalog on a bookshelf behind her. "Do you want a veil?"

"She does," Mary Alice confirmed.

Out. Of. Control.

"Are you sure?" Wanda asked. "You don't strike me as the veil type."

"I am, but no. No dress. No hall. Nothing." She

had to put a stop to this or she'd be married by that very afternoon.

The women paused for a split second.

"Eloping?" Liz asked.

"Justice of the peace," Mary Alice said wisely, nodding. "I can perform the ceremony." She pulled her phone from her cleavage and opened its calendar app. "I can fit you in most anywhere. I've performed over a dozen marriages in the past year and there are references on my website." She handed Olivia a warm business card.

Liz's phone was pinging with incoming messages, and Olivia began to feel anxiety build inside her.

"We want low-key," she emphasized, trying to slow the train without hurting anyone's feelings. "Simple."

"You'll still need a dress," Ginger said. "You are wearing a dress, right?"

"Nothing too fancy," Liz said, joining her in poring over the book. "And not white. Nobody does white anymore. But there's no time to order one."

"Or design one," Ginger added.

"Oh, you design?" Liz asked.

At the same moment, Wanda stated, "Cream." She pointed to something in her catalog. "Ivory would wash out her complexion."

"I just...I need to talk to Devon," Olivia said weakly, backing away from the impromptu planning that had begun around her.

"Don't wait too long. He's going to be so busy after the election. Best to have your wedding before he's sworn in, since there's not enough time before the election."

"The mayor's wife," another agreed. "Very busy."

"Best to hurry this along."

"It's a good thing she's got us!"

One of the women held up the gown book. "What about this one?"

The gown was gorgeous. Almost perfect. But not quite right. Olivia closed her eyes and spoke without thinking. "I'm a designer and I'll be designing my own." She wanted this *her* way. On her terms. "And I'll be the one showing you the kind of dress I want."

Devon was feeling antsy, unable to concentrate on a basic land transfer contract for the town. He rubbed his eyes and yawned. He was spent from the emotional drain of last night. Completely wiped.

He finished his fifth cup of coffee and stretched, trying to focus on the twenty-page document in front of him. He kept thinking about Olivia. The engagement party. How hot their kisses were. How being with her felt like he was an integral part of something big, strong and important. And when he held her close, his body responding to her generous, soft curves pressed against him, it felt like home. The only place he'd ever felt fully himself was with her.

Which meant he needed to have his head checked. She still loved that proper, upper-crust world, had shone at the party, shone every time she pretended to be the fiancée of the possible mayor-to-be. She was going to walk away, return to her family just like they'd agreed.

But this time it was going to be even worse than the first time.

He found himself ditching work and walking to Ginger's store, Veils and Vows, where he figured Olivia would still be, ensconced in the things she used to love best.

Halfway there, he ducked into the flower store that his sister used to live above before marrying Frankie. He picked out a bouquet of roses, fingers tapping against the countertop while the woman behind the counter tied a ribbon around their stems.

"Olivia is a lucky woman," she said.

"I'm a lucky man."

"My husband and I will be voting for you!" she called, as he left the store with his bouquet.

"Thank you!"

He smiled, dodging a small group of kindergarten kids on their way to a field trip at the fire hall.

"Election day is coming!" one of the parent helpers said as she passed him. "My husband's going to run a shuttle from the downtown businesses so they can slip out to vote. He figures it'll earn you an extra twenty to thirty votes for sure."

Devon smiled. "Tell him thanks in advance."

"No, thank *you*. And anyway, it was Olivia's idea!" She beamed and hurried to catch up with the kids.

Devon stopped to look up at the pure blue sky and count his blessings. Him as mayor could really happen, and all because he'd taken a chance and found the woman who'd once broken his heart. Now they were healing, forgiving.

Go figure. Mayor and more.

Wait. He was considering Olivia, wasn't he? Really considering her.

Yesterday in the hospital he'd been hoping to find love and start a family…yet when he paused to think, he realized he already had the start of some of that. But how would he turn a fake relationship into something real?

He dragged a hand down his face. It *was* fake. This wasn't what he was looking for, even though it felt real.

Wanda met him at the door to Veils and Vows, taking one quick glance at the flowers before tipping her head toward the fitting room. "She's in there creating magic."

"Thanks."

For guys there were man caves and for women there were bridal shops. And as Devon headed to the large room done up in cream colors, flowers and ribbons—basically, a room so feminine it lowered testosterone levels simply by looking at it—he realized he was more than happy to give up his man card if it meant being closer to a woman such as Olivia.

He walked through the expansive arch that joined the salesroom and fitting area, and came to a halt. There on the stage in front of massive three-way mirrors was a bride. She was in charge, pointing out various parts of the dress, bunching handfuls here and there, creating an image for the women surrounding her. There was something about her that made his blood stop moving. Something…electrifying.

The bride straightened and the air left his lungs. It was Olivia.

She was in a wedding gown, looking radiant

and absolutely stunning. He wanted to walk up to her, drop to his knees and propose for real.

He had to blink emotion from his eyes as the flowers went slack in his grip.

Last night they'd let go of the grief, letting each other in. But their charade…it was going too far. He was in too deep and someone was going to get hurt.

And he knew it was going to be him.

OLIVIA HAD GOTTEN a bit carried away with the gown of her dreams, as she now referred to the pretty-close-but-not-quite-perfect gown. She loved that everyone around her was on board, thought she was good for Devon, thought the dress was beautiful. And after last night things seemed different, as if enough of it was real that the two of them could skirt by, build something new.

She caught a glimpse of herself in the mirror. Her cheeks were flushed with excitement, like a real bride.

One day.

One day, she was going to marry the man of her dreams: Devon.

There was a flicker of movement behind her in the mirror.

It was her fiancé, his jaw hanging low.

He looked as though he was fighting whether to be awed or to give in to dread.

He didn't want this. Any of this, and Olivia felt her heart roll down onto the floor.

"I'm not supposed to see the bride," Devon said, his voice choked.

Ginger, who'd been fussing with the hem of Olivia's dress, gasped. "Devon! Out! Now!"

"But I brought flowers." He came closer, despite Ginger's attempts to shoo him away. "It's beautiful. I mean, you are. It's…" He cleared his throat and raised a fist to his mouth, just about whacking himself in the face with the roses.

Olivia giggled, loving how she'd knocked him off center. Maybe, just maybe he felt it, too. That special something they had when they were together. That dizzying feeling as if she could do anything as long as he was her man.

That wasn't something they could pretend. That wasn't part of the act.

Devon offered the flowers, but Wanda plucked them from his grip. "We don't want to soil the dress."

"Devon needs a cummerbund," Mary Alice said, furiously flipping magazine pages. "Periwinkle? Powder blue? No. Aquamarine?" She held up a page.

"Definitely aqua," her sister agreed.

Devon paled, taking one step back, hands raised. "We're waiting until after the election before we get into planning."

"If we don't start now you won't be getting married for years!" Mary Alice cried.

"We're…eloping," Devon said.

Olivia nodded. "It's true."

One of the women held a fabric swatch up to Devon and nodded. It was so ridiculous, so out of hand that Olivia began laughing. She'd never seen Mr. Aloof so scrambled before.

"It's not funny," he said hotly, and she bit down on her laughter.

She knew it wasn't funny. It really wasn't. But she'd felt so light and full of love all day…why couldn't he just play along? Be him? Fun and loose and free? Nobody was going to get hurt. Let the ladies have their fun. All the two of them had to do was drag their feet for a week, then slowly break up.

Or stay together.

"If you're worried about the cost, I get discounts all over town and it'll barely dent your wallet." Ginger was prodding at Devon. "Don't you love her? Give her what she wants. What she deserves."

Devon looked up, locking eyes with Olivia. She

felt that special current run through her. She knew he truly saw her, that they were connecting on a level reached only by those who were truly soul mates.

"Livvy claimed my heart back in school," he said, "making it useless to anyone but her."

Olivia's eyes welled. "Oh, Devon." She could barely speak, she was so choked up. She just wanted to hold on to him and never let go.

"That had better be waterproof mascara!" Wanda cried, waving a tissue at Olivia. Mary Alice was there in a flash, digging through her bra for more, despite Wanda having an entire box at her disposal.

Ginger sighed happily. "You two are the most in-love couple I've seen in a long time."

Olivia rolled her eyes. Her friend might be taking the act a bit far with that one.

"And that's saying something," Wanda said, handing Olivia a fresh tissue.

"Would you consider moving up the date if you had help?" Mary Alice asked.

Olivia looked to Devon. He opened his mouth and she feared he was about to reveal the truth. She took a step forward.

"Ladies," he said, "I love and appreciate your support, but we all know how much time and effort goes into wedding planning. We just want to spend time together before things get truly crazy." He reached out, giving Olivia's hand a squeeze, leaving her heart a mushy mess in her chest. His smile wavered. He paused, then skipped up the two steps to where she was standing and kissed her hard and fast.

All she could think was *I love you.*

CHAPTER 13

"What on earth is going on out there?" Ginger asked. She was facing the front of the store, where massive windows overlooked the street. "Grandma? Did you plan another sale without telling me? There's a mob out front." She lowered her voice and muttered, "I swear, even though it's my name on the deed she's never going to fully give up control."

Devon shared a look with Olivia, who stepped down from her perch where she'd been showing off the gown. Outside, the noise was growing exponentially, keeping pace with the horrible feeling in Devon's gut.

He stepped into the main salesroom, where it became instantly obvious what was happening. And it wasn't anything good. Olivia was right behind him and he heard the air escape her lungs in a gut-wrenching gasp.

Protesters and reporters alike were out front, some of them banging on the glass.

One of the reporters came in, her perky smile in place. "Hi! We're here to talk to the mayoral candidate's fiancée. Oh! There she is." She turned to the cameraman behind her. "Get a shot of that."

Devon was on the man in a flash, hand in front of the lens.

This had to be the work of Barry Lunn. Had to be. Devon had heard a rumor the man's mother had been pushing on him to take the race seriously, and that morning Logan's old pal Zach had discovered Barry was doing some digging into Olivia's past. Extensive digging.

"What do you have to say about your sister's illness, Olivia? Doctors say it was caused by her constant exposure to the toxins in Carrington Cosmetics."

Devon went slack, his hand falling from in front of the lens. Barry had found pay dirt and had set his lasers to Destroy.

Ginger stepped up, trying to shepherd the reporter out of her store. The cameraman took his shot of Olivia as the reporter pushed Ginger back with an arm, holding out her microphone so she'd catch anything Olivia uttered.

"Don't say anything!" Devon said. Olivia was smarter than that, and by the looks of it, too traumatized to let out even a pained croak.

Logan came storming into the store, looking like a bull about to take out a china shop. He picked up the reporter and carried her to the threshold, placing her outside. He glowered at the cameraman, who hustled out after her. Logan finally snapped the lock on the door and faced the room, his shoulders lowering only when he'd confirmed that Ginger was okay.

Olivia was behind a rack, still in the beautiful gown, looking as though someone had just crashed into her crystal dreams.

Rich, raw emotion rolled through Devon and he stepped to where she was trembling, trying to act tough, brave. His heart tumbled like a loose boulder.

Seeing her glowing in her gown had felt real. Like destiny. The woman he loved in a white dress. A bouquet of roses. His ring on her finger.

It was all he wanted.

Her body language changed and he immediately knew she was going to go confront the protesters and reporters for her sister's sake. Devon wanted to protect her, tell her to stay put, not engage the disaster waiting to happen. But he also knew Olivia wanted to protect her sister. She was going to do what she felt was best, but it also meant she was going to choose her family—Emma—over staying in Blueberry Springs with him. His campaign, his affection, weren't enough to hold her here.

He needed to do something, say something. Convince her to stay put and ride this out.

He strode to her, words and emotions locked in his throat. He hooked her arm, pulling her to him, kissing her mouth like he used to when they'd been in their twenties. Possessive and full of everlasting love.

OUTSIDE THE STORE the mob kept growing. Olivia needed to do something. Anything. She couldn't just sit here and let them send Carrington down in flames, as well as Devon's campaign.

Everything she cared about.

Devon had just about kissed the living daylights out of her a moment ago and now held her hand in his. Solid support.

He had her back.

She needed to solve this, protect him, even if it meant pushing him away, shutting him out until the coast was clear. He would understand. They were different now, stronger. They'd lie low so her mess wouldn't taint his campaign, then find a way to come back together.

That's what she'd planned to do with their baby. Let things settle down with her parents, then give her parental rights to Devon when their child was born. Let him raise her, not a stranger. And then maybe, one day, she'd find a way to come back to him as well.

This time, though, she wasn't going to fail. They understood each other better and she was an adult with more choices. She was going to win. She was going to have Devon. She wasn't going to let a love like theirs slip away twice.

But what could she do? How could she stop this insanity without making it worse? Someone wanted her to fail.

She looked up, spying a familiar form through the window. Olivia looked again. It was her sister, face pinched with worry, her tall, elegant form weaving through the crowds. People were yelling. At her, at the store. At Olivia.

What was she doing here?

"My sister's out there," she said, moving to Logan.

Before she could say anything more, the body-guard darted out and drew Emma inside. Olivia met them at the door.

"What are you doing here?" she asked Emma.

"Luke said there was a problem."

"Luke?" That made no sense.

"He said you were acting differently and he was worried."

"I'm trying to save the company while keeping this craziness under control," Olivia muttered. She gathered the skirt of the large wedding gown, and pushed her way out onto the sidewalk. The sun was hot, the crowd noisy.

She was in PR and trained to handle this. She scanned the gathered group. Muriel was standing proudly, eyes narrowed in triumph as she lifted her sign in rhythm to the other protesters' chanting.

So that was why she'd been happy enough to meet later—she had plans to skewer Olivia beforehand.

"What are you doing?" Devon asked, reaching her. Microphones were aimed in their direction as reporters jockeyed for position in front of the protesters and curious townsfolk.

"I'm going to turn this." It was her job, her responsibility. She had to protect Emma, protect Devon.

"This isn't a good idea."

"And since when did I ever listen?" she said lightly.

He dropped her arm, stepping back.

"You wanted to speak to me?" she hollered over

the shouting. Her back was to a beautiful window display of a poufy dream gown, similar to the one she was wearing, veils pinned in the window all around it. It was light, airy and everything the angry crowd in front of her wasn't.

Logan was at her side, urging her back toward the door. She planted her feet with a solid "no." Devon gave Logan a reluctant nod, siding with her.

At the end of the block Olivia spied Barry talking to someone, one eye on her and the store.

Reporters were asking her a million questions, the protesters chanting in front of her. People were banging on the store's windows and it wouldn't be long before things got broken. Things she might not be able to repair.

"Carrington Cosmetics is killing the Carringtons!" they chanted. Olivia's gaze slid to her sister, who had joined her outside, along with Mary Alice and Liz.

Emma was pale, angry. Seething, actually. Her arms were tightly crossed, her gaze steely. Olivia gave her a small shake of the head, trying to communicate that she hadn't been the one to cause the leak.

It had to have come from somewhere else.

Her attention moved back to Barry. He looked pleased.

Too pleased.

Out in the crowd were nameless protesters, but also faces she'd come to know over the past few days. People who had gathered to support her. People like Mandy, Todd, and even Vintra.

But she didn't know how to fix this.

Her mind scrambled for a company party line.

She grabbed a nearby reporter's microphone and gave them the spiel. "All of Carrington's cosmetics fall within the federal guidelines and exceed the standards set out by the industry."

"Isn't your sister's recent health issues due to toxins found in your lipsticks?"

"There is no direct link."

"Is it true you're marrying Devon Mattson, current contender for the mayoral seat of Blueberry Springs, in order to secure nontoxic ingredients—ingredients that will prevent Carrington Cosmetics users from becoming sick?"

Olivia was still in the wedding gown. She looked like a fool, trying to deal with the pointed questions.

What did everyone think of her right now? She'd come here trying to help and had only made things worse.

"I'm marrying Devon because..." She looked down at the dress, then over at Devon. He was trying to act calm, but she could see his body vibrating, his need to take over was so strong. "Carrington Cosmetics and the town of Blueberry Springs have an agreement providing the company access to all valerian within the vicinity. There is no need for me to marry Devon Mattson in order to secure access."

Barry frowned, hands on his hips. At the outer edge of the crowd, Olivia saw her father, his expression stern. He had several men in suits flanking him.

"Valerian simply brought me back to my—"

Someone jostled her, a cluster of reporters pressing closer, a microphone accidentally whacking her chin. Immediately, Logan and Devon were at her side.

She was running out of time to get her message across, her father's men drawing closer.

"As for Devon, he would make a great mayor. He has foresight and integrity and cares for his hometown."

"I think your engagement is a ploy!" shouted Barry. "A publicity stunt. A sham!"

"I think you're mistaking our relationship for your vision for the town," she said, pleased with her redirect. "That's the true sham here. Your dam is dangerous and will put Blueberry Springs under tremendous financial strain. It's going to cost the town, not help all the struggling families and small businesses. Devon understands that and is looking for safe alternatives that will bring industry and jobs to this town. He cares about helping local enterprises and the folks who run them."

"We need to get you out of here," Devon said in her ear.

No. She was not running away, not going to let a man like Barry Lunn push her out when she'd finally found what she wanted. She belonged here and this time she wasn't going down without a fight. This was her life.

The protesters had quieted, listening, her father's men waiting.

"Yeah, of course he cares about those firms and their owners," Barry scoffed. "His siblings own three of the five food businesses in town." His words were met with a few laughs. "And what about your family?"

"My family, Carrington Cosmetics, is looking forward to working with the people of Blueberry Springs and has signed an agreement to hire locally whenever possible."

See? She totally had this.

Devon's grip tightened on her arm. "*Now.*"

"I meant *your* family."

Olivia swore the sky suddenly swung to the left. She blinked, realizing it was her swaying with the shock of Barry's implication. He could *not* have meant what she thought he did.

"What about my family?" she called back, with more strength than she thought possible.

Devon began tugging on her arm and her frustration grew. He wasn't trusting her to take care of this, to protect them. She *had* this. She was *trained* for this. She was proving she loved him, standing up for him as well as their relationship, instead of letting someone else take over, call the shots.

"We need to clear out," he said.

"Devon…"

"Nope. Time to dance right on out of here."

"Your illegitimate child," Barry said. "Tell me how you getting pregnant out of wedlock shows a strength in family values."

Olivia felt her jaw unhinge and she turned to Devon, trying not to kill him with her glare. But he was pale, his expression entirely closed off. Behind him her sister was staring at her in shock. Then her eyes shut tight in what was clearly a feeling of betrayal topped with disappointment.

Her rejection hit Olivia like a slap.

She was alone.

"There was no child," Olivia said quietly and the microphones were shoved closer. Devon pushed them away. "I had a miscarriage. Is that all, Barry? Have you proved to the town what a caring soul you are yet?"

The crowd was silent and Barry looked down.

Obviously whatever tidbit had made it to him hadn't included the story's ending.

She felt decimated. Exposed.

She was shaking with shame and humiliation.

She tried to push her way through the crowd, seeking the solace and safety of the nearby helicopter. People parted to let her pass, as Logan commanded them to, her father's assistants coming to join them.

But Devon's rival wasn't finished yet. He moved closer, his voice carrying over the crowd's silence. "You're in PR, Olivia, and we see what you've done with Devon—pretended to be engaged, dressed him up. But we can spot the truth. You can put a spin on Devon's campaign, just like you will with the toxins, but Blueberry Springs isn't fooled. We know who you really are and you're not welcome here."

Shame leeching deep within her, Olivia kept blindly moving toward the machine that would lift her out of this humiliation.

She didn't want to fathom what people must be thinking of her and Devon right now. She'd tried to protect him, but instead she'd aired all their secrets, destroyed his life and his image alongside hers—just like before.

As she reached the edge of the crowd, she glanced back, seeing Emma. The pain of being lied to, shut out from the truth was there like a knife in her sister's side.

Logan ushered her along before she could find Devon in the crowd. She might love him, but there wasn't much for him to love back. She was nothing but a liar, protecting a company that hurt others, failing every time she tried to make things good.

But worst of all, she'd forced him to lie to the people who loved him most, and now he was going to lose it all.

DEVON DIDN'T KNOW what to say, what to do. He felt gutted.

Olivia had done the unthinkable, letting everything explode like a watermelon dropped from a skyscraper. He knew Barry, had recognized that glint in his eye, but she'd ignored his warnings, had pushed him away. Turned into Miss Carrington, cool and businesslike, confident her way was The Way.

And now she was marching toward her father's helicopter, ready to get out of Dodge because everything had crashed and burned.

The end.

He didn't care what everyone thought. He

didn't care that they knew about the baby, about the toxins. He only cared about Olivia.

He caught up to her, the silence after all the shouting feeling strangely loud.

"Olivia."

"I need to leave."

"Livvy, please."

"Devon, I've made a mess. I need to go."

"Stay. It's okay. We can fix this together."

She turned, facing him. Her expression was soft but determined. She laid a hand against the side of his face. "Devon, this has been an incredible few days with you, but we both know it's best that I leave. I'm no longer helping, I'm hindering. I'm nowhere near perfect enough to not make this worse. You need to win and you won't if I stay." Her eyes, filled with sorrow, gazed out at the crowd behind him. They were already dispersing, the drama over.

"You said you wouldn't run from them." He pointed toward the protesters, knowing he'd already lost her, knowing she'd already made up her mind. And who could blame her? Barry Lunn had just slaughtered her, run her out of town.

"I said my piece and fixed things the best I could. I no longer enhance your image, so it's best that I go while everyone still likes you." Her hands were flexing. Open. Closed. Open. Closed. Ready to run, ready to fight. Her voice had developed a tremble and he wasn't sure if it was from anger or anguish. "A company that's killing its own family? A woman who—"

"Don't say it," he pleaded. She needed to stop punishing herself. "The people who matter know the truth about us."

"That we're in love and about to go through with that wedding they're planning? I don't think so, Devon. He showed them the truth."

She turned away, her expression unreadable, her shoulders drooping as if she was trying to hold up the entire town on her own.

"*We* can show them the truth. We're a team, remember?"

"I need to be with my family," she said quietly. "I need to fix this with Emma, with the company. I have to leave before we lose what we've gained—if we haven't already."

He reached for her hand, playing with the ring.

He wanted her to stay. Stay until their children were grown. Stay until they were both in a nursing home with no remaining memories of anything other than that they had once loved someone so intensely that it overwrote everything else. A love that wove its way into the fabric of their lives, their very beings, for they weren't themselves without each other.

Olivia looked out beyond him, at the town and the mountains beyond. Her eyes were damp.

"Stay." They could fix things by sticking together.

She sniffed, her face wrinkling as she tipped her chin upward. "Tell them I had to take care of business. Tell Ginger I'll mail the dress back to her."

She kissed him, slow and sweet, and he knew it was over. That he'd never really had a chance and would always live with a hole in his heart where Livvy should be because she was already gone.

OLIVIA ARGUED with herself as the helicopter lifted her out of the town of Blueberry Springs.

She'd made a promise to Devon not to shut him out or run away.

She wasn't running away. She was protecting him.

But that's what she'd called it last time, too.

This time was different, though. Barry Lunn had laid out everything she'd tried to hide, from Emma's illness to the fake engagement to her and Devon's baby, a public feast of shame and humiliation. There was no way that her staying in Blueberry Springs would make any of it better.

Last time, she'd been protecting herself, her family. This time she was protecting Devon.

We see what you've done with Devon—pretended to be engaged, dressed him up. But we can spot the truth.

Blueberry Springs isn't fooled. We know who you really are.

The town still loved Devon Mattson, and she didn't want to be the one who changed that fact.

She had to leave.

Surely he understood?

"You made a royal mess of that," her father said. "We'll be lucky if we still have a company come tomorrow."

Beside her, Emma sniffled. Olivia reached for her hand, but her sister pulled away.

"What a bunch of lies," he muttered. "Making people sick?"

At Olivia's side, Emma stiffened. "I am sick, Dad," she said. "I'm sick and it's from the toxins in our cosmetics."

The cab of the helicopter grew silent and Olivia kept her gaze averted, watching the small town below grow smaller, wishing she had a parachute, a do-over.

Her father kept clearing his throat, a sure sign he was having trouble keeping it together. "You sure?"

"Yes. It's not terminal."

"Thank the heavens for that…" He cleared his throat again.

Below, Olivia could see the meadow. The downtown, even Devon's house, her Porsche parked outside.

"I need to get my dog," she said, finally looking away from the window.

"Ricky's taking care of it."

Olivia nodded. Of course. Her father had set up a protective perimeter around her like always, taking care, taking charge. She was doing the right thing, leaving. She was protecting Devon from even worse publicity, because she knew things like this didn't die down overnight and he still had days before the election. It would be best for him if she disappeared, stayed out of sight and out of mind. And anyway, she'd just splashed every bit of dirt Carrington had across the media and she had to spin this before they lost every-thing. And before she found herself in a position where she could no longer help Blueberry Springs.

"I'll issue a press release. We have to put our re-sources into doing whatever we can to make sure Devon wins this election."

"Olivia…" her father began.

"I love him, Daddy. Just like I always have. But this is about the valerian. If he loses, we lose. Even more so now that this bit about the toxins has gotten out."

"You promised me you wouldn't let the valerian go!" Emma said, bursting into tears, her earlier stoicism gone.

Olivia pulled her sister to her and Emma collapsed in her arms, a surprisingly heavy weight.

"I'm so sorry," Olivia whispered. "I wish I'd done better out there. I wish I'd convinced them we're the good guys." If Devon lost...

Stop thinking!

She was doing everything she could, including avoiding Devon so her dramas wouldn't taint him. All he had to do was say she was home dealing with the media hailstorm, and maybe, just maybe, the town wouldn't think about whether or not Barry had been right about the fake engagement, and they'd continue to favor Devon right up until election day.

It was a long shot, but it was all they had.

"Do I still have a job?" Olivia asked her father.

"Olivia Dawn," her father replied on a sigh.

"Do I?" She needed to know if he was planning on kicking her out of the company. She had work to do.

"Yes. Fine. But everything goes through me. You understand? No more shenanigans."

"Yes."

"I'll help," Emma said.

"Are you sure?" Olivia asked.

She rolled her shoulders in a shrug. "My health issues are already out there. Why not leverage them to create some exposure into our upcoming product line changes?"

Her father leaned forward, pinching his nose. "That's incredibly risky."

"That's life."

He sagged into the seat as though exhausted. "I swear I will never understand you two no matter how long I live."

He might not, but Olivia hoped Devon would, and that he knew how hard it had been to walk away from him moments ago. And that she was doing it for him.

Because like always, with just one kiss, he had turned her life upside down and made her his. And as a result, she'd taken everything good, her snow globe of a life in Blueberry Springs, and smashed it on a concrete floor. And along with it, Devon's.

But maybe this time it would land on a pillow of love and trust and would be okay.

DEVON RAN FASTER on his basement treadmill. He hit the incline button, punishing himself with a more difficult run.

He hadn't been enough to make Olivia stay. He hadn't been able to shelter that seedling of their renewed connection, protect it, cherish her in the right way. And so she was gone.

She had what she wanted—the valerian. Plus she now had a media storm she could manipulate to highlight her upcoming organic, safe cosmetic line, if she so chose.

That's what she'd come for.

Like the fool he was, he'd opened his arms, exposing himself to the pain, knowing it was coming. But knowing it was worth it if he could have even one more minute with her in his life.

He tried to laugh at himself for falling for her again, but his chest hurt.

One of her company's minions had cleared out Devon's guest room, collected her dog.

Mr. Right.

He supposed the dog's name was correct, seeing as no human seemed able to step into that role for Olivia.

He'd been a fool to think it was different this time, that sharing their mourning would matter.

Instead it just hurt.

Devon ran faster, his feet thumping the treadmill with quick precision, his blood pumping.

Such a fool.

And he still had a mayoral race to win—without
his fiancée at his side. No, not his. Never was.
Never would be.

He had to refocus. Take what he still had and
shape it into something that mattered.

Nothing mattered.

He'd lost it all.

She had to go fix the company, soothe her family. He knew that. But he was certain she could
have done it from here. They could have faced
Barry together. It would have been better—
standing up to the bully, kissing in public to prove
it wasn't all fake. Running away made them look
guilty.

What was he going to say when people asked
him where Olivia was? He could say she was just
taking care of business back home, but the truth
was she had left him. This was the breakup stage.
The first few hours of the drawn-out "we couldn't
make it work long-distance" plan.

He'd thought he would have another week. He'd
thought he'd have more time.

He stumbled, grabbing the treadmill's railing
until he could get himself back on pace. He kept
running, but his rhythm was off, jagged, and when

he nearly fell again, he yanked the emergency stop cord, bringing the machine to a sudden halt. Breathing hard, he bent over. He'd run too hard, too fast, kept the warm-up too short. His muscles were screaming and he felt like his lungs were going to explode, but it didn't come close to the level of pain in his heart.

He stepped off the treadmill and paced the room, trying to get his breathing back under control. He shoved a hand into his hair, but there wasn't enough to grab onto. Nothing felt right any longer.

Frustrated and angry, he stormed up the stairs to the main floor. He spied a discarded silk tie hanging over the couch and he swiped it up, then banged open his bedroom door. He pulled the new shirts off their hangers, dumping them into a pile on the floor along with the tie. Grabbing his briefcase, he dumped it upside down, scattering contents across his unmade bed, which still smelled like Olivia's perfume. Everything new went into the heap before he bundled it up, tossing the whole kit and caboodle into the trash bin in his garage.

What a desperate sucker he'd been to let her waltz right in and dress him up, believing it was real. That she'd meant it. That he belonged with her and that this time their worlds would join as one.

CHAPTER 14

*H*is last gift from Olivia. Devon pretended his smile was real as he joked with the crowd gathered in the community center to hear the election results as the votes were tallied.

He'd won.

Devon Mattson, mayor of Blueberry Springs.

Devon Mattson, dumped before he reached the altar.

What did he have to do to get it right with Olivia?

And why wasn't he excited about the win? He'd got exactly what he'd asked for from Olivia—a deal to stop the dam, creating industry and jobs in his hometown. The mayoral seat.

He had everything he'd reached for.

Despite it all, he knew why his win felt empty. It was because Olivia wasn't there at his side to laugh, say "good job," hug him and take him home. She would have made this all feel worthwhile.

"I thought there was supposed to be a wedding?" his grandfather asked, looking around the community center's ballroom, his brows furrowed in confusion.

It took Devon a moment to catch up. "For Jen and Rob? They both got a nasty flu. It was postponed. It'll be this weekend instead." In fact, the very date Mary Alice had reserved for him and Olivia. He supposed it was cool the way that had worked in Jen's favor. Which reminded him. He needed to call Olivia, set up an official breakup date, because he couldn't go on like this much longer—acting like they were together when his heart was broken.

Ethan shared a look with Devon as if to ask if Gramps was losing a few marbles. The man hadn't even been invited to that shindig.

"No," protested their grandfather. "You and that woman. Where is she?"

"Olivia?"

"That's the one."

"Right. Well..." Devon felt uncomfortable with the old line he'd been using since she'd left Blueberry Springs five days and seven hours ago. "She's taking care of business stuff back home, setting up things so her family's company can come work with Blueberry Springs."

He wasn't certain if that was still true or not. Her father might have kept his promise and turfed her out of her position as PR manager after all that had gone down outside Veils and Vows last Wednesday. The media fallout had been huge.

The parts about her sister had been horrible, coverage of their unborn child even worse as reporters turned to speculation about toxins and miscarriages.

But the people of Blueberry Springs had stayed by his side. Hers, too, if she'd stuck around.

Devon had picked up his phone to call her, ask if she was okay, but he'd feared she would take it the wrong way—him calling only to see if their valerian deal was still valid. And if it wasn't, he hadn't wanted to know before the election, so he didn't have to lie about one more thing.

Barry Lunn came across the busy room, hand extended. His son was at his side, looking at Devon hopefully.

"Well, my boy, you did it." Barry clapped a palm on Devon's shoulder while he shook his hand. Devon resisted the urge to deck the man in front of Peter. The last time he'd seen Barry the man had been slamming Olivia in front of the press, and

Devon had taken several rage-fueled runs on his treadmill since then, trying to burn off the residual anger. "The town is full of smart people."

Devon said nothing, afraid if he spoke it could get nasty. He sufficed with a curt nod.

"My mom's already gone home to dry her tears." Barry gave an affable shrug. "I was hoping to retire as mayor, because where do you go from here in a small town like this?"

"I have a catering business for sale," Ethan said at Devon's side.

"Ha! Me, cooking? I'd kill half my customers in the first week." Barry added to Devon, almost like an afterthought, "It'll be nice not to have to deal with you in chambers."

Devon had been edging away, watching Trish and his father approach. As overbearing as they sometimes were, they were still two of his favorite people. At Barry's words, he stepped back in surprise. "Sorry?"

"You scare me, boy. You don't back down when you know what you want."

Not totally true. Take Olivia, for example. He was still waiting for her to call, instead of chasing after her.

"Never once did you think about giving me the gears over contracts." He emphasized his point with a raised fist. "You'll be good for this town. It needs an advocate who'll stand up for it and knows what should be done." He nodded once, as though trying to figure out if his words had made sense.

"Excuse me," Devon said, pushing past him.

The former mayor caught him by the arm. "I'm sorry, Devon. I know you're mad. Wednesday wasn't my finest moment and my desperation showed."

"It's not that. It's about who you hurt," Devon said, his voice hard.

Barry hung his head and Peter took the opportunity to hold a magazine page in front of Devon's face. He tried to avoid it, but the woman depicted there caught his eye. It was Olivia in an old Carrington ad.

Peter grinned and held up several more folded pages along with a pen. Devon touched the first worn picture. It was autographed by Olivia, who was radiating happiness right off the page. She was beautiful and glowing, looking exactly the way she had back in college. Happy and free.

His.

Their love had been real. Both times.

He had to do something.

Peter waved the pen and Devon shook his head. "Sorry, Pete. She's not here."

He turned away, stepping right into the outstretched arms of his stepmom who, teary-eyed, engulfed him in a massive hug. He let her hold on for as long as she liked.

"Our boy," she said, her voice choked.

And he realized that he was indeed their boy—hers, too. She might have been unprepared to step into a mothering role for him as a teen, but he saw it now. She *was* a mother. She'd taken him in for just as many stitches as his own mom. She'd grounded him, baked him cookies, and had always had an ear at the ready, his biggest advocate and protector, glad to celebrate his biggest triumphs.

"You're a good woman, Trish. Dad's lucky to have you. As am I."

She pulled away, took one look at Devon and broke into happy sobs. He had to admit he was feeling a little choked up himself.

"Thanks for being there," he added. "For all of us."

He'd left her speechless. That was a first.

Behind her, his father smiled, his own eyes wet. He moved around his wife and yanked Devon into a tight hug that almost made Devon worry about cracked ribs. "You make me so proud."

"Thanks, Dad."

"Ethan, old coot, take me home," Gramps said, turning to Ethan. "It's getting too sappy in here for me."

"I agree," Ethan replied. "And for future reference, you're older than I am."

"You limp more."

"I was paralyzed for a month. Was in a wheelchair for years. I had to learn to walk again."

"You did it once, why not do it twice? Quit your complaining," Gramps grumped.

Ethan smiled slightly and gently took their grandfather by the arm, supporting him while he tugged overshoes over his dress shoes. Completely unnecessary on the beautiful June day.

Ethan turned to Devon. "Oh, and congratulations, butthead. Don't screw up the town."

Devon had a million comebacks, all biting. He sufficed with a simple dig. "Either or, Ethan snores. Can't wait until you start dating so I can taunt you with that one. I'm sure Trish could get Mom to share some baby pictures, too."

Trish had a mischievous twinkle in her eye. "I already have some stockpiled."

Ethan glared, but everyone knew it was just for show. "You know I don't date."

"That's because he's Oscar the Grouch," Mandy said, joining them. Trish and their dad excused themselves to go accept offered congratulations as the proud parents.

"Oh, look, it's Fluff." Devon gave Mandy a hug, sticking up for Ethan while impeding his sister's attempt to give him a good shove for using her old nickname, which came from the way Trish and Dad treated her—like she was fluff, incapable of taking care of herself.

"Why aren't you smiling? You won!" Mandy declared. Nicola joined them, her babies at home with Todd.

"I am smiling, see?" Devon gave an exaggerated grin, fairly certain he looked similar to Jack Nicholson playing the Joker.

"Olivia broke up with you," Nicola said with a gasp. Mandy's eyes expanded and her jaw dropped.

"My cue to leave," Ethan muttered. "You ready, Gramps?" Their grandfather was still fumbling with his shoes.

"Women," Gramps grumbled.

"Tell me about. They leave at the first signs of distress."

The two went limping off, commiserating.

Nicola and Mandy were still staring at Devon in shocked surprise. He took a step closer in case he had to muzzle them, then looked around for eavesdroppers even though their horrified expressions had probably already given everything away.

Mandy's gaze turned sympathetic. "You need to go to her. Seriously, Demon Boy. I thought you were happy until I saw you engaged."

The first time he and Olivia had broken up he'd

wished he'd tried harder, let her know he still loved her, still wanted her.

And hadn't he promised himself not to repeat his past mistakes?

OLIVIA HAD SPENT days in her hotel room writing press releases that often skirted around her personal life and instead focused on dealing with details related to the All You product line. She couldn't wait to return home and have her real office back, be in her own space. But her father had decided that the core group from Carrington needed to spend another few days on retreat, brainstorming and having breakout sessions on how they could get the new line to market as soon as humanly possible. And then cut a few months off that schedule.

Thank goodness for Emma. She was amazing, taking on incredible amounts of detailed tasks and timelines, contingency plans and more—all stuff that made Olivia's brain hurt, leaving her to deal with PR and marketing. Which felt…well, lackluster and boring.

She missed Devon. She was only hours away and every night she had to force herself to stay away.

But the worst was that with every release she wrote, trying to cover up the disaster, she realized just how much she'd let him down, how undeserving she was.

So instead of going to him, she cried herself to sleep. Instead of calling, she mentally begged for his forgiveness, prayed he understood why she was staying away.

She was so tired of her job. Spinning webs, creating images that weren't fully accurate. When exactly had she become someone who directed everyone to look away from the issues? And even worse was the fact that Luke's company, Cohen's Blissful Body Care, had taken an image hit over the whole disaster as well. He'd stepped up, defending Carrington Cosmetics which had only served to have the media take a closer look at Cohen's products' ingredient lists.

Olivia had been grateful to have Jen's wedding dress to work on for the first two nights. Something to absorb herself in, take her mind off the real world. When Olivia had left, right after the fitting, she'd had Ginger ship the dress to her so she wouldn't leave Jen in the lurch. She told herself it would help Devon's campaign—keeping her promise to the bride-to-be—but in reality she'd just wanted something creative to distract her, wanted to do something that would help a woman who was getting her happily ever after.

So she'd gone out and bought needles, thread and a stitch ripper, and had spent several wonderful hours in her own little world, doing the alterations by hand before sending it back in the nick of time for last weekend's wedding.

However, the rush had been for nothing, as Ginger had communicated the news that the young family had come down with the flu the night before their big day. However, this weekend they would tie the knot—thanks to Olivia, who'd insisted the family take the reservations Mary Alice had indeed made on her and Devon's behalf. And so, by the sound of things, the town was being its usual accommodating self and taking the last-minute change of plans in stride. It made Olivia want to be there.

Of course, with a change of plans there were a few hiccups, such as one of the bridesmaids not being able to make the new date. She just hoped it didn't impinge on Jen's courage to walk down the aisle. Olivia looked at her own ring, realizing the dream of her and Devon being together was over. She slipped off the ring and set it on her desk with a sigh.

She swiped at her eyes and refocused her thoughts on the new product line instead of what was happening in Blueberry Springs. All You was going to happen. Really happen.

That should excite her. Just like the news of Devon winning the election had excited her. He had sent a text after she'd fallen asleep last night, letting her know he'd won.

It had been a disappointingly short message, but even so, she'd been truly happy for him. Not just because it meant that Carrington's source of valerian was secured, but because Blueberry Springs would be in good hands. He was the right choice.

She looked at her phone. She wanted to call him, pass on her congratulations, hear his voice, find out if it was okay for them to be seen in public together.

But he hadn't called her or reached out other than the one text, which suggested to her that things had been quite bad for him after she'd left, and he needed to keep his distance. They had definitely been bad for her in the news, so she completely understood.

Both of them were in damage control mode.

Still, she'd been hoping she'd be the first one he called when the votes came in. Carry the facade of them loving each other just a little further into his new life.

Feeling dejected, Olivia called her dog and

leashed him, determined to shed her mind of everything.

In the lobby she bumped into Emma who was talking with Luke, heads bent over something he was holding.

"Luke!" Olivia came closer. "I thought you'd gone back with the rest of your company."

"I missed you."

"Me?" Olivia laughed in surprise.

"Is that so funny?"

"Just unexpected." They were friends; it was ever so clear to all that they were nothing more. The companies didn't need them to marry now that she'd secured the ingredients for All You. And Cohen's had never really needed Carrington Cosmetics, anyway. It had been more a case of one old family friend trying to help out another. And in fact, much to Olivia's chagrin, her recent bout of not-so-great publicity had given Cohen's a bit of a black eye as well—thanks to Luke trying to defend Carrington to the press and instead resulting in the toxin light being shone on some of their products as well.

"We were just talking about…work," Emma said blithely.

Olivia sent her a warning glance, and in reply, her sister's gaze slipped to Olivia's bare ring finger. She gave Olivia an expectant look.

The past few days had been intense as the two sisters reconfigured their relationship. Emma had been disappointed and hurt that Olivia hadn't told her about the pregnancy. But having her illness spread in the news, Emma seemed to understand why Olivia had kept her mouth shut. In a strange way, the week had forged a stronger bond between them.

Luke raised his brows in invitation while tipping his head toward the outer doors.

Olivia joined him, asking Emma over her shoulder, "Did you want to come?"

She shook her head, scrunching her nose while giving Olivia an odd look that seemed almost wistful.

As Olivia walked the hotel's grounds with Luke and her dog, Luke took her elbow as he often did. He was easy to be with, kind and polite. In some ways Olivia was surprised that he and Emma had never hit it off. They weren't exactly alike but there was something about the two of them together that just felt right. Weird, but right.

"How are you doing?" Luke asked.

"Fine. And yourself?" Despite having apologized to him and his family, she still felt bad for the way his company had taken an image hit for standing up for her and Carrington.

He paused, really looking at her. She wondered what he saw.

"I'm sorry things didn't work out with Devon," he said.

"It worked out fine," she replied, raising her chin. She didn't need pity. She needed Devon to reach out to her so she'd know it was safe to take up their...whatever it was they'd had.

"I heard a funny joke," Luke said at last. They sat near a fountain in the midst of a hedged-in garden near the hotel's small, private lake. Around them birds sang and a few people passed by. Mr. Right growled intermittently as though he was checking an incoming signal.

"A funny joke?" Olivia repeated in surprise. Luke didn't normally crack jokes. He was typically Mr. Serious CEO.

"Why didn't the panda bear become a bear? No. Why did the...hang on."

Luke was trying to make her smile and she appreciated it, but he really wasn't a comedian.

He collected her hands in his, concentrating on the punch line. "Okay. I've got it. Why isn't a koala bear a bear?"

"It's not?"

"It doesn't have the right koala-fications."

Olivia broke into laughter at the unexpected pun. "Well done, Luke." She let her shoulder bump into his. Mr. Right suddenly perked up, whining and tugging on his leash. Luke slid off the bench and onto one knee.

"Are you okay?" she asked, while trying to calm her dog. "I hope you're not having a heart attack."

"Olivia Dawn Mary Carrington, would you do me the honor of becoming my wife?"

DEVON STOOD on the grounds overlooking the lake at Olivia's hotel. He'd thought he'd seen her walk behind a hedge when he'd pulled into the parking lot moments ago. Devon began walking again, inhaling the sweet, innocent scent of a honeysuckle hedge. He scanned the greenery, finally spying Olivia. With Luke.

They were walking together as though they belonged side by side on the other side of the garden. Their outfits were well-tailored, her shaggy dog behaving on his leash—the only thing out of place in the perfect scene.

They sat down companionably on a bench. Luke clutched Olivia's hands and she let him. Then her laughter broke over the sound of the water splashing in the picturesque fountain. Rich and free, warming Devon's heart.

Then Luke got down on one knee.

One. Knee.

Devon felt as though the weight of a tanker truck fell on his chest.

Awesome Dog began barking and whining, suddenly lunging on his leash, as he sensed him nearby, but Devon turned and broke into a run. This was not where he wanted to be right now.

He had been stupid coming here. Stupid to have thought there was something more beyond their ploy to get him elected. It had worked and now he had to live with the lie he'd told, he'd believed, the truth falling upon his conscience with sharps daggers, leaving a bitter taste in his mouth.

He started his car, the alternator belt squealing in the sea of Cadillacs and Lincolns. The Honda's tires followed suit as he pinned the gas pedal to the floor, taking the corners too fast, desperate to get away.

CHAPTER 15

Olivia parked her car just off Main Street in Blueberry Springs and inhaled the fresh mountain air. She had missed this place in the days she'd been away. It had been a week and a half, but felt so much longer.

She'd heard from Ginger that the protesters had left town after the election results, moving on to protest another proposed dam a few states over, and today Jen would be getting married in the newly quiet town.

Olivia checked the time. She would be meeting Emma in an hour or two, but wanted to borrow an alteration kit from Ginger, as she'd promised to do a last-minute fitting for Jen at the community center before the three o'clock ceremony. Plus she had to meet up with Vintra, who'd set up a small lab in one of the buildings just off the downtown.

And then there was Devon. They needed to break up.

The very thought brought tears to her eyes.

She hadn't seen him. Hadn't talked to him.

She'd just about lost it when Luke had proposed. She didn't want *him*. She had left Blueberry Springs only to give Devon the space he needed to win. He was the only man she'd ever loved and she couldn't imagine wanting anyone else.

Olivia stepped onto the curb and crossed the sidewalk into Veils and Vows, blinking quickly to ensure she didn't look teary-eyed. Her engagement ring from Devon weighed heavy on her hand as she played a few more hours as his fiancée.

"Now that's the person we need," Ginger said, immediately drawing Olivia into the store's fitting area as though she'd been hovering at the door, waiting. Jen was sitting in one of the chairs, looking distraught. "Jen needs another bridesmaid."

"I heard about that. Do you need me to fit a dress?" Olivia asked.

"She has to fit into *that* dress." Jen pointed to a gown being held up by Ginger. It was very similar to the one Olivia had been wearing as her dream gown, only it was a pale blue.

"It's beautiful."

"And it would fit perfectly over Olivia's curves," Ginger said to Jen.

She nodded.

Why did Olivia feel as though she was being set up? She looked to Jen in question. They'd had a nice hike together, but surely the woman had more options than someone who still fell in the acquaintances category.

Jen got up and came to her, saying, "Please! You know how stressed I am."

Olivia considered her. Saying yes would be the right thing to do.

"You want me to try it on?"

OLIVIA HUSTLED into the community center at two-fifteen. She had a dress to slip into—Ginger had worked quickly to set her up with shoes and all the accessories after Olivia had agreed to stand in as a bridesmaid—as well as her hair to do.

Olivia was nervous. She'd been a bridesmaid before, but she hadn't faced the town since fleeing. Sure, she'd bumped into a few people while checking in on Vintra and then meeting up with Emma, who was with her now, looking as though she was hiding a secret.

The one person Olivia hadn't found was Devon.

And maybe that was a good thing. It would have been awkward if they'd planned their breakup and then she'd had to come here and act like they were still together.

Man, she missed him. Everything in this town reminded her of him.

"You okay?" Emma asked.

Olivia's held-back tears came to the surface. She nodded and looked up, hoping to somehow get them to defy nature and sink back into her eyes again.

"Aw, hon." Emma gave her a hug. "Is this about Devon?"

"Weddings just make me emotional."

Ginger came rushing in, her curly hair done up in a bun. She snagged Olivia by the arm. "Come on! Hurry! We have so much to do!"

Olivia's anxiety picked up a notch at the stress in her voice. "Is everything okay?"

Her friend gave a slightly demented laugh and plunked her in front of a woman armed with hair spray, bobby pins and a brush.

"Hair. Makeup. I'll be back in ten minutes."

Emma hadn't followed Olivia, and she worried her sister felt ditched. The hairdresser set to work with a speed that astounded Olivia, and before long, Ginger was back, wearing a pale pink dress, whisking her into a room where gowns and bins of accessories were laid out.

"Why so many dresses?" Olivia asked. Surely the others weren't getting ready here, too.

"Put this on."

"This isn't the one I tried on," Olivia said. It was cream, not blue.

"I know, I know. Blue was a problem."

"Why?"

"I spilled something on it."

"Ginger…" Olivia said in warning.

"Trust me."

Olivia sighed and put on the dress, worrying that she was going to outshine the bride, not serve as backup. She caught sight of her reflection in the mirror, and her heart stuttered.

She looked like a real bride.

She wanted this to be her wedding day.

To Devon.

Ginger appeared moments later. "Do you need help with the zipper?"

Olivia shook her head. There had been a zipper helper, the device reminding her of the time Devon had had to help her with her Chanel dress. The rain, the mud. The trust.

She wished he'd call her, wished there was a way to keep the relationship they'd had.

"You'll need this." Ginger handed her a bouquet.

"What's this for? Where's Jen?"

Ginger took a deep breath. "Don't kill me, but it's you who's getting married today."

"What?" Olivia's loud exclamation had likely wakened half the town, but she didn't care. She wasn't engaged. She wasn't even in a real relationship. She'd given her wedding day to Jen for a reason. How was this happening?

Ginger handed Olivia a pair of diamond earrings. "Your mother's. Something borrowed."

"But...to who?"

"To Devon," her friend said quietly, giving her a funny look.

"Devon? Devon Mattson?"

She might need to sit down.

Now.

Feebly, and with shaking limbs, she sat herself in a hard plastic chair and put a palm against her forehead. Fever dream. Had to be. Only she wasn't sick.

Who planned a surprise wedding? Especially for a couple who hadn't even had a real relationship? This was a nightmare.

She began sobbing, unable to keep it in.

Ginger crouched in front of her, looking alarmed.

"It was fake." Olivia hiccupped. "We were never really engaged."

Her friend's brow furrowed. "But…"

Olivia swallowed the hard lump in her throat. How had Ginger not known? How had she not seen through it all?

"But you two are in love."

"I love him, but he's not…he's not…"

"Well, I don't know what to tell you," Ginger said soberly. "But we already wrangled him into waiting at the altar for you." She pinned a veil in Olivia's hair.

"What?"

Ginger gave a secret, self-satisfied smile.

"Are my parents here?"

"Yes. And Emma's a bridesmaid."

How on earth had they managed that?

"How long have you been planning this?"

"Since the moment that ring hit your finger. You're both runners. You let stupid things come between you instead of trusting each other and your love. I figured if I didn't plan it superfast you two would break up again. Which apparently you didn't need to do, because it wasn't ever real. Except for the fact that you two are totally head over heels for each other."

"He's here? Really here?"

Ginger kept nodding.

Olivia couldn't wrap her mind around the whole idea that Devon might actually love her, love her enough that he was truly waiting for her. No games. No ploys to fool anyone. Just…love.

"He knows…knows he's supposed to—marry me? Here? Today? For real and forever and ever?"

"Wow, you're babbling."

Olivia nodded vigorously, gulping air.

"It's a lot to take in," her friend said matter-of-factly. "I'll give you a minute. Oh, and by the way, I made myself one of your bridesmaids. I hope you don't mind." She let herself out of the room, but Olivia was already on the move.

She had to know what Devon was really thinking, really feeling.

<hr>

DEVON WAS SWEATING bullets at the front of the church.

He thought he was supposed to be Rob's best man. It turned out he was actually the groom.

Him.

Devon Mattson.

Olivia had said no to Luke. *No.*

The happiest word that had ever been relayed back to him. Ever.

As for Rob and Jen, they'd eloped and had the wedding they'd truly wanted, leaving him and Olivia to be set up with a surprise wedding.

Who did that?

Obviously, Blueberry Springs.

And the funny thing was that despite the pain of a possible massive, public rejection by her...he was okay with it all. Because left to their own devices, he wasn't certain he and Olivia would ever make it this far on their own.

Assuming she didn't walk out today.

What if she didn't love him? He turned away, his doubts beginning to gnaw at him like hungry piranhas.

Liz, who was at the piano, began playing, and Devon's eyes zagged to the doorway.

Bridesmaids tried to hustle into position, jockeying to head down the aisle before Olivia, who was pushing them all out of the way.

She strode down the aisle, making a "cut" signal to Liz. The community center was packed and it grew silent, all eyes watching her as she marched toward Devon. She was beautiful. Her dress showing off every dangerous curve of her heavenly body. Her skin clear and glowing.

Her eyes flashing with something he couldn't quite catch.

Uh-oh.

His feet angled toward the door. But as she neared and he got a better read on her expression, his muscles relaxed and he let out a slow breath.

"Hey," he said.

"Did you know about this?"

He shook his head, watching her. "But I'm game if you are."

"Devon…"

"Liv, I know I didn't get to propose to you properly, so maybe this would be a good time."

She gave him a surprised look and he carefully got down on one knee, taking her hand.

"Olivia, you are the most courageous woman I know. You protect others above yourself. I love you and I don't know what I'd do without you. Sharing my home with you as my fiancée were some of the best days of my entire life. I know I'm not perfect, and neither are you, but I think that's what makes us perfect for each other. Somewhere between your world and my world is our world. One that is made up of our in jokes, our laughter, but most of all our love. I've never loved anyone the way I love you, Olivia, and I can't live without you in my life.

"Could you find it in your heart to fall in love with me again and be my wife?"

Olivia looked out at their audience. Everyone was waiting for her reply, perched on the edges of their seats, leaning forward.

"No," she said softly, shaking her head.

Devon felt cold. He couldn't move, couldn't speak.

This was not how it was supposed to go.

Olivia continued, "I can't fall in love with you again because I never once stopped loving you, no matter how hard I tried. And I don't think I ever will. It's not in my nature to stop loving you."

Devon let out a shaky breath of relief. Man, she'd really had him going there for an excruciating minute.

"So, yes. I will be your wife, because I love you, Devon Mattson, and nobody else. For real."

He popped to his feet, finding her lips, claiming them with a deep kiss so full of love he nearly keeled over on the spot.

"I love you," he whispered.

Olivia's eyes welled with tears. "I love you, too."

Mary Alice, resplendent in a bright yellow dress, began their vows. Devon, unable to resist, pulled Olivia into another kiss.

Mary Alice cleared her throat. "This is important legal stuff, you two."

He came up for air.

"Do you, Devon Adam Mattson, take Olivia Dawn Mary Carrington to be your lawfully wedded wife?"

"I do," he said with a smile.

"Do you, Olivia Dawn Mary Carrington, take Devon Adam Mattson to be your lawfully wedded husband?"

"I do," Olivia replied breathlessly.

She grinned wide as Mary Alice said, "With the power invested in me by the town of Blueberry Springs, I now declare you husband and wife!"

The audience cheered, whooped and hollered. Devon collected Olivia in his arms again, dipping her backward as he gave her a long kiss that promised of many more to come.

CHAPTER 16

*D*evon stretched, watching the town celebrate his love in a room full of fairy lights and streamers. Sweet love, he was married. The confirmed bachelor wedded. To the woman he'd never once stopped thinking about. Life didn't get much better, and he owed the town for making it happen, for taking his and Olivia's fears out of their hands and making the choice simple.

You love each other? Yes? Then get married. Here you go. Done.

"Congratulations," Mandy said, coming up behind him to give him a hug.

"Who'd have thought, huh?"

"Surprising you with a wedding? That's Blueberry Springs for you."

"Another reason to love my town."

"*My* town, huh? This mayor business is going to your head."

Mandy took Olivia's empty chair at the head table and they watched Nicola and Todd for a moment. The two were smiling, looking like the most awake couple in the hall as the reception wound down. Something about being up crazy hours with twins had them fully prepared for an impromptu wedding.

Mandy was smiling in that soft way of hers whenever she saw babies lately, and Devon watched her. Her gaze flicked to her husband and best friend, Frankie.

Totally in love. He wondered if he looked that sappy whenever he glanced at Olivia. He had a pretty good idea that he did. In fact, he couldn't wait to get her home and out of that gorgeous gown.

"You're so lovesick," Mandy said, nudging him.

He grinned. Coming home had never been as sweet as when Olivia had been there waiting for him, and he looked forward to many decades of doing so.

"Speak for yourself," he retorted. "I saw you ogling the twins. What's that about?"

Mandy turned somber, her gaze finding its way back to her husband.

"What? What's wrong?" Anxiety built inside

Devon. He knew how devastating a miscarriage could be, and it was something he'd never wish upon his sister, no matter how big a pain in the butt she was.

"We're adopting."

"What?"

"Yeah." She smiled. "But shh. It's not totally firm yet and you know how these things can go."

"That's awesome, Fluff."

She growled. "Don't call me that, Demon Boy."

"Why not?"

She swung her arm back to slug his arm and he leaned away, laughing. Life was good, and his sister would make an amazing mother.

Olivia's father strode over, looking stern as usual, and Mandy scooted off while Devon straightened his bow tie in anticipation. He stood, shaking his father-in-law's hand. He still didn't know how anyone had convinced his new in-laws to come to the surprise wedding.

"I'm taking Joan back to the hotel," Mr. Carrington said gruffly. He turned to look out over the dance floor, where Olivia was strutting her stuff with Ginger, Logan's daughter Annabelle, and Emma, the three of them laughing like they didn't have a care in the world. It looked a lot like they were doing the Funky Chicken. In other words, it was undignified and horrible. And it brought a wistful smile to the businessman's face.

"She's happy," Mr. Carrington stated.

"I intend to keep her that way."

"Good."

They shook hands again, this time Mr. Carrington giving Devon a slap on the biceps with his free palm, letting the contact linger in as much of a man-hug as he'd ever give. With a curt nod, and looking as though he wanted to say more, the man was off.

"They offered to send us on a honeymoon," Olivia said, coming to join Devon after hugging her parents goodbye.

"Really?"

"I told them no. I'm not taking their money."

Images of a luxury vacation fell from Devon's mind. "Oh."

She hooked a finger in his aquamarine cummerbund and gave him a wicked smile. "But as a gift, I said we'd be happy to accept."

He pulled her tight to him, kissing her ear, ending with a playful nip that made her growl.

"Be careful or we'll be consummating this marriage in the coatroom."

"Works for me." He pretended to stand. "Because I haven't seen a stitch of 'something blue' on you and I have a feeling it's a special lingerie treat meant for my eyes only."

She laughed in delight, yanking him onto the chair beside her and in the process pulling the head table's white linen tablecloth askew. He slung an arm across her shoulders, bringing her close enough that he could inhale her perfume and that special scent of hers that brought back a treasure trove of wonderful memories.

"How did they manage to pull all of this off?" she murmured in wonder, taking in the room.

The space had a magical glow from the tiny white fairy lights strung above. Black material behind them gave the effect of a night sky, and there were flowers everywhere. Elegant and simply gorgeous. Just like his bride.

She bit her bottom lip, her eyes sparkling as much as her mother's borrowed diamond earrings as she leaned forward and kissed him. "I love you."

Devon stared into the depths of her warm brown eyes. "I love you, too, Liv."

The bride and groom smiled at each other.

"So how did they convince your parents to come to this?" he asked.

"Emma threatened them."

"It was that easy?"

"Not quite, but my father...he just wants what's

best for me and I think her illness has made him realize the truth—life's short."

Devon kissed her nose, taking in the implications of her statement.

"What do you think?" Ginger demanded, interrupting their tête-à-tête. "Did we do okay?" She was standing at their table with Wanda, Mary Alice and Trish, glasses of champagne mixed with orange juice in hand.

"Amazing," Olivia and Devon said at the same time.

"You'll send us a bill?" Devon added.

"We'll figure it out eventually," his stepmom said. "Maybe." She was smiling, happy. For all the teasing they'd given her as teens, she wasn't half-bad.

"Thanks. For everything," Devon murmured.

The women scattered and Nicola came by, baby in her arms. "Can you hold her? I need to use the ladies' room."

Olivia popped up, arms extended for the hand-off, and Nicola shuffled the sleeping baby into Olivia's care. Devon felt the familiar sting of their lost infant once again, more pronounced in the natural way Olivia was cuddling the child. The light in her eyes was soft, her expression one of consummate love.

"She's adorable," she whispered, taking her seat beside Devon.

Devon tickled the baby's chin, stunned by the tender feelings the child evoked.

"Maybe we should have a few of these," he whispered, feeling slightly choked up.

Olivia nodded. Her expression wasn't one of pain, as he'd expected, but rather one of curiosity and longing. She met his gaze. "Think we could do this? For real?"

He slipped an arm around her shoulder, tucking a strand of hair behind her ear, even though he knew the tendril had been intentionally left out of her blond twist.

"Yeah, I do."

"I'd like to do some work for Ginger. It was fun working with dresses again. But I need to finish up things with Carrington—hand the project off to Emma and see if she can get things back on track. Then maybe finish my minor in fashion. Have it all."

"Yeah?" He loved it when she dreamed big, and in his mind there was nothing sexier than the woman in his life following her heart, her dreams.

Her lip got tugged into her mouth again as she stared at the sleeping child. "But we're already in our thirties. The doctors said I'm okay after what happened with my pregnancy…but I'm not getting any younger."

"We'll figure it out."

"What if there isn't time to do it all?" Olivia asked. Her expression turned hopeful. "Maybe you could be a stay-at-home dad and we could have a baby right away?"

"I could tote around a mini mayor?" he joked.

"Would you do that for me? Be a stay-at-home dad?"

"How would we afford it?"

"If I came up with a plan, would you trust me to follow it?"

He watched her, knowing she was asking for more than just a parenting plan. She was looking for him to trust them, trust her.

"For you, I would resign."

Olivia frowned. "That doesn't feel right, either."

He pulled her close, kissing her temple. "We'll get it figured out," he repeated. "We don't have to have everything planned today. And if you do find a way for us to have it all, just tell me where to show up and I'll be there."

"Hey, congratulations," Ethan said, sitting beside Devon. He looked out across the room and frowned. "What's Gramps doing? He doesn't drink sherry."

Devon followed his gaze and laughed. It looked

like Gran was filling their grandfather's glass with some special blend from her handbag.

"Has Gramps seemed...off...to you lately?" Ethan asked, massaging his bad leg.

"He's eighty. He's not the same spring chicken he was when he was seventy-six."

"Ha," Ethan said humorlessly. His brother was one of the few in the family who could handle spending time with Gramps, a man almost as curmudgeonly as Alvin Lasota.

"Want to buy a catering business?" Ethan asked, breaking into Devon's thoughts.

"Nope. I have a job."

"Seriously? Not even for a steal of a deal? Do it part-time while running the town? Come on. Please?"

"Seriously."

"You know who should take it over?" Olivia asked, leaning forward, the baby still sleeping in her arms. "Lily."

"Lily who?" Ethan was a horrible actor. His brow had furrowed in fake confusion at the mention of Lily Harper.

"She's just finishing chef school and is thinking about coming home," Olivia announced.

"Totally your type." Devon smiled at his brother and clapped him on the shoulder. "She likes grumpy apes." He tossed his head back and laughed, enjoying the way he was torturing his brother with what could maybe one day bloom into love.

———

"Devon? Where can I put this?" Olivia had a rare abstract print in her hands from a well-known New York artist. It was fairly small, but she'd still have to move something on Devon's walls—sorry, their walls—in order to hang it.

"That's hideous," he said, his body pressing into hers as he glanced over her shoulder. She leaned into him, savoring the fact that she could.

"It's very expensive."

"Sorry. Expensive *and* hideous."

Olivia gave the print another look. He was right. "I'll put it in the garage sale pile."

"You sure?"

"Our world, remember?"

She set the print in the growing stack of things they were parting with. Devon cupped her chin, smiling at her as if he couldn't quite believe they were truly together.

"If you like it, it doesn't matter what I think."

"Maybe I like how you break the mold in my head."

"What does that mean?" His blue eyes narrowed in confusion.

"I have certain ideas about what's right or proper or good. Sometimes it's limiting. I like that you accept me for however I happen to be in the moment. You, my dear, are more than enough for a woman like me."

His mouth grazed hers, sending electric shocks through her body. Her fingers went flying up, knotting in his hair as he took her mouth with an urgency that had the two of them knocking into the couch as they struggled for equilibrium.

Their dogs began barking, thinking it was all a game.

Devon's kisses were consuming, his mouth fully over hers. She could barely breathe, barely think. It was just like college. Consuming. Rapid-fire kisses, brain meltdowns and seduction in one small touch that ignited everything. It was just like before, only hotter, because now they were married, their love enough to conquer everything that came across their path, their worlds united as one.

Finally, Devon Mattson was hers.

GET MORE BLUEBERRY SPRINGS!

Want to find out how sweet matchmaker Ginger McGinty snagged her husband and got her title as a matchmaker? Read all about it in *Sweet Matchmaker.*

Need to meet the man baby Finn was named after? He's the movie star hero in Jean's book *Falling for the Movie Star*!

And keep reading Veils and Vows with the next book in the series: *A Pinch of Commitment*—Ethan Mattson and Lily Harper's story. Dive in today and continue the adventure!

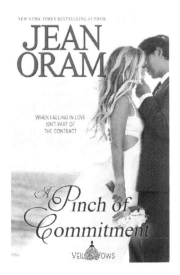

When falling in love isn't part of the plan.

VEILS AND VOWS

Find love in unexpected places with these sweet marriage of convenience romances.

The Promise (Book 0: Devon & Olivia)

The Surprise Wedding (Book 1: Devon & Olivia)

A Pinch of Commitment (Book 2: Ethan & Lily)

The Wedding Plan (Book 3: Luke & Emma)

Accidentally Married (Book 4: Burke & Jill)

The Marriage Pledge (Book 5: Moe & Amy)

Mail Order Soulmate (Book 6: Zach & Catherine)

ALSO BY JEAN ORAM

FREE EBOOK

Read, Dream, Laugh & Love
Sweet, Laugh-out-Loud Romances

Have you fallen in love with Blueberry Springs? Catch up with your friends and their adventures...

Book 1: Whiskey and Gumdrops (Mandy & Frankie)

Book 2: Rum and Raindrops (Jen & Rob)

Book 3: Eggnog and Candy Canes (Katie & Nash)

Book 4: Sweet Treats (3 short stories—Mandy, Amber, & Nicola)

Book 5: Vodka and Chocolate Drops (Amber & Scott)

Book 6: Tequila and Candy Drops (Nicola & Todd)

Companion Novel: Champagne and Lemon Drops (Beth & Oz)

THE SUMMER SISTERS

Taming billionaires has never been so *sweet*.

Falling for billionaires has never been so sweet.

* Available in paperback & ebook & audio! *

One cottage. Four sisters. And four billionaires who will sweep them off their feet.

Falling for the Movie Star

Falling for the Boss

Falling for the Single Dad

Falling for the Bodyguard

Falling for the Firefighter